PRAISE |

ISRAELIS AND PALESTINIAN VOICES: A DIALOGUE WITH BOTH SIDES

Standing in the shoes of those who face each other daily across this dangerous divide forces us to see beyond media stereotypes often reduced to terrorist and victim. This fast-paced narrative and compelling interviews brings to life a conflict whose complexities Americans must try to understand."Janice Harayda, Minneapolis StarTribune

Sarah Harder, President, National Peace Foundation

A BEIRUT HEART

There is nothing like an intelligent woman, spouse and mother of small children, to carry one into the midst of war, with its horrors as well as its capacity for soul-building. Sultan's narrative enfleshes our disjointed 'news' of the Middle East.

David Burrell, C.S.C, Hesburgh Professor in Philosophy and Theology, University of Notre Dame; Director, Tantur Ecumenical Institute, Jerusalem

...a view drawn from a camera obscura that moves behind the screen of invading armies, détentes, and broken treaties...a compelling story of survival that settles for no less than the promise that this family will remain together and safe at all costs...

Colleen McElroy, Professor of English, University of Seattle; author of 14 books including *Over the Lip of the World: Among Storytellers of Madagascar* and *Queen of the Ebony Isles*, which received the American Book Award

THE SYRIAN

In *The Syrian*, Cathy Sultan has achieved a master trifecta of political thriller, historical fiction and romance. This wickedly smart novel reminds us that politics is all about relationships and dares us to conceive that women are just as capable of sexual power plays as the men who have made careers by them for millennia. Sultan's expertise about the contemporary Middle East brings a breathless authenticity to the surprises that come at every turn.

Antonia Felix
New York Times Bestselling Author

TRAGEDY IN SOUTH LEBANON: THE ISRAELI-HEZBOLLAH WAR OF 2006

Tragedy in South Lebanon provides vital information about a topic often misreported by the mainstream media. I particularly liked the interviews with both Hezbollah and Israeli soldiers describing the same battle. This is an important book that should be read by anyone interested in Israel and Lebanon.

Reese Erlich, foreign correspondent and author of *The Iran Agenda: The Real Story of US Policy and the Middle East Crisis*

As someone who works with other organizations to ban the use, sale, and transfer of cluster bombs, I applaud Cathy Sultan's discussion on the effects of these lethal weapons on Lebanese civilians, many of them children, who continue to be killed and maimed by these odious, unexploded Israeli cluster munitions.

George Cody, Ph.D., Executive Director, American Task Force for Lebanon

Finally, finally, finally, there is a book that looks at the complex issues in Lebanon for what they are—complex. And even more importantly, Sultan has taken her experience and transported all of us into the region to better understand the complexities from the people themselves. We have had enough of the bumper sticker slogans and five second sound bites. Great.

Jack Rice, journalist and former CIA officer

Sultan gives a fair and accurate account of what went on in South Lebanon. As a UN official who has spent 24 years in South Lebanon, I say she also lends refreshing voice to those who would otherwise never be heard.

Timor Goksel, Senior Advisor and Official Spokesman for the United National Interim Force in Lebanon

Omar's Choice

CALUMET EDITIONS

Minneapolis

FIRST EDITION SEPTEMBER 2024

OMAR'S CHOICE. Copyright © 2024 by Cathy Sultan.
All rights reserved.

This is a work of fiction. All of the characters, names, incidents, organizations, and dialogue are either the products of the author's imagination or are used fictiously.

10 9 8 7 6 5 4 3 2 1

ISBN: 978-1-962834-23-0

Cover design by Sue Stein
Book design by Gary Lindberg

Omar's Choice

Book 4 of The Syria Quartet

Cathy Sultan

CALUMET EDITIONS
Minneapolis

To the people of Syria, that they may be left alone to choose their own leaders and solve their own problems without Western and regional interference

"In a time of universal deceit, telling the truth is a revolutionary act."

–George Orwell

"War is manufactured by political leaders who then must make a tremendous effort-by enticement, by propaganda, by coercion-to mobilize a normally reluctant population to go to war."

–Howard Zinn

"A nation that is afraid to let its people judge the truth and falsehood in an open market is a nation that is afraid of its people."

–John F. Kennedy

Also by Cathy Sultan

Nonfiction

A Beirut Heart: One Woman's War
Israeli and Palestinian Voices: A Dialogue with Both Sides
Tragedy in South Lebanon: The Israeli-Hezbollah War of 2006

Fiction

The Syrian
Damascus Street
An Ambassador to Syria

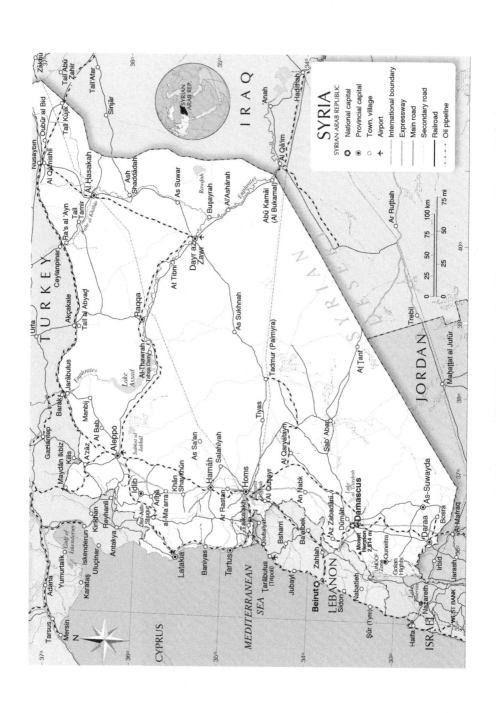

PROLOGUE

He wanted to spare the old priest, but that would have been impossible. Escape was not an option either. His minder was there to make sure that did not happen. Commander Abbas may have befriended and guided him through his training, but he was still a formidable presence, not to be disobeyed. As his assignment mandated, the two had left Raqqa for Homs' Old City, a pile of still-smoldering rubble after a three-year-long siege, and the priest—loyal and stalwart as always—would be at the wrecked church, ministering to the few remaining Christians.

He led Abbas through a maze of narrow cobblestone alleyways and lanes cluttered with fallen debris, broken mortar, twisted metal and burned-out shells of vehicles; past shops, their metal shutters ripped off, their wooden shelves stripped, their safes blown open and looted and the owners, despondent, sitting on sidewalks, desperate to sell whatever they had salvaged. Around another corner was the Old City's major market-place, or what was left of it. They entered, walking over crushed glass fallen from the cylindrical roof overhead. They stopped and glanced around, likely imagining the bustling scene of market day—a sea of people shouting at vendors who were selling vegetables, fruit, baked goods, textiles and hardware, all frantically haggling for the best prices.

When they emerged from the souk into a narrow lane, they saw a sickening plume of smoke rising into the sky. In the distance, through the stagnant fog of vapors, they could see the church and rectory. It was the vile sweet smell that hit their nostrils before they saw the bodies, dozens of them, some poking through the remains of the burning building, others ejected by the blast and strewn across the red-stained ground, the blood already curdled into thick blobs. And there were the flies, great hordes of them, nibbling on open flesh and literally covering the bodies black. The stench, not just from burning limbs but from open bowels and decaying flesh, was unbearable.

The two men took quick, shallow breaths, hoping the stink would not pass to their lungs, but bile rose in their throats. They gagged repeatedly, and each of them bent over and vomited. Drained, they sought a place out of the hot sun and away from the smells where they sat and drank from their bottled water until they recovered enough to continue to their destination.

The old church in the Bustan al-Diwan neighborhood of the Old City was in ruins, its walls crumbling, its furnishings long since looted or vandalized, its ornately carved wooden ceiling and wall panels thrown into a nearby heap of garbage. Behind the church, enclosed within a stone wall, was a garden of blooming narcissus and hibiscus. Intertwined against the back wall, a row of white jasmine was trying to climb to the top, an extraordinarily defiant feat of nature, bright green leaves stubbornly poking their heads up from under fallen stones. There was a peculiar-looking tree in the middle of the garden, too, one neither man had seen before, its oblong leathery green leaves and reddish-purple flowers in striking contrast to the drabness of gray everywhere else.

They heard voices and stopped before they reached the garden gate. The old priest, his back to the men and seated on a white plastic chair, was dressed in a short-sleeved black polo shirt and black jeans. He had a white band of hair around the base of his head. A woman knelt on the ground before the priest while the other two stood silently along the back wall reciting the rosary.

He had grown up near a Catholic neighborhood in Dearborn, Michigan, and knew these women were there to say confession and ask forgiveness for their sins, whatever those could have been for such brave souls who had steadfastly remained in the Old City. Their drawn faces and weathered skin suggested they had been long deprived of the most basic human needs.

When the priest finished hearing her confession, he blessed the woman with a sign of the cross and sent her on her way. She in turn bowed her head, stood and left the garden, filing past the two men, acknowledging their presence with a nod of her head.

The men waited until the three women had left the church grounds before they advanced toward the priest.

"Greetings, Frans," he said in English, the language he and the priest had spoken in past encounters. He was shocked by how much Frans had aged, but then he had endured the siege, and dark circles under his eyes, deep crevices in his cheeks and sagging clothes were all symptoms of near starvation. But there was also his age. Quite a toll for a man he knew to be in his eighties.

"There you are, Omar," Frans answered, his voice weary. "I wondered when you'd come." With a motion of his frail arm, he waved his visitor closer. "Come, take a seat. Who is your friend?"

"His name is Abbas."

"Should you be telling me his name?"

"It doesn't matter," said Abbas.

"No, I suppose it doesn't," Frans said, slowly nodding his head. "Tell me what you've been up to, Omar. You sneaked out of Homs without a goodbye."

"I moved to Raqqa."

"Raqqa? ISIS is in Raqqa."

"Yes, I've joined them."

"So, you've become a head chopper. Shame on you! What about your friend here? Is he one too?"

"That's none of your business," Abbas snapped.

Frans said, "You professed anger toward infidels like me, Omar, but behind that bravado, I never pegged you a killer."

"My pledge to Allah comes with certain rites I must perform."

"You were also a sentimental man. I saw how you treated your men, your friends Andrew and Hassan, the Somali man from Minneapolis. How does such a person become a killer?"

Omar looked at Abbas before he answered. "I thought ISIS would want me for my media skills rather than... other tasks."

"How could you have been so naive? They cite passages from the Quran that explicitly promote violence. 'When you encounter the unbelievers on the battlefield, strike off their heads until you have crushed them completely.' Yes, I've read the Quran. I know all the passages that promote such acts. There are many. I should think death preferable to a life of shame."

Frans did not wait for a response. "So instead, you kill others, is that it? How many?"

"Too many to count, Father. We have hundreds of prisoners. They're our live fodder. We use them for target practice. It's not that hard to put a gun to someone's head and pull the trigger after you've done it dozens of times. It's the beheadings that are more difficult."

"And have you perfected the technique?"

"Yes, I have."

"So, I won't suffer?"

"No, you have my word."

CHAPTER ONE

Over the past year, while she recovered from a major brain trauma, Mary O'Brien studied not only Levantine politics but also how their controversies, internecine feuds and proxy wars played out across the greater Middle East. This awareness not only altered her perception of the region, but it challenged everything she thought she knew. She became aware of certain facts so controversial that they would never see the light of day in any American newspaper, even if the research was factually accurate.

A good journalist's job was to challenge the halls of power, but that was not always easy when it came to the Middle East where perceived, ingrained biases steadfastly held. Fiction, however, existed for a reason. So, why not fictionalize all this information, incorporate it into a storyline, and begin the novel with two women, both journalists, on their way to investigate the horrific murder of a priest named Father Frans? Mary found the idea liberating.

* * *

The taxi dropped Mary and her friend Sonia off within walking distance to what had once been Bab Amr, their old neighborhood adjacent to the Old City of Homs. To get any closer by car would have been impossible. The damage was so widespread that even buildings seemed unsure whether to crumble or remain standing. On others, walls *had* crumbled, stone pillars the only things left to support the floors that stretched back into dark, haunting symmetry. Fires still burned randomly. Their dark plumes obscured the sun and cast a somber shroud of gray over a city that had already taken on the color of death. The streets were still strewn with blocks of fallen mortar and twisted metal, and from the putrid, pungent smell that stung their nostrils, there remained far too many as-yet recovered bodies still buried in the massive piles of rubble, rotting in the suffocating heat.

How tragic that a city that had existed since ancient times, with its mercantile souks and cobblestone alleyways, should succumb, in the twenty-first century, to senseless, wanton Western warfare. This great city had once smelled of cedar and musk, incense and myrrh, and had seen traders selling their wares to Persians, Babylonians and Greeks, possibly even Cleopatra.

"Look," Sonia said as they approached a building. "That's where we used to live."

Mary tried to identify some previous landmark. "I don't see anything I recognize."

"That's because the building that once stood next to ours is gone," Sonia said, pointing in that direction.

"It's surreal. The sheared-off walls, the dangling balconies, the hollowed-out buildings. It looks like the remains of a nuclear explosion. How the hell did we survive this?"

"Do you remember the day we were coming back from market and saw a bomb hit the top floor? We were sure Frans had died in the blast."

"And now he has, poor man," said Mary.

And all she could do was write about his death in the dullest, most noncontroversial manner possible so her American editor would not find fault or deem it too far outside the prevailing "moderate rebel" narrative. Over the past year, when Mary had uncovered new information, Sonia would be at the center of it all, barging into her room late at night, usually in her nightgown, with two glasses and a bottle of wine. Before she had even uncorked the bottle, Sonia would have already begun by saying, "There are some things you need to know about what just happened." And she'd be off talking about the CIA working with the al Qaeda affiliates in Syria, revelations Mary knew she could never use, except in fiction.

By the time Sonia had finished the rest of the bottle, Mary was still on her first glass. Sonia would have already jumped into the sordid history of the CIA across the Middle East, whether it was their suitcases full of dollars to bribe Lebanese politicians into voting for Bachir Gemayel or Operation Cyclone in Afghanistan where they armed the mujahadeen to the tune of a billion dollars with state-of-the-art weaponry and training. By sunrise, she would finally conclude with something profound like, "…and such actions turned Afghanistan into a petri dish for international jihadists."

Mary had come to expect such exuberant outpourings from her friend. Sonia was an Arab journalist, proud and well versed in her region's history. She knew its leaders, many of them personally. She had covered their wars and sympathized with their complicated political and religious fault lines. She held a deep-seated animosity toward any Western power that deemed it their right to interfere in regional affairs, and she freely expressed her feelings in explicit Arabic vulgarity.

But now, and going forward, Mary was no longer the journalist constrained by her editor's dictates about what was and wasn't permissible. She was a novelist writing a book inspired by the real-life murder of a Jesuit priest who had served Syria's Christian community for fifty-six years.

Mary still shuddered when she thought of Frans and his last moments. His brutal murder had unsettled her because, as Sonia suspected, the West had tacitly given the go-ahead to their regional allies to weaponize and train the men who had killed the priest.

From her own personal experience, Mary had come to the same conclusion. She knew some of these men, a certain Omar among them. She had embedded herself with them in Homs, been their mouthpiece to the outside world, and in so doing had tacitly supported al Nusra, one of the uglier offshoots of al Qaeda.

Mary began her investigation at the scene of the crime, the garden behind a crumbling church in the Old City of Bab Amir. What better way to jog a witness's memory and flush out some trivial detail not previously remembered? Her witnesses were three nuns. She knew from the authorities where Frans had been seated in the garden, where the witnesses stood while waiting for him to hear their confessions, and she had set up the murder scene accordingly.

At the designated hour, she and Sonia had arrived at the church with the three nuns, Colonel Yakob—who headed the official state investigation—and his assistant, Yousef, both of whom were friends from Homs.

Mary was familiar with the inside of the church. She, Frans and Sonia had sought refuge there during the Syrian Army's siege. At the time, in her haste to escape the ongoing shelling, she had never fully appreciated the beauty of the church's architecture. On this occasion, she examined its prominent Mamluk black and white stone facade and its three wide arches through which worshippers entered the church. She imagined the splendor of the red tile roof on a sun-filled day, now but a hint of its former brilliance, its colors faded, its once-glazed clay slabs covered in grime.

Mary suspected her witnesses might still be traumatized. At the very least, they might fear, as did Mary, that the killers could still be in the Old City and on the prowl for witnesses who dared come forward. The killers had known where to find the priest. They could just as easily find the nuns. Mary reasoned that at least one of the men had to have been familiar with the layout of the Old City and the location of the church, which meant they could have also found a secure place to hide and wait.

Mary asked Yousef to sit in the chair Frans had occupied, then asked the three nuns to stand against the back wall. Eventually, she asked each of the nuns to kneel for confession, then stand again and exit the garden. She had Sonia and Yakob sit alongside her, all of them facing the nuns.

The older of the three women, Sister Marie, the mother superior of the convent, volunteered to go first.

"Do you mind if I question you in English?" Mary asked.

The nun shook her head, "I not speak good English. Arabic, please, or French."

"Yes, of course, then I yield to my colleague," Mary said, turning to Sonia. "She'll ask you some questions, if you don't mind."

Sister Marie nodded.

"Sister, please describe the afternoon. You had just arrived. Who did you see?" asked Sonia in Arabic.

"Father Frans, of course. He was seated where the officer is seated now, facing the garden. I was there no more than ten minutes when my two younger sisters arrived. As was the custom, if someone was already in confession, the others would wait against the back wall until it was their turn. I finished, Father blessed me and I left."

"And there was no one lingering near the garden when you left?"

"No, and had the others seen anyone suspicious when they entered, they would have said something to me or to Father. You see, we consider this our private garden. We plant the flowers and trim the tree and often come here to pray, so we're leery of any strangers who might lurk about."

"Thank you, Sister Marie," Sonia said. "I have no further questions. You're welcome to stay while we talk to your sisters."

"I will leave if you don't mind. I'm needed back at the convent."

Sister Sophie, the next witness, spoke fluent English.

"When you arrived for confession," asked Mary, "did you see anyone near the garden?"

"No, it wasn't until I left that I saw the two men."

"Describe them for us, if you will."

"They weren't men who would have stood out in a crowd. They had beards, but then so do most men in Homs these days, especially after the long siege. They wore polo shirts and khaki pants, standard Western attire, except for the combat boots. At the time, I didn't think anything of it. Now, of course, with Father's murder, maybe the boots should have raised a red flag in my mind."

"Why?" Mary asked.

"Call it social conditioning, but I associate boots with combat."

"Did they act strangely?"

"No, but I did find their presence a bit odd. As mother superior just said, we considered these our private grounds, and to find two men standing there surprised me. But for all I knew at the time, they were there to pay Father Frans a visit. One of the men turned as I left and nodded. That's probably why I let my guard down, because I considered that an amiable gesture on his part."

"Nothing in their actions suggested they were there to harm the priest?"

"The furthest thing from my mind... I never even glanced back to look at them as I walked away. God forgive me for being so negligent."

"Were the men Arabs?"

"Judging by the color of their tanned skin and black hair, I'd say yes."

"Thank you, Sister Sophie. You've been very helpful," Mary said, before turning to the last nun waiting against the back wall.

"Sister Madeline, please come forward. Are you comfortable speaking English?"

"Yes, I'm quite proficient. I studied it at university."

Mary nodded. "Can you add anything to our conversation?"

"The two men were already there when I arrived. I found their presence curious. My instinct told me they were not there for confession. I can't tell you why I thought that. I just sensed they weren't friendly."

"But Sister Sophie just told us one of them nodded at her as she left."

"I know, but I sensed a boorishness about them. Maybe they just felt clumsy in the presence of a woman dressed in nun attire, but then maybe they were uneasy about the nasty business they were there to conduct and eager to get the job done."

"What happened next?" Mary asked. "Did you report your suspicions to the authorities when you left the church grounds?"

"No, because I didn't leave," she blurted out, bursting into tears. "Had I gone looking for help I might have saved Father's life."

"That's not a given, Sister. And had you tried, you might have put your own life at risk."

"Well, I did leave the garden after my confession, as the others had done. I nodded politely to the two men as I passed, and they did the same. I pretended to walk away, and when I knew I could safely turn to look back, they had already entered the garden. So I doubled back and hid inside the church. I know every inch of the church because I'm in charge of keeping it as tidy as possible. Not an easy job, given all the destruction, but I do my best."

Mary knew the inside of the church too. During the siege, she, Frans, and Sonia had shared the space with three annoying families who shamelessly begged for their food until Father Frans, generous to a fault, gave away every last lentil and bean, leaving them with nothing to eat.

Sister Madeline continued. "On the left side of the altar, there's a window close to the garden. From there, I could safely sneak a peek without being seen. More importantly, I could hear bits and pieces of their conversation."

Mary fought back tears. She knew that window too. It was from there that she could glance out at her lover Joe Lavrov's grave under the tree in that garden.

"If you were that close, why couldn't you hear the entire conversation?"

"It depended on where they stood at any specific moment, and whether they faced in my direction. There was a bit of a breeze that day, and wind tends to project voices in odd directions."

"If you don't mind, I'd like to concentrate on what you saw from the church window."

"Father Frans didn't turn when he heard someone enter the garden. He must have assumed another nun had come to confess, but even when the younger man said, 'Hello, Frans,' he still didn't turn around, which made me think Father recognized the man by his voice. They spoke at length, which only confirmed my assumption that they knew each other. During the entire conversation, Father sat there seemingly unafraid, looking at the young man who then was standing in front of him. In an instant, the atmosphere changed when the older man opened his backpack, pulled out a knife and handed it to the younger man."

The nun's voice cracked, and she cried openly. Mary waited until she had settled down before she continued her questioning.

"Do you want to rest a moment before we continue?" she asked.

"No, I'll be fine," Sister Madeline said, as she pulled a Kleenex from her pocket and blew her nose.

Mary waited another minute before she continued. "What happened next?"

"From then on, I could only hear bits of the conversation, but I can say with certainly that whatever was said, Father remained calm. He had to have known he was about to die, and yet… no reaction. When he tilted his head back, I did hear him ask, 'Will I suffer?' And then, he said something else. Perhaps a prayer? When the younger man took the knife and approached Father's neck, I pressed both of my hands over my mouth so I wouldn't scream and give myself away. As scared as I was, I must confess I couldn't stop watching. I studied nursing at university, so I'm familiar with the body's anatomy. Once the younger man slashed Father's throat, I knew he was dead."

"Did you leave the church then?"

"Heavens, no. I was too scared. Besides, the older man started shouting, and I got even more frightened."

"So, you did hear them."

"A few words, but I could also read their body language. The older man made a fist as if he intended to punch the younger one, but he didn't. Instead, he shouted repeatedly and pointed to the knife, which the other had dropped. At this point, Father's head was still attached, and his blood continued to gush like a river, down his shirt and his pants and shoes. It collected in a ghastly pool around his chair. It was only when the older man poked the younger one on his shoulder and shouted again that the young man picked up the knife and began to cut through the sinew. It takes an enormous effort to reach the spinal column and get to the other side of the neck. When he finished, the young man let the knife slide from his hand and fall to the ground."

"Did the two men leave at that point?"

"No, they hadn't finished. The older one shouted again, but the younger one stood there as if frozen, like he was in shock. Maybe this was his first beheading. In the end, when he didn't budge, the older man poked him hard. He stumbled and almost fell into the slimy mess. Finally, he picked up the knife, wiped it off as best he could along the side of his slacks, and put it in his backpack. The older man shouted another order, and the younger man lifted Father's head off the ground and placed it atop a grave under the terebinth tree."

It wasn't just any grave, Mary thought. *It was Joe's, with his beautiful body which she had once thought would be hers forever.*

"It was at this point that the older man grabbed the younger's arm and led him out of the garden?" Mary asked. "Then what happened?"

"As they were leaving, I dropped to the ground so they wouldn't see me, but I accidentally kicked over a metal trash can."

Mary gasped. "Oh my God. What did you do then?"

"I knew I only had seconds to hide before they came rushing into the church. Luckily, I know the inside of the church, and they didn't. When you enter, there are a dozen rows of pews with an aisle down the middle. I assumed they'd look in between the rows first before looking elsewhere. That gave me time to rush to the other side of the altar and squeeze in behind a pile of wood panels that had fallen from the ceiling. Why they didn't look behind the pile, I'll never know, especially since they came within feet of discovering me. By some miracle, at that very moment, there came the sound of something crashing on the marble floor. I was sure the noise was God-sent to save me until I remembered leaving a glass vase on top of the altar, and then I heard a meow. The cat saved my life because the men turned and headed in the direction of the noise."

"Did they find the cat?"

"I heard them say '*qut*,' which is the word for cat in Arabic. I assumed the cat had hopped on the chair near the open window and jumped out."

"After the men left, did you follow them?"

"Certainly not. I stayed behind the pile of wood, too terrified to move. I kept thinking they might return. It was only when I heard Sister Sophie's voice calling out my name that I burst into tears and answered her."

Sister Sophie spoke up. "When Madeline didn't return to the convent, I got worried and came looking for her. After she explained what had happened, I went to the garden and saw Father Frans's beheaded body slumped in the white plastic chair, his head propped up on the grave. I returned to the church and grabbed hold of Madeline's hand. I pulled her up from the floor and led her outside. We went directly to the army post to report the murder. Everyone knew Father Frans. He was our local saint. He never abandoned us during the army's siege. I knew his death would cause great agitation, and people would come to view the crime scene, so I thought it urgent to notify the authorities as soon as possible so they could cordon off the area to protect Father's body."

"Sister Madeline, what can you tell me about the men's accents? I realize you were only able to hear parts of their conversation, but in your opinion, were they from the area?"

"The younger man spoke to Father Frans in English. When he and the older man exchanged words in Arabic, I could tell it wasn't his native tongue. As best I could tell, the older man was local, or at least from the region."

"Thank you for your cooperation. This couldn't have been easy for you," Mary said, holding Sister Madeline's warm hand in hers. *Such a lovely young woman,* Mary thought. *Why would she have ever wanted to be stuck here as a nun? Maybe that's why I'm not a Catholic anymore. I've lost my faith and any appreciation for such sacrifices.*

With admiration, Mary watched Madeline walk away, then suddenly stop as she brought her hands to her face and sob. What she had seen was horrific. Instinctively, Mary wanted to rush to her and comfort her, but Sister Sophie did so instead, gently putting her arm around Madeline's shoulder.

Sonia waited until the nuns had exited the church grounds before she spoke. "I've no doubt the younger of the two men was Omar."

"I agree with Sonia for two reasons," Yakob said. "Omar knew where to find Father, and if we're to believe the witnesses, the older man literally commanded Omar to behead him. The crime is quite extraordinary. It's as if Father had been waiting for him to show up and take his life."

"As much as I dislike Omar, I find it hard to believe he joined that band of savages," Mary said. "We can speculate about what he did or didn't do, but in order to bring charges we need proof of guilt."

"When I first met him in Daraa in 2011," Sonia said, "he swore to me and Frans, as infidels, that our time would come."

"That doesn't mean he became a head chopper," insisted Mary.

"We could argue this till hell freezes over, but I'm done for the day," Sonia said. "I'm tired, and I'd like to go back to the hotel."

"Allow me to accompany you," Yakob said.

"We won't hear of it," Mary said. "You've already done a great deal to help us. You've agreed to head the official investigation, and you helped us organize this meeting with the three nuns. We will, however, allow you to find us a taxi."

"Of course. Where are you staying?"

"The Safir on Ragheb al Jamali Street."

"Nice," he said, nodding.

"Luckily, it's far enough from the actual war zone that it didn't suffer structural damage. And in this heat, and if given a choice, who wouldn't choose a hotel with air-conditioned rooms?"

* * *

Sonia plopped herself down on the soft bed as soon as she got back to the room and let the air conditioning cool her body. Mary, leaning against two large pillows, closed her eyes and wondered if the past year had just been one long nightmare. The siege of the Old City, their repeated brushes with death, her lover Joe killed, and then the unthinkable—Frans beheaded. How could such things have happened?

And then there was Omar, the man she had briefly worked for. Had he really become a head chopper? According to Yakob, he was nowhere to be found after she and Sonia left Homs. And when his men were evacuated to Idlib in northwest Syria, he hadn't boarded the bus. Where had he gone? Al Nusra had all but dissolved by then.

With limited options, Yakob assumed he had joined ISIS. But Mary still was not convinced. The nuns had described the two men as having trimmed beards and Western-style clothes. Not exactly the image one had of ISIS fighters, yet two ordinary-looking men had shown up in Homs at a time when the city was in complete upheaval, with people returning to check on their apartments while others were fleeing with their few remaining possessions, and no one had paid attention to the strangers.

That was the perfect cover, and Omar would have known that too. He was a chameleon. Hadn't Sonia said Omar had a long, straggly beard and unkempt hair the first time she'd met him? When Mary was introduced to him a few months later, he had trimmed his beard and worn a clean shirt and pressed trousers. In hindsight, he had wanted to impress her and make sure she agreed to work with him in his media center.

How naive she had been at the time. Sonia had tried to warn her about Omar and his affiliation with al Nusra. She had refused to believe it and instead had accused Sonia of being pro-Assad. To her credit, Sonia insisted she was not so much pro-Assad as anti-al Qaeda and its ilk. More than anything, she abhorred the idea of a Western power coming in and taking out their leaders. That was a job for the Syrian people if they so chose—no one else.

Mary was about to ask Sonia something when she heard her snoring. She desperately wanted to close her eyes too. She was exhausted, but instead she opened her laptop. She knew only that Omar was from Dearborn, Michigan, but she needed more details. The population of Dearborn, she discovered, was ninety-one thousand, forty thousand of them Arab Americans.

Given that high percentage, it was not surprising that the largest mosque in the United States, the Islamic Center of America, was in Dearborn. The majority of the Sunnis, like Omar, were from Iraq, while most of the Shiites came from south Lebanon. According to one article she found, the younger generation was fervent in their religious and cultural beliefs and were offended by the attention their community received from the FBI any time an Arab anywhere committed an act of terrorism. More importantly, they strongly condemned their elders for their collaboration with both the CIA and the FBI, working as informants, translators or agents.

All interesting tidbits, Mary thought, *but none of it led to Omar*. She assumed he was in his mid-twenties, so she pulled up every high school in the city and looked at their student body photos going back five or six years. When she found Fordson High School, she took notice. About 90 percent of the students were Arabs.

When she couldn't find any class or yearbook photos, she pulled up the school's sports teams. She did not think Omar would have played baseball or football because of his height and build, so she looked for a soccer team. Fordson High School had a soccer team. Its coaches had Arab names, but neither the names of the players nor their photos were listed, so she searched through newspaper articles on soccer matches, and there he was. Only his name was not Omar. It was Kareem, and he was captain of the varsity soccer team.

What a stroke of luck, thought Mary.

"Sonia, wake up. I found him."

Sonia turned over in her bed and looked groggily at Mary. "Who?"

"I found Omar. Look," she said as she leaped off her bed, computer in hand, and slid in next to Sonia.

"The photo's probably about five years old, but look, it's him. No doubt about it."

"Oh my God," Sonia said, studying the photo. "It *is* Omar. What did you say his real name was?"

"Kareem."

"I wonder how many men like Kareem joined ISIS."

"I looked that up too," Mary said. "Officially, some three hundred Americans joined or attempted to join ISIS, with some rising to senior positions, but only a dozen or so were from Michigan."

That number represented 1 percent of the estimated thirty thousand foreign fighters who had joined ISIS. Mary found the photo of one of those men, from Dearborn, who had been captured in Syria and returned to the United States to stand trial. In all, fifty Americans were arrested as they tried to leave the country. When put on trial, they received harsh sentences, while those who reached Iraq or Syria received lighter sentences. Mary thought that counterintuitive until she realized those caught on the battlefield would have had information to trade or could, at the very least, have shed light on ISIS's structure in exchange for more lenient sentences, but that would not apply to Omar. His crime was far too egregious.

"So, what do we do with this information?" Sonia asked.

"I suggest we call Yakob in the morning and ask him to arrange a meeting with Sisters Sophie and Madeline."

Sonia nodded. "And if they positively identify Omar, he'll tell us how to proceed."

"According to one of the articles I read, any foreigner caught working for ISIS on Syrian soil is turned over to his country's authorities for prosecution."

"Yakob will likely suggest some official in Damascus," Sonia said, "and that would be perfect timing since we'll be there tomorrow to hear the final UN report on Assad's chemical weapons use."

* * *

"Thank you, Sisters, for agreeing to meet with us again," Mary said. "Last night, I did some research and came across a photo of a man who may have beheaded Father Frans. Would you be willing to look at the photo?"

"Will we be asked to testify in a court of law?" Sister Sophie asked.

"I don't know," Mary said.

"Will our lives be put in danger if we identify the man?"

"He will be prosecuted in the United States and sent to prison there."

"Given the gravity of the crime," said Sister Madeline, as she turned to address Sophie, "we have an obligation to help. Show us the photo."

Sister Sophie nodded. "She's right."

Mary pulled the newspaper article from her purse and put it on the table in front of the two women. She watched as they examined the photo. They took their time, which she appreciated, and more importantly, they did not consult one another.

"I recognize this man," Sister Sophie said, pointing to Omar. "He was one of the two men I saw standing outside the garden as I left."

"I can unequivocally say this is the man who beheaded Father Frans," said Sister Madeline.

"Thank you both very much," Mary said.

* * *

In addition to discovering the identity of an American jihadist, Mary knew it would be a remarkably satisfying feat of journalism if she could also produce a well-documented story about Bashar Assad's alleged use of chemical weapons. All the evidence she and Sonia had collected pointed to a false flag operation. And what was she to do with everything she had learned about the origins of al Qaeda? And the CIA's role in arming jihadists in Afghanistan to fight the Russians and empowering men like Osama bin Laden to attack the World Trade Center on 9/11? Or the US attack on Iraq that produced a fertile seedbed for ISIS by intentionally dismantling the Iraqi army to promote Sunni-Shiite warfare?

It was not enough to know these things—she needed to understand why the US, along with the UK and France, would want to produce this kind of mayhem across the Middle East, knowing it would provoke the Russians and Iranians into action. Why would the US collaborate with France to initiate an attack on Libya and create yet another Iraqi-style failed state and then go after Syria, demanding regime change?

None of it made any sense. Or did it? When a belligerent country adopts a military objective but lacks the capability to achieve its goal, as had been the case again and again, was it arrogance or sheer incompetence that drove such foolish actions, or was it something more insidious?

CHAPTER TWO

"Why are you giving me the silent treatment?" Omar asked as he and Abbas walked away from the church. "You haven't said a word since I beheaded the priest."

"Because you did a lousy job. A donkey could have done better. You acted like you were being forced to do something you didn't want to do."

"Of course I didn't want to do it. I knew the man. He wasn't my enemy."

Without another word, he followed Abbas's lead as they retraced their tracks through the cobblestone walkways of the Old City to the city center, where they boarded a bus back to Raqqa. Abbas shoved Omar into a seat toward the rear of the bus and settled in behind him, while Omar sat there fuming and swearing revenge on Abbas for his insulting behavior.

When Omar and his friend Hassan had met the swine Abbas on a rickety old bus on their flight from Homs to Raqqa a year earlier, he had pretended to be their friend. They and the other ISIS recruits had been rudely ushered onto the bus by men with assault rifles, which had, as Omar recalled, greatly offended Hassan, who insisted he and the others were volunteers, not prisoners and deserved better treatment. A man seated opposite Omar on the aisle spoke up and took their side. Sensing a possible ally, and desperate to pass the four-and-a-half-hour journey across the Syrian desert conversing with someone other than his disgruntled friend, Omar turned to the man and introduced himself.

"Know anything about the place we're going?"

"Yeah, it's a stinking hellhole in the middle of the fucking desert," he laughed. "By the way," he said, extending his hand, "my name's Abbas. Where are you from? I don't recognize your accent."

Omar thought him friendly enough, and so he confessed, "I'm originally from Iraq, but I moved to the US at an early age. I practice my Arabic every chance I get, but as you can tell, I'm not very good."

To honor his mother, Omar had tried to keep up his Arabic, but like many young boys, even those who settled into predominantly Arab-American communities like Dearborn, Michigan, he felt the need to fit in and feel American. English began to filter into his conversations, making it harder to keep up his native tongue.

"No worries. I understand you well enough. It's just that your funny accent gives you away as a foreigner."

Omar asked uneasily, "Does it matter if I am?"

"Not at all. We welcome anyone who's willing to fight for our cause. No favoritism given, no prejudice or discrimination, no useless questions asked about anyone's background."

That's a relief, Omar thought, *because you probably wouldn't want to know that I'm a homosexual and that I've spent most of my life denying it and only recently indulged in such pleasures for the first time with my friend Hassan, seated alongside me. I've spent my whole life in internal conflict, denying my homosexuality to shield my mother from such a social stigma in our Arab community. I never blended in with my American classmates either, as I wasn't allowed to go to parties and drink and smoke and always felt like an outcast.*

And now, riding on the bus with Abbas back to Raqqa, Omar began musing again. He wondered why he had beheaded a very good man, why he hadn't broken loose of Abbas's hold and punched him in the face. Instead, he was drowning in remorse for all the people he had beheaded in practice runs and wondered if they had been fine people too.

He'd blindly followed orders, too scared to question who the targets were and why they had to die. Had he had a choice?

"Oh, Omar," as his friend Andrew would have said, "you always have a choice. Sometimes it comes with serious consequences, a risk of punishment or worse, but you always have a choice."

Omar continued his self-deprecating monologue. *I chose to abandon my mother and my education, my community and religion, and in so doing, dishonored the memory of my father. Simply and sadly put, my actions turned me into an instrument of ISIS and, before that, a tool of al Nusra, an offshoot of al Qaeda. I have no one to blame for these decisions but myself. If I could change any of it, and return to my former life, I would, but there is no way out, no turning back.* Teary-eyed, he thought of Hassan. *If I hadn't coerced him into joining ISIS, he would still love me.*

And reflecting on his years in Dearborn, Omar suspected it had been the ambiguity of his unacknowledged gayness that had confounded his classmates. Even he did not know how to define himself. Maybe it was because most of his acquaintances were also Arab and would not have assumed he was gay. He'd never had a girlfriend, a telltale sign for sure, if anyone had taken notice. He claimed his studies took priority, but he was in the top tier of his class and didn't need those extra study hours. He was an exceptionally good athlete, a trait that his mother said he had inherited from his father. He had chosen to play soccer, and because he was good at it, he had become his team's captain.

"Abbas," Omar asked, "what'll happen to us recruits once we get to Raqqa?"

"To begin with, you'll be enrolled in some religious training courses, which will take some months."

"But I've already spent six months in Saudi Arabia in a madrassa studying the Quran and Wahhabism before I was sent to Syria. Is there more I need to learn?"

"Does one ever learn enough about Islam?" Abbas asked.

"Of course not, but it isn't as if I'm looking to become an Islamic scholar. I know enough about my religion to be proud of it. Isn't that enough?"

Even in his early teens, when his mother might have expected his religious beliefs to have conflicted with his new American life, Omar never gave her reason to be concerned, for she had instilled in him a sense of self-pride as a young Muslim man. His religion had, after all, come from a land not far from the Sinai where Judaism was born, and near enough to Jerusalem where Christianity originated—the three of them desert religions, all People of the Book who shared the same God, the same ideas on morality, and Abrahamic traditions. And wasn't it the Muslims who had conquered the Christian lands of the Levant and North Africa and invaded Europe and ruled Sicily, Spain, Portugal and parts of France?

And yet, Omar thought, *for all your pride in your religion, you've shamed it by beheading not just a good man but a man of God who had served the Christian communities in Syria for many years.*

After 9/11, Omar hardly knew what to make of all the political strife attributed to Muslims and their religion. The atmosphere in Dearborn began to change too. Arabs were kept under tight FBI surveillance. The younger generations were upset at their elders for working with the US government. His mother dissuaded him from joining others in any overt display of discontent, insisting he keep his eye on his academic goals.

At its foundation, Omar knew Islam to be a beautiful religion. The word itself means peace and tolerance, and its tenets forbid the killing of another human being. When such violence did occur, as happened on 9/11, he and others were quick to attribute it to a few misguided individuals on the fringe of society. When the West initiated its wars across the Middle East, referring to them as holy crusades, Muslim jihadists took note and rebelled, turning to the Quran's "sword verses" to justify their war of revenge on the Western infidels even if those verses were radical interpretations not endorsed by most of the faithful.

Historically, Omar knew acts of violence were not specific just to Muslims. The Mongols had used them to great effect in the thirteenth century to conquer lands stretching from the Pacific to the Mediterranean, massacring entire towns that refused to surrender. According to the Bible, the ancient Israelites did the same in their conquest of Canaan. Later, Israeli religious zealots repeated the same atrocities when they distorted biblical verses to brutally expel the indigenous population from their land. And those Christian soldiers who believed they were fighting a holy crusade in Iraq, as proclaimed by their president? What was one to make of them and their misguided beliefs?

It was in the initial days of the US invasion of Iraq, when the American officials deliberately ordered the dismantlement of the Iraqi army to ignite conflicting polarities within Iraq's Shiite and Sunni communities, that Omar began to pay closer attention to the news. When the inter-religious war spread from Iraq to Syria during his second year at the University of Michigan in Ann Arbor as an engineering major, secret chat groups started popping up, motivating young Sunni men to come fight the infidels.

That was when Omar knew he could no longer ignore the carnage. He had a responsibility to respond to Allah's call, especially since it was a war directed against Shiite infidels, the ones who had killed his father and raped his mother. When an online televangelist from Saudi Arabia urged these men to "grind the flesh" of the Shiites and "feed it to the dogs," his message appealed to Omar. It had all seemed straightforward at the time. Without weighing the consequences of his actions, he abandoned his studies, changed his name to Omar to protect his mother, and responded to the call. He was referred to a recruiter on an online chatgroup and, within weeks, was issued a passport and plane ticket.

He had been six years old when he fled Iraq after the American invasion. This was a time when Shiite militiamen roamed undeterred through Baghdad's Sunni neighborhoods, and young boys watched innocent men being slaughtered, his father among them. Despite the passing of years, his grown man's heart still carried a deep vengeful hatred for Shiites.

His Iraqi-American mother from Dearborn had met his father on a family visit to Baghdad. They married and settled down in what was then a thriving, cosmopolitan city, he a well-paid engineer and she a psychologist. Under the American occupation, when the city descended into unimaginable horror and the killing spree continued with unabated force, his mother made the painful decision to abandon Baghdad for Dearborn where she had relatives.

Omar was nudged back from his musing as Abbas continued explaining the recruits' requirements. "Once you've completed your religious education, you'll move on to a six-month, military-style training course."

"That's a long time," Omar complained. "During my stay in Saudi Arabia, I underwent a grueling jihadist training camp. It was hotter than hell, with unbearably long hours endlessly repeating the same exercises and drills. By the end, I knew I never wanted to experience that again, and now you're telling me I must endure the same kind of torture?"

"If you'd volunteered for the US military, you'd have had to perform the same requirements."

"I'd never have done anything so foolish. Maybe I'm not making myself clear, Abbas. I don't want to be a fighter. I saw enough war during my two years in Homs. Many of my men were killed or rendered disabled for lack of adequate treatment."

Omar had done his research on ISIS, and despite what Abbas claimed, he knew that not all its members were obliged to become fighters. Some were tasked with office and administrative work, while others were placed in factories as laborers. So why couldn't he and Hassan work in media and recruitment?

"I know there are many honorable ways to serve Allah," Omar insisted. "I want to do my part by using my skills. And Hassan, here…" he pointed at him, still fast asleep, "…he's a highly talented recruiter. Why can't we be allowed to do what we do best?"

When Omar arrived in Syria in 2011, he was put in charge of al Nusra's media center in Homs, a critically important job during the Syrian army's siege of the Old City. It was urgent that his team relay the message to the outside world that an evil government under

Bashar Assad was oppressing a heroic civilian population, and that Western-backed rebels were fending off the army's onslaught. Perception was crucial.

There were few foreign journalists anywhere in Syria due to visa restrictions, and even fewer in Homs, aside from the starry-eyed Mary O'Brien, whom Omar had smuggled in through the city's water sewage system to be his spokesperson. Her willingness to report al Nusra's version of events enabled Omar and his crew to run a highly sophisticated media operation, proffering immediate coverage of every incident thanks to compelling and carefully selected YouTube footage. Though his rendition of events was heavily biased, Omar was both surprised and relieved to see his narrative so readily and naively regurgitated. But then, that was what high-quality propaganda was supposed to do.

Omar's disinformation campaign became an even more effective tool when a young, bearded, twenty-year-old Somalian immigrant from Minneapolis, Minnesota by the name of Hassan joined his team as a recruitment specialist. Hassan came to Omar's attention when he sought Omar's advice about persistent diarrhea, a common affliction for newcomers not used to drinking unfiltered water and eating unwashed, raw food. It was not a subject most men felt comfortable discussing, but Hassan was different. He was affable and tender in the way he addressed Omar, and he felt an immediate affinity with him.

Omar admired the men under his command for their bravery and willingness to take up arms. Yet, he was unable to connect with them socially and was ashamed he could not match their battlefront bravery. Omar found Hassan to be a tender and vulnerable companion who had answered the call to serve Allah but shouldn't have, because, like Omar, he wasn't by nature capable of killing another human being. Gazing at nothing special from his bus window, Omar smiled as he recalled their first conversation.

"How did you end up here, Hassan? You're not tall, and you don't look particularly strong, and like me you'd be of no use to anyone on the battlefield."

Hassan laughed freely. "When I told the recruiter that same thing, he insisted I only needed to be a well-rounded believer." When Hassan began to fail his classes at university, his father threatened to take away his social privileges, but it was too late. Hassan had already decided he hated both school and his father's strict rules. He felt trapped, and online private chat groups became his lifeline. He spent entire days reading updates about the conflict, and soon he was getting messages from fighters encouraging him to come to Syria. He was put in contact with a man who arranged everything, including a passport and money—as had been done for Omar—and eventually Hassan hooked up with other recruits on the Turkish-Syrian border.

Omar remembered discreetly asking if Hassan had left a wife or girlfriend behind. When Hassan shook his head shyly, Omar was pleased. If Hassan had asked Omar the same question, he would have said yes, his mother, whom he had betrayed. *God have mercy on my soul*, he thought.

Over the following months, he and Omar worked alongside each other. In front of others, they showed nothing more than a professional relationship. It was only when Omar's men went to their families at night and the two of them were alone that he and Hassan began to explore their relationship intimately. It was the happiest of times for Omar. He finally had someone to talk to, sometimes late into the night. Neither of them felt it was unnatural, a gentle caress slowly turning into a more physical display of affection. And then there was no turning back.

"You're right, Omar," Abbas said, nodding. "There are many ways to serve Allah, but when it comes to ISIS, I'm afraid there are agreed-upon procedures and practices that must be followed. You see, ISIS didn't search you out for your skills. You and your friend joined of your own free will, so according to our policy, you must be treated like the others and undergo its training requirements. After you've completed all your assignments, the hierarchy will decide where you and your friend will be most useful. In the end, maybe you'll be assigned to the media and recruitment departments, but I'm not in a position to promise you such a thing."

"What is your position, then?"

"I help transition young recruits like you through the program."

"What does the military training involve?" Omar asked.

"You'll be taught how to handle a variety of weapons, from a simple handgun to rifles to RPGs. Once you've gotten good at those skills, you'll learn how to launch surface-to-air missiles and rocket launchers."

Omar had rolled his eyes and shaken his head. He knew it highly unlikely he would advance beyond a handgun or rifle. "After we're put through a full year's worth of training," he'd asked, "will we finally be declared full-fledged ISIS members?"

"Aside from a few other requisites in the second year, that's pretty much it. And those other skills aren't something you have to worry about right now. Just concentrate on the coming year. Don't worry, I'll be by your side the entire time and offer help whenever you need it. That's my job."

All these months later, Omar could still see Abbas's cynical smile as he blatantly lied to his face.

"What do you know about Baghdadi and ISIS?" Omar had asked.

He had been told Baghdadi had become radicalized while he was a prisoner in the US-run Camp Bucca in Iraq. According to Abbas, that was not true. Baghdadi was a civilian detainee who never got tortured, unlike so many men from Saddam's former military and security units. Abbas referred to Camp Bucca as The Academy where prisoners were waterboarded, along with other unspeakable atrocities, and hated the Americans for what they had done to them. As a result, most prisoners joined al Qaeda in Iraq after their release, then ISIS.

Baghdadi joined, too, but only after he had bided enough time to assume leadership and declare himself Caliph. Many people believed Baghdadi owed his success to the men who served in Saddam's military. Whether their allegiance to Baghdadi was won or coerced, Abbas seemed to insinuate it was the latter. Omar wondered if it mattered. The result was the birth of ISIS and its Caliphate.

Baghdadi had gone from declaring the formation of ISIS to establishing his Caliphate in Raqqa and calling himself Caliph.

"How did that happen so quickly?" Omar had asked.

From his research, he knew that Raqqa was a city of about three hundred thousand people. It sat on the northeastern bank of the Euphrates River, ninety-nine miles from the Iraqi border. *A sizable population*, Omar thought, *yet so easily swallowed up by ISIS. How was that possible?*

"Let's see. Where to begin…" Abbas explained that once Baghdadi got established in Raqqa, his men went about training ten- to twelve-year-old boys to carry out clandestine suicide bombing missions, which not only terrorized the local population but also the police who promptly abandoned their posts and left the city wide open for ISIS to move in and establish itself.

Curious about this, Omar asked, "Why would a youngster agree to do such things? These are hideous acts of savagery."

"These kids have lived all their lives in a war zone. Their parents, siblings and friends have all been killed. They have no one left. They're not only traumatized but many of them are probably psychopaths and don't care if they live or die, so they're fodder for us to use when we need suicide bombers."

Omar thought it cruel of Abbas to refer to those young boys as no more than human flesh to be used as live bombs. Surely, ISIS had put them through some hideous indoctrination program to make them do such things. Omar had suffered war trauma, and he was not a psychopath. Or was he? Wasn't he on his way to becoming an ISIS member? What did that say about him and his state of mind? He knew he still suffered from PTSD and recurring nightmares, but that didn't make him want to put on a suicide belt and blow himself up.

Yes, he still had his mother, and those suicide kids had no one, but Omar's nightmares were awful. In them, he was dragged from his home and made to stand in front of his father, who was kneeling on the ground with a gun pointed at his head. In these dreams, he saw his father's terrified eyes looking up at him, tears streaming down his cheeks, and he watched helplessly.

And after his father had been shot, his brain matter and blood had splattered across Omar's face, clothes, bare legs and shoes. He had run into the house to seek comfort from his mother only to discover one of the Shiite militiamen raping her as she screamed in horror.

Rather than accusing Abbas of lying, Omar thought it wiser to keep asking questions to keep the conversation going. There were still many miles to go before they reached Raqqa.

"How did the people in Raqqa feel about ISIS encroaching on their city?"

According to Abbas, the aim, however deceptive, was to win over the people. The first thing ISIS did when it moved in was repair roads, stock grocery stores, open more hospitals and offer food and free medical care. Only when they had won over the locals did ISIS start to impose their rules. If anyone did something they did not like, they waterboarded them in the town square. If a woman wasn't wearing her *hijab,* they flogged her. If someone was caught stealing, they cut off their hand.

"I bet the people fell in line after seeing such atrocities," said Omar.

"Yes, ISIS was right when it said atrocities worked. No one in Raqqa dared open their mouth after that. ISIS then went on to implement a new conscription law. Every family had to agree to hand over one of their sons to ISIS for training. The remaining children were ordered to attend an ISIS-run school. They forbade smoking, too, even though the ISIS hierarchy smoked."

"Do as I say, not as I do," commented Omar.

Abbas leaned in toward him and whispered. "You want to hear the latest? It's another of those rules that apply to everyone else. A member of ISIS's top command just got caught having sex with a fifteen-year-old boy. ISIS claims homosexuality is forbidden and punishable by death, yet it appears there's a double standard when it comes to the ISIS higher-ups."

Omar knew the tradition of adult males engaging in sexual pleasure with pre-pubescent boys had existed well before the creation of Islam.

While commonplace, it was still not easily accepted in most cultures and was why he and Hassan would need to be extremely careful. ISIS punished gay men by throwing them off tall buildings, and if they were not dead by the time they hit the ground, they were stoned to death. All of which would have made living in a tent sweating in the heat and freezing in the winter in Idlib, as Hassan had suggested, a far better alternative than joining ISIS. If only he had listened to Hassan and hopped on that bus for Idlib in northwestern Syria.

The best part about Raqqa, according to Abbas, was an abundance of women to choose from since all unmarried women were required to marry ISIS fighters, a law imposed on the women of Raqqa. If forced to marry to prove his manhood, Omar would be as respectful as possible to any woman. His mother had been doting and loving yet intolerant of any sign of disrespectful behavior. He adored the woman who had raised him single-handedly and had worked long hours to provide him with a comfortable life. In homage to her, he would never mistreat a woman.

Abbas explained the religious and military training requirements that recruits were obliged to complete, but he failed to mention the final and most important stage in their training, which he and Hassan only learned about when they met the camp commander face-to-face.

"What initiation rites?" Omar had asked.

"Executions and beheadings."

Omar and Hassan had exchanged anxious glances.

"You mean put a gun to a person's head and kill him?"

As the officer spoke, Omar could hear Andrew's voice in his head. *Under all that gruffness, you're a softy, Omar. You couldn't kill anyone.*

"What if we don't want to be fighters and kill people?" Omar had asked. "We were told we could serve Allah in other ways."

"Yes, there are such positions available," said the commander, "but they're reserved for special cases."

Without spelling it out, Omar understood this to mean that people with clout and money could buy their way out of certain obligations, and neither he nor Hassan had either. The commander insisted that executions played a vital role in the life of ISIS. Not only did they intimidate the enemy, they demonstrated a commitment to ISIS and its goals. It was only under certain circumstances that ISIS needed to call attention to itself with something as shocking as a beheading, a form of execution all ISIS members were expected to perfect as part of their training.

This shocking news was followed by an order to hand over their passports for safekeeping, which Omar understood to mean that he and Hassan were now essentially ISIS captives, albeit well-paid at a thousand dollars per month. Additional benefits included supervised internet access, food, lodging, and women for their sexual pleasures.

When they were alone, Hassan ripped into Omar for getting him into this mess while Omar, feebly trying to apologize, promised to find a way out.

"From the fucking middle of nowhere and without our passports," Hassan had complained. "Are you delusional?"

"I've heard of people escaping. With the kind of money we'll be earning, we'll have enough cash to pay our way out of this mess… and get new passports. Trust me."

"Trust you?" Hassan shouted. "Never again. And if I haven't already told you I hate you for getting me into this mess, I'm telling you now."

* * *

In his mind's eye, the vast, hostile Syrian desert Omar saw from his bus window was the reflection of what he had become and what he had lost—possibly the very essence of his humanity. By beheading Frans, he had reduced himself to nothing more than a hollowed shell, or maybe something as grotesque as the bloated, rotting corpse of the dead camel he had just seen lying along the road.

Despondent, he mused at the irony of his situation. He and his al Nusra team had fought Assad's army for two years while serving American interests. And now, as an ISIS fighter, he would again be working for the same power that had initially trained and equipped him.

CHAPTER THREE

Mary and Sonia arrived in Damascus late morning. Their taxi dropped them off at the gates of Bab Touma, the entrance to the Christian Quarter of the Old City, the neighborhood closest to Douma, the rebel-held suburb in Eastern Ghouta. It was also the site of the sarin gas attack in August 2013. Mary grabbed her carry-on from the taxi. As she waited for Sonia to do the same, she stood transfixed, as she did every visit, by the intense commotion of one of the oldest continuously inhabited cities on the planet. This was where the mighty Hittites, Assyrians, Babylonians and Greeks had once walked, where both the muezzin in his minaret and the peal of church bells called their faithful to prayer, where car radios blared guttural, passionate Arabic songs and everywhere people indulged in idle chitchat while street vendors shouted out their wares and the smell of spit-fire grilled chicken from a nearby café reminded Mary how famished she was.

As she followed Sonia through the maze of ancient souks and passed by merchants trading in everything from gold jewelry to brass trays, tiles, Persian carpets and Damascene inlaid mother-of-pearl furniture, she rubbed her hand along the stone walls and imagined the ancient smells of cedar, musk and myrrh. She pictured traders selling their pottery and bronze art and women in brightly colored silk garments haggling over which gold and silver trinkets to buy.

"You're upset, aren't you," Mary called out to Sonia ahead of her, "because I told John we'd be in Damascus."

"Yes," Sonia replied without turning around.

"But why?" Mary asked when she'd caught up with her friend.

"Because I don't trust him."

Mary had met John Murphy, security officer to Ambassador Robert Jenkins, a year before at a luncheon hosted by Nadia Khoury to celebrate Dr. Andrew Sullivan's release from captivity in Homs. Omar had kidnapped Andrew from Beirut the previous year, sneaked him into Syria, and forced him to run a medical clinic for al Nusra during the Syrian Army's siege of the Old City.

Just as dessert was being served, and to the surprise of everyone present, the ambassador had suddenly fallen forward on the table. Initially, no one suspected foul play. It was only when they saw the blood pour from his head that they realized he had been assassinated.

"John and I corresponded this past year," Mary said to Sonia. "You knew that, so why the fuss if I told him we were coming to Damascus? He was upset about his boss's assassination and wanted someone to talk to. I was there, and just as shocked by the murder."

"You make him sound like some innocent schoolboy. The man's security with top-level clearance, Mary. He's trained to expect such things."

"This assassination was personal for him. He had shadowed Jenkins twenty-four-seven. He genuinely liked the man and felt guilty that he'd been killed on his watch."

"I'm just advising caution. We've put ourselves into a very dangerous situation, and I don't think it prudent to open yourself up to someone until you know which side he's on. Jenkins was CIA. Likely John is too."

"You don't know that."

"My dear Mary, you may be well versed on Middle East politics now, but you're still a neophyte when it comes to detecting spies and covert ops, or for that matter, choosing men."

Mary gave her a startled look. "Where do you, of all people, come off saying such a thing? You've slept with more men than I can count."

"You admitted as much, too, when we first met."

"Christ, those mistakes were made long before I met Joe. You do recall that we were a thing?"

"Yes, you were, but he was an exceptional human being, and if I hadn't already fallen in love with Fouad, I'd have snagged him long before you came along."

"Aren't you the bitch."

They both burst into laughter.

"Look, I just want your eyes wide open, that's all. We're two women researching a messy situation in a dirty war in the Middle East, and our findings could get us into a lot of trouble."

"Should that deter us?"

"Certainly not, but it requires us to be suspicious of everyone, and that includes John. I hope you didn't tell him where we'd be staying."

"Afraid I did. And he's probably already there waiting for us."

There were several boutique hotels scattered about the Old City, but Sonia had decided on the Shahbandar Palace Hotel on Qeimariyeh Street. Mary pushed open the massive front door and stepped inside to discover an anteroom covered with Old Damascene tiles in typical Arabesque patterns—clusters of fruits, tendrils of vines, and leaves—all in vivid cobalt blue, deep turquoise and sage green. When she walked into the former courtyard-turned-hotel lobby, she discovered a collage of white and black marble with high arched alcoves, red cushioned divans, gurgling fountains etched with Arabic motifs, and above it all, a retractable glass ceiling.

As she glanced around, she saw John approaching her.

"Welcome to Damascus, Mary," he said, taking her luggage from her hand and kissing her cheek. "How nice to see you again."

She had forgotten how intense his blue eyes were and that his dark brown hair was wavy and untamed in a sexy kind of way. And, of course, it mattered that he was Irish like her and that his self-confident manner and ready smile reminded her of her father, a man she greatly admired for his social graces. She and John had both grown up in

Washington, DC, attended elite high schools in the same northwest neighborhood, and had probably attended the same sporting events. Mary assumed their politics were different. He, by profession, was probably an interventionist. She, quite the opposite, having experienced war first-hand and seen what it did to people and their lives. Did such differences make them likely foes, as Sonia had suggested? Mary intended to find out.

"Thank you, John." As she turned, she said, "surely you remember my friend, Sonia Rizk."

"Yes, of course," he said, extending his hand. "How nice to see you again."

"I'm surprised you're still in Damascus. Your ambassador died a year ago."

"His death created a bureaucratic nightmare across two borders. There were official inquiries both here and in Lebanon."

"Standard protocol since he died on Lebanese territory," Sonia said.

"I accompanied his body to Boston, and his girlfriend, Nadia, flew in for his funeral, which ended up being a huge affair with dozens of dignitaries in attendance. Quite the gathering, but then he and his father had both served under several administrations. Robert's father was inconsolable, poor man. Thankfully, Nadia was there to comfort him. They spent hours taking walks, sitting in the garden and talking about Robert and his work. By the time Nadia and I left, he seemed much calmer, even eager to begin writing the book he and Robert were to have written together. I've no doubt it was Nadia who encouraged him. She knew how eager Robert had been to begin the project."

Sonia interrupted John.

"Did you know Nadia and Andrew had recently married?"

"No, I didn't."

Mary noticed his puzzled expression, but then perhaps he was unaware of their long-standing relationship. It was not something the ambassador would have necessarily shared with John since he and Nadia were romantically involved.

"Sonia, you wanted to know why I was still here," John said. "The embassy's closed but the consular office is open for visa applications. They're short-staffed, and Washington gave me the green light to stay."

"You don't seem eager to get back to the States. And yet, as I recall, you were going to resign and run the ambassador's senatorial campaign."

"That was then, and truth be told, I love it here. In fact, I was due to leave today for Petra and Aqaba in Jordan, but when Mary told me you were coming, I delayed my departure. Turning to Mary, he said, "And I'm awfully glad I did."

"We were just about to check in and then go to lunch," Mary said. "Would you care to join us?"

"With pleasure. It's not every day I get to escort two beautiful women around Damascus."

A tired cliché, Mary thought, *but maybe he meant it.*

To reach the restaurant from their hotel, they chose to walk through the al Hamidiyah souk, the most ancient indoor souk in the world. Its main thoroughfare was lined with clothes emporiums and handicraft shops, its narrow side streets crowded with stalls selling everything from spices and dried fruits to gold jewelry, cashmere and silks. Between the main entrance and the Omayyad Mosque at the opposite end was the famous Bakdash ice cream parlor, which had made its delicacy since 1885 from the roots of orchids and orange blossoms. Even more ancient was Straight Street, the old *decumanus maximus*, or main Roman Road, which ran east to west through the Old City and where, under a massive Roman arch on the west end, they found Naranji, a favorite Damascene restaurant.

It was the end of lunch rush hour, so the maître d'gave them the choice of where to sit. There was an open-air balcony on the second floor that overlooked Straight Street, but after the experience of watching the ambassador get shot at the restaurant on the Corniche in Beirut, Mary remained cautious. How strange to hear John say the same thing, insisting they choose a corner on the street level where they could see both entrance and exit. On one side of the restaurant, tall arched windows faced Straight Street, allowing the curious a chance to glance inside while giving the leery diner the advantage of eyeing any suspicious outside activity. The walls were white, as were the table linens dressing each table.

Once seated, the three of them silently perused the menu until Mary said, "Do you mind if we order right away? I'm about to faint from hunger, and I know what I want." She put up her hand to call the waiter. "A chicken shawarma and a cold beer, please."

"That sounds delicious. I'll have the same," said John and Sonia at the same time. They laughed at their silliness.

"You two were just in Homs. What were you doing there?"

"Investigating the beheading of a Jesuit priest by the name of Father Frans."

John sat forward in his chair. "I read about his horrific death. You knew him?"

"For many years," Sonia said. "He was a dear friend. Mary and I stayed with him during the army's siege of the Old City."

"Do you have any idea who killed him?"

"According to eyewitnesses who saw the two assailants," Sonia said quietly, "Frans knew his killer, and that could have only been the man who goes by the name of Omar. I first met him in Daraa in 2011 when the Syrian uprising began."

"And I know Omar too," Mary said. "At my editor's insistence, I embedded with his al Nusra team and helped him run a successful propaganda campaign against Bashar Assad."

Sonia raised a finger and said, "When Omar didn't leave Homs for Idlib with his men after the siege ended, we concluded he'd fled to Raqqa to join ISIS—the only other place he could have gone. Otherwise, he would have risked being captured by the Syrian Army and remanded to US custody."

"What else do you know about him?"

"He's an Iraqi American. His father was killed when he was six. His mother had family in Dearborn, Michigan, so they moved there."

"What do you plan to do with this information?" John asked.

"Hand it over to the Syrian authorities," Mary said.

"Why go through the Syrians? Give *me* whatever information you have. I'll handle his transfer to US authorities and save you the trouble."

"Thanks, but that won't be necessary," Mary said. "We'll have Yakob take care of it."

"Who's Yakob?"

"A colonel in the Syrian Army who saved our lives during the siege," Mary said, glancing at Sonia's nod of approval.

"As you wish."

When their waiter arrived with their orders, a momentary calm fell over the table. Each of them was content to savor the flavor of grilled chicken served in a tahini-garlic sauce, dressed with pickled vegetables and wrapped in pita bread.

"This is so good," Mary said, dabbing the sauce from her mouth with her napkin. She picked up her bottle of beer and offered a toast. "*Sahha.*"

"You speak Arabic?" John asked.

"I wish."

"Mary told me that you not only speak Arabic but read and write it," Sonia said. "That's impressive. It's not an easy language to learn."

"I like languages—always have. I picked up Arabic in college, but when I got accepted into the foreign service, I was put into a special language program."

"Something else about Omar," Sonia said, "Before he joined ISIS, he was part of al Nusra, one of the so-called moderate rebel groups financed and armed by the US and its regional allies."

"Says who?" John asked.

"Says anyone who's done their homework," Sonia said. "Don't try to defend what the West and its allies are doing here, John. Your ambassador had it figured out. It's probably what got him killed."

"Are you suggesting it was the American government who killed him?"

"I have no proof, but the Americans are high on my list of suspects, as are the Lebanese, the Syrians, the Saudis, the Israelis and the CIA."

"Everyone on your list has dirty hands," John said. "Going back a century, it was the Brits and the French who carved up the Middle East with their Sykes-Picot Agreement for their own political gains. Now, it's the Americans and their regional allies tearing it all apart."

"Has your government issued an official statement about the Jenkins assassination?" Sonia asked.

"There was a total blackout after his death."

"So there was no investigation?" she asked.

"By the Syrian and Lebanese governments, yes. Both the FBI and the CIA came here—the protocol when someone of Jenkins' stature is killed abroad. They asked me some mundane questions, but they didn't seem interested in any of the details surrounding his death. I was the only person from the embassy who had driven him from Damascus to Beirut that day. I had been with him when he died and had worked closely with him every day. Their questions didn't make any sense until I realized they hadn't come to investigate a murder. They had come to close the case."

"That makes no sense," Sonia said. "Who were they protecting? Surely not the Syrians."

"It would have been the perfect opportunity to blame Hezbollah, and yet they didn't do that either," Mary said. "Why not, I wonder."

"I don't know."

"What do you mean, you don't know?" insisted Sonia. "You throw us some crumbs about an investigation that went nowhere, and then you pretend you don't know anything. You speak Arabic, and considering your specialized training, I assume you learned classical, not colloquial, Arabic, which means you understand everything that's going on regionally. So please don't sit here and tell us you know nothing... when in fact, you do."

John interrupted. "Okay—I knew Jenkins had committed crimes in Lebanon and that the Lebanese government would have wanted to see him stand trial. But the Lebanese didn't kill him."

"What makes you so sure?" Mary asked.

"I have to agree with John," Sonia said. "It's not something they would have done."

"How do you know that?" Mary asked.

"They're more apt to let someone else come in and do the job."

"You know that for a fact?" Mary asked.

"Just speculating."

Mary wondered if Sonia had inside information from her boyfriend Fouad Nasr, Deputy Director of Lebanon's Internal Security Services. Or maybe Sonia was trying to push John into admitting something he shouldn't.

"To set the record straight, John," said Sonia, "Jenkins committed more than just a few crimes in Lebanon. There was the murder of a top Shiite cleric and the attempted assassination of a high-level Hezbollah official. The explosion killed fifty-five people and only wounded him. Jenkins was his government's number two man in Iraq in charge of recruiting and training terrorist units from Turkey, Jordan, Saudi Arabia and Libya. Quite a sordid list of crimes, not to mention the assassination of Syria's former intelligence czar."

"Which means the Syrians had a legitimate reason to want him dead," Mary said.

"Bashar's much too intelligent to do something so stupid as murdering an American ambassador," Sonia said.

John sat with his elbows on the table glancing across at Mary. "I think we've pretty much surmised that everyone in the region has something to hide, which means they're all guilty of one crime or another."

"That's the stuff of spy novels," Sonia said. "Is that the club you belong to?"

"No, and not because I didn't try to join."

"Well, there's a straightforward answer if it's true."

"Look, I knew what the ambassador was doing here. I was with him when he met with the rebel leaders of al Nusra. On orders from Washington, he gave them the green light to bring down Assad, but it wasn't my job to interfere."

"Do you always do what you're told?" Mary asked.

"No," John said, smiling at her and evading any more questions by asking one of his own. "Now tell me why you two are in Damascus. This isn't the safest place to be right now."

"Our business concerns the chemical weapons attack that took place in Douma in Eastern Ghouta back in August 2013," Mary said. "An OPCW official is giving a press conference later this afternoon to announce their findings. We plan to be there. You're welcome to join us."

"I'm afraid I can't. I have a few things to clear up at the embassy before I leave town. Was that August attack the first sarin gas attack?"

"No," Mary said, "there was an attack five months earlier in a town called Khan al-Asal near Aleppo. The rebels killed twelve Syrian soldiers with sarin gas, but it was the Ghouta attack that caused the greatest fury in Washington."

"That's when Obama wanted to bomb Damascus," Sonia explained, "even when his director of national intelligence warned him that his case against Assad wasn't a slam dunk. Surely you already know this, John."

"I'm not always privy to what happens in Washington."

"Well then, listen up," Mary said. "Obama had already boxed himself in with his 'red line' policy. This was essentially an open invitation to rebel groups to carry out a false flag operation. I know how easy it is to establish a successful public relations campaign, especially if it demonizes Assad. And I know that anyone on social media can post photos of so-called victims breathing into oxygen masks. Simply put, the opposition has a monopoly on the flow of information because there are so few foreign journalists on the ground to challenge false allegations."

Mary was on a roll. "And when the 2013 attack happened, the president was apparently pressured not only by staff but by Israel, Saudi Arabia and the UAE, proponents of regime change in Syria, to do something. In a hastily prepared intelligence report, he blamed the Syrian government for the attack."

Their waiter arrived to clear their dishes. "Would you like coffee or perhaps some dessert?"

John looked around the table and saw two nods for the first option. "Three coffees, please, and I'll have the check."

"Thank you, John," Mary said.

"The least I can do for allowing me to join you."

"General Martin Dempsey, Chairman of the Joint Chiefs of Staff, also agreed it wasn't a slam dunk," Mary said. "So did the UK's General Sir Peter Wall and the chief general of the Russian Army, Valery Gerasimov."

"How do you know all this?" John asked.

"Seymour Hersh wrote about it in his article in the London Review of Books. These three generals were friends. During their careers, they consulted one another. The sarin gas attack in Ghouta was an example of their collaborative efforts to steady the waters and right wrongs before something catastrophic happened."

John laughed out loud. "Hersh was mocked as a raving lunatic over that article, and not for the first time. Please tell me you aren't basing your findings on his research."

"Not at all," Mary insisted. "There's plenty of evidence that proves the rebels had chemical weapons and were using them."

Sonia nodded and said, "When Father Frans and I first met Omar in Daraa in March 2011, he confirmed that sarin gas supplies were being shipped to them from Libya. I'm surprised you know none of this, John. You and the ambassador were already in Syria at the time."

Mary cast a stern look at John and added, "And you just admitted you knew what the ambassador was up to."

"Apparently, there was a lot I wasn't privy to," John replied.

"But you knew about the Hersh article," Mary insisted.

"Knowing about the article and believing it as fact are two different things."

"Then allow us to enlighten you," Sonia said, taking over from Mary. "In June 2013, the Defense Intelligence Agency issued a warning that Turkey and Saudi-based chemical facilitators were attempting to obtain sarin precursors in bulk, likely for an anticipated large-scale production effort in Syria. Fortunately for Assad, Obama got no support for his intended military strike on Syrian infrastructure from the UK... or from members of his own Congress."

Mary continued the history lesson. "This prompted Sergey Lavrov, the Russian foreign minister, to get Assad to agree to dispose of his entire stock of chemical weapons under the supervision of the OPCW. By doing so, Lavrov let Obama save face.

"It was a calculated but brilliant move on Lavrov's part. He not only boosted Russia's image on the world stage, but he also helped Assad unload his stockpile of chemical weapons and ward off a US-led military strike. It was a rare example of how easy it is to de-escalate tensions if the will is there. It's not every day we see such statesmanship."

"Ladies," John said, raising his hands as if in surrender. "I commend you on your research. It's quite thorough and seems irrefutable."

The coffee arrived along with a platter of fruit. They served themselves from a selection of watermelon, apricots and cherries.

Between bites, Mary continued. "Shortly after the chemical weapons were collected, Sir Peter Wall took a sample to Porton Down, a science park in Wiltshire, England, where chemists sampled the sarin gas from Assad's stockpile and found it didn't match the sarin used in Ghouta in August 2013. It turns out that al Nusra had a stockpile of the precursor to sarin gas all along. General Dempsey knew it and informed Obama, but the president chose not to go public with these findings."

"That's unsettling," John said. "I would have thought better of the man."

"What's even more disturbing is that Obama never cleared Assad's name," Sonia said. "He let that bloody libel remain on the public record."

Mary took note that John made no comment, then looked at her watch and at Sonia. "We'd better leave if we want to get to the conference hall in time."

"Allow me to accompany you part of the way," John offered.

"Of course," Mary said.

When they neared the hall, John stopped rather abruptly and said, "Goodbye, ladies. I enjoyed our visit, but I must leave you here. Best of luck with your investigation." And he walked off.

"That was a rather odd parting, wasn't it?" Mary said as she watched John disappear into the crowd.

"What did you expect? We showed him up."

Mary nodded. "Yes, we did."

* * *

Mary followed Sonia into the auditorium. The hall was filling up with other foreign and domestic journalists as well as foreign embassy staffers, some of whom Sonia recognized from years of covering wars and regional upheavals. Also attending were the obligatory Syrian military intelligence agents, always present during such gatherings. Undeterred, they walked past them and grabbed two front-row seats.

Mary settled in and was about to type something into her iPhone when she felt a tap on her shoulder. Thinking it was a fellow journalist, she turned to discover Fouad in the seat behind her.

"I thought I'd surprise you and Sonia," Fouad said. "I was in Damascus on business, and I remembered the conference."

Okay, Mary reasoned, *it was easy enough for Fouad in his official capacity with driver to cross the Lebanese/Syrian border hassle-free and be in Damascus in less than two hours, but Sonia had spoken to him last night from Homs, and he had said nothing about coming. What made him change his mind?*

The hall fell silent as a tall, gray-haired gentleman in a suit walked up to the podium. Fernando Lopez had been the former Argentinian ambassador to Syria in the mid-nineties. During his career in multilateral diplomacy, he had also served as the Permanent Representative of Argentina to the United Nations. Addressing his audience in English, he began.

"Good afternoon, ladies and gentlemen. My name is Fernando Lopez. I'm Director General of the Organization for the Prevention of Chemical Weapons, and as such it is my job to review inspection reports, ensure confidentiality of sensitive information provided by member states and ensure effective governance and leadership. In that capacity, I'm here today to present the results of a thorough investigation into the sarin chemical attack that took place in Douma in the Ghouta province on the outskirts of Damascus in August 2013."

He stopped awkwardly, referred to his notes, then continued.

"According to our findings, significant quantities of sarin were used in a well-planned, indiscriminate attack targeting civilian-inhabited areas and causing mass casualties. The available evidence concerning the nature, quality and quantity of the agents used in the attack on August 21, 2013, indicates that the perpetrators likely had access to the chemical weapons stockpile of the Syrian military plus the expertise and equipment necessary to safely manipulate large amounts of chemical agents. The OPCW is confident in the robustness of its scientific work and the integrity of its investigation into the Douma attack. I realize there are a lot of questions concerning the final report, and I would be happy to take any questions you may have."

Mary raised her hand, earning a nod from Lopez. She spoke loudly so all could hear her question. "Sir, laboratories working with the OPCW compared samples taken by members of your UN inspection team after the August attack to the chemical weapons handed over by the Syrian government for destruction in 2014. They did not match the chemical weapons found in the Syrian arsenal. Because of this new evidence, some of your own inspectors are now calling into question the OPCW's official findings. Can you comment, please?"

Lopez nodded and said, "Most of the analytical work, including some seventy samples used to produce this final report, took place in the last six months when the dissenting inspectors were no longer part of the Douma fact-finding mission. The Scientific Advisory Board of the OPCW concluded that the original inspectors had relied on incomplete information when they produced their findings."

"Sir," Mary insisted, "unless the OPCW somehow failed to report dozens of analyzed samples, the claim of seventy samples appears to be an inflated number. Your final report shows that just forty-four samples were analyzed throughout the entire probe, and reports on only thirteen of those samples made it into the final report. And this was after the dissenting inspectors were out of the picture. If the OPCW somehow failed to report dozens of analyzed samples until now, wouldn't that suggest a false picture of the final report?"

Lopez appeared irritated as he said, "The power to revisit the results, or question any discrepancies, is now in the hands of the Executive Council, the rotating group of forty-one member states who govern the OPCW. As director general, I have no authority to reopen this investigation to discover if, in fact, an error did occur."

"Sir, are you suggesting you would have no objections to reopening the investigation?"

"It is not uncommon for the Scientific Board to agree to a review of OPCW inspectors' findings or even a return to the scene of a chemical gas attack."

Mary spoke quickly so as to not be interrupted by another journalist. "It is my understanding, sir, that no one is suggesting that. Those questioning the final report are simply asking the OPCW to hear from the Douma probe's own inspectors, and address their complaints, including what they consider to be the doctoring of the mission's original report."

Another hand shot up, and Mary recognized it belonged to the reporter from Agence France-Presse, who said, "Sir, Carla Del Ponte, head of the UN independent commission of inquiry on Syria, oversaw an investigation into a sarin gas attack that took place in May of 2013. They collected testimony from doctors and victims that strongly suggested it was the opposition, not the Syrian government, who had used the sarin gas. Doesn't that throw into question the results of your investigation, or at the very least suggest the possibility that the Assad government did not use sarin gas?"

Lopez looked like he wanted to be somewhere else as he answered, "In that particular instance, there was no irrefutable evidence—which is what we base our findings on—to suggest it was the opposition forces who used sarin gas."

"I understand that, sir," the French reporter said, "and I agree that the idea has been promoted by both the Syrian and Russian governments suggesting there was some political bias, but the inspectors who were sidelined are completely non-political scientists. They've worked for the OPCW for years and feel dismayed that their professional conclusions in the final report were set aside to favor the agenda of certain states. They said, and I quote, 'Most of the Douma team felt the two reports, the Interim and the Final Report, were scientifically impoverished, procedurally irregular and possibly fraudulent. Our request for an internal investigation was refused, and every other attempt to raise our concerns has been stonewalled.'"

Another hand shot up. Mary recognized the Agência Brasil reporter.

"Sir, I'd like to follow up on what my colleague from AFP just said. An esteemed diplomat from my country—in fact, he was the first director general of the OPCW, Jose Boustani—recently tried to defend both the integrity of the OPCW and the dissenting inspectors. He was prevented from doing so in a public forum. Since he was not even allowed to ask questions, let me ask you, Mr. Director General, why you never met personally with the dissenting inspectors or with the entire Douma team who went to Syria to investigate the chemical attack. Not only were the dissenters censored, but they were all replaced—except for one—by a core team of people who had never set foot in Douma."

"I was not responsible for many of those decisions," Lopez said.

"Maybe not, sir," the Brazilian continued, "but wouldn't you agree that it would have been far better—for the prestige of an organization that won the Nobel Peace Prize last year—to reopen the investigation, let the inspectors be heard, and let the public hear the evidence they felt was suppressed? Especially, sir, since it was John Bolton, National Security Adviser to President Trump, who had overseen the bombing of Syria in 2018— the same John Bolton who led a delegation to the OPCW headquarters and pressured the inspectors into reaching a conclusion that justified the bombing raid on Syria. In light of such findings, isn't it only right to show that the organization is capable of undoing something that had been wrongly done? I respectfully suggest that every inspector general has his own view on how the organization should be run, and I hope you can find a way to defend the OPCW from such political interference and restore its stellar reputation."

Lopez glanced around the auditorium and said, "Ladies and gentlemen, I think this is an appropriate place to conclude this afternoon's conference. Thank you for your comments and questions."

Before Fernando Lopez left the podium, Sonia turned to address Fouad, but he was no longer in his seat.

"That's odd," she said. "Where did he go?"

She and Mary stood and scanned the room until they saw Fouad in serious conversation with a man Sonia did not recognize. And then, as Mary was about to say something, Sonia saw John, who had claimed he could not attend the conference, talking to Muhammad Jolani, the leader of al Nusra.

This caught Sonia's attention. Jolani was the man she had seen being photographed alongside Senator John McCain when he visited northern Syria in May 2013—the same man who was reportedly on the CIA payroll even though the US State Department had declared him a designated global terrorist in 2013. Jolani was also a man who now ran an enclave for Islamic terrorists in Idlib in northwest Syria.

Unlike his appearance in the photo with the senator, Jolani had trimmed his beard and donned a suit for this occasion. Was that because Jolani was positioning himself as an influential force in Syria's future? Since what happened in Syria often affected events in Lebanon, this explain Fouad's presence, especially if he had been forewarned that Jolani would be there.

But why was John present? Where did he fit into this whole picture?

CHAPTER FOUR

Omar had decapitated the old priest and thereby proven his loyalty to ISIS. Still, Abbas had accused him of being sloppy. *A goat could have done a better job.*

Omar said nothing, but he spent the five-hour bus trip from Homs back to Raqqa counting ways he would take revenge on his minder, in each instance using the same knife he had used to decapitate Father Frans.

At various times during the trip, Abbas had tapped him on the shoulder trying to chat him up. Omar ignored him until finally Abbas said, "Don't take what I said back there so seriously. It didn't mean a thing."

Omar thought about that for a second. Was that an apology? Too late, if it was.

When the bus finally lumbered into Raqqa's city center and the passengers exited the bus, Omar remained seated. From behind him, Abbas zippered up his carry-on, pulled himself to a standing position and leaned into Omar's seat with a hand on his shoulder saying, "*Yallah,* let's go."

Omar shook off Abbas's hand.

"Suit yourself," Abbas replied and walked on. Omar, glaring at him, stroked the outline of the knife inside his carry-on. The last to disembark, he slung his bag over his shoulder and headed toward the apartment he shared with Hassan in a neighborhood east of downtown Raqqa.

This was a city of little renown other than for its loyalty to the Syrian government before the arrival of ISIS. It sat quietly along the northeastern banks of the Euphrates River. Its half-million residents—mostly Sunnis, former tribesmen and Bedouins—lived in nondescript, sandstone apartment buildings that lined litter-free, poplar-lined boulevards. These were simple people who worked in agriculture or at the local electric company.

The residents had probably assumed their predictable lives would continue, but then ISIS had moved in, and suddenly young men with long black beards and sweat-stained T-shirts and AK-47s started marching through their quiet neighborhoods imposing ISIS rules of conduct. After unexpected knocks on doors, apartments were inspected and anything deemed illegal like radios, televisions and computers were confiscated. The local cinemas and bookstores were closed, books thrown into the street and burned. Even more horrifying was the religious police force, an all-woman squad that subjected any female violator to a public thrashing for failing to cover her head, wear a full-length black coat, or for daring to wear makeup or nail polish.

Omar and Hassan shared a one-bedroom apartment on the second floor of a building located on a quiet street far from the city center, secluded enough to resist the grim changes Raqqa had begun to endure. It overlooked several unique, green-shuttered houses with gardens crowded with herbs, flowers, citrus and olive trees, some wide and tall enough to give shade to these small dwellings. They had probably been built at the turn of the twentieth century. On any given day, Omar could pull up the shades and open the window to bright sunlight. If the winds blew in their direction, he could enjoy the scent of citrus, marjoram, basil and Damascene roses in full bloom.

Omar turned the key to his apartment and entered. As was his habit, he dropped his bag near the front door and walked to the bedroom where he knew he'd find Hassan. Without the usual greeting in English to his Somalian lover, he threw himself on the bed next to Hassan's and sighed, rubbing his face with his hands.

"I did everything that bastard Abbas asked me to do," Omar complained, "and he rewards me with insults. Doesn't he know how difficult it is to kill someone you know?"

"Do you hear yourself, Omar?" Hassan asked. "You lay there and complain about some silly insult when you should be blinded by shame."

"You don't think I am? I see the terror on Frans's face every time I close my eyes."

"You should. You came here to kill Shiites, not Christians, and you chopped off the head of an innocent man. Allah will damn you to eternal fire."

"Enough already."

"No!" Hassan shouted. "Frans wasn't your enemy. You should have refused. Why didn't you?"

"That was my assignment, Hassan. I had no choice."

"You always have a choice, Omar."

"No, Hassan, not if saying 'I refuse to comply' means a bullet to my head. And yes, I've crossed the line and done the unthinkable, but there's no turning back to beg forgiveness."

"Your decision, Omar. I hope it haunts you for the rest of your life."

"What's going on with you, Hassan? You're going to keep rubbing it in? You think I feel good about what I did? Yes, it probably will haunt me, but I'll learn to live with my crime. Just like you will, Hassan, when your turn comes, and you're ordered to cut someone's head off."

"That's not going to happen," Hassan said, springing to his feet.

Omar swung around on the bed to face him. "You're talking nonsense. I couldn't bear to see you shot for insubordination."

"You don't get it, do you, Omar? If it comes to that, and I do get killed, and that's my only option, I'll gladly die. I'll take death with honor any day. It's far better than becoming a head chopper."

"When did you decide all this? When I left for Homs, you promised you'd go to class and practice. What happened?"

"I changed my mind."

"Just like that? You've already refused one assignment. What if they don't give you a second chance?"

"So what if they don't? At least if I'm dead I won't have to listen to your nagging. 'Do it this way, Hassan. Work harder, Hassan.' I'm not you, Omar, and now I'm glad I'm not."

"All I wanted was for you not to fall behind. When we volunteered, I envisioned us succeeding at every stage of the initiation, then celebrating together. I meant no harm, Hassan."

"Correction! I never volunteered, Omar." Hassan's voice was shrill. "You know that."

"Okay, you agreed to come with me. That's practically the same thing."

"No, it's not! And you promised me a way out if I didn't like it. Well, I want out and you'd better arrange it, or else."

"Or else what, Hassan?"

"I'll denounce you as a homosexual."

Omar laughed. "You're not making any sense. You'd also be denouncing yourself."

"Not if I take a woman."

"You're upset, Hassan. You're saying things you don't mean."

"No, I mean every word, Omar. From now on, I'll decide what's best for *me*. I'll have a talk with the commander, one on one. We're finished, you and me. And if you bully me, I might have to tell the commander your dirty little secret. You've ruined my life. And for your information, that wasn't an idle threat I just threw out. I've met a woman."

Omar looked at him incredulously.

"Yes, and if all goes well," Hassan said, smirking, "she'll be moving in with me very soon, so you'll have to move out. And if you ever come near me again, I swear I'll kill you."

"Are you sleeping with her?"

For one fleeting second, Hassan made eye contact with Omar then quickly looked away.

"Are you, or aren't you?"

"That's none of your business."

"But it *is* my business," Omar snapped. "We are lovers. Tell me. Who is she? Is she Somali? Is she a convert to Islam? How did you find her? I have a right to know."

"All rights are canceled as of now."

"You're scared, Hassan, and overreacting. I get that. But you can't just go from being gay to sleeping with a woman. I may have to do the same thing, but the thought terrifies me."

"It's you who made me think I was gay."

"But that's not—"

"There are no buts, Omar. We're done. Go find another partner. And while you're at it, watch your back. It would be a pity if you were to accidently get shot in one of our live-fire exercises."

"This is crazy, Hassan. I've shared my secrets with you and the most intimate of moments, and suddenly you're saying you want me dead? How is that possible?"

When Hassan did not respond, Omar continued. "I understand you're afraid of getting caught, but there's no need for threats. We've both been under tremendous stress. Too many long hours of training, and the pressure to perform that one final act of loyalty to ISIS. I get it. Regrets? Certainly, but I respect your decision. I'll move out tomorrow."

"No, you want to stay another night so you can get me one more time. I'm not doing that anymore. I want you to leave now."

Omar avoided Hassan's silent, cold stare. Hurt and angry at Hassan's death threats, he collected his belongings and threw them haphazardly on top of the blood-stained knife in his carry-on. Without a word, he placed his house key on the table near the door and walked out.

As he left the neighborhood and walked toward Abbas's office, Omar knew he would miss the tranquility of this quiet part of Raqqa. He even allowed himself to wonder what would happen to the lives of those peaceful people who still sheltered behind their garden walls. He felt ashamed, for he knew that with the presence of ISIS in their midst, and its brutally repressive measures, they risked floggings for not being properly dressed and possible execution by crucifixion or beheading. They would be told what they could read and study. Music, cinema and all form of entertainment would be forbidden, their every freedom severely curtailed, their lives forever altered. And he felt sorry for them.

After Abbas's insult, Omar hated the idea of asking him for help, but he had no choice. He was homeless and in need of a woman to cover his sexual orientation. He was prepared to swallow his pride and suffer the dreaded, squirm-inducing encounter with a woman if it meant staving off Hassan's threat of exposure. Abbas had offered him women in the past, and each time he had refused, claiming they would be a distraction from his rigorous training schedule. But now, post-beheading, it seemed an appropriate time to be wanting a woman, and not just any woman. Omar wanted her to be a younger version of his mother—slim, attractive, energetic and loyal.

***

Abbas occupied an office on the first floor in what had been Raqqa's local seat of government before ISIS had taken it over. When Omar opened the door and looked in, Abbas informed him he was unable to see him immediately but invited him to have a seat on one of the chairs along the corridor. As he waited, Omar noticed a number of people freely entering and exiting Abbas's office. He took this to be a snub but was in no position to protest.

Abbas, now head of ISIS's Legal Counsel, oversaw executions. Omar wanted what Abbas had—an important position inside ISIS and an office of his own. He had studied the organization and knew that Abu Bakr al Baghdadi, head of ISIS, had copied the American military's counter-insurgency mantra of "clear and hold" to win territory, establish control over an area and then give it back to the locals to govern. In a remarkably short period of time, Caliph Baghdadi, the name he had bestowed upon himself, had managed to unify militant groups, raise an army of jihadis from across the globe, and seize a chunk of land the size of Pennsylvania that stretched from Raqqa in northeastern Syria to central Iraq which he referred to as his Caliphate, treating it as one state with two administrative governments.

Baghdadi's challenge was not only to put a governing and military structure in place there, but also to build a system that could provide basic services. Baghdadi, himself a former Iraqi military officer, oversaw the Caliphate along with his cabinet advisers and two key deputies who had also served under Saddam Hussein.

The Shura Council was the Caliphate's religious monitor charged with making sure all the local councils and governors adhered to ISIS's version of Islamic law. Unlike Saudi Arabia's authoritative religious police, the same Council also had the power to censure the leadership if it ran afoul of its interpretation of Sharia law. ISIS had a financial department that handled weapons purchases and oil sales, a Military Council that defended the state, an Intelligence Council that tracked ISIS enemies, and a Media Council that regulated print and social media, a position Omar coveted.

After what seemed an endless wait, Abbas finally opened his door and gestured for Omar to enter. In contrast to the noisy corridor, the room was surprisingly quiet except for an outmoded fluorescent light along the ceiling that flickered intermittently, emitting an annoying hum. On one of the dull, gray walls hung the obligatory portrait of Abu Bakr Baghdadi preaching in his black robe, his arms outstretched. An oriental carpet in fair condition covered most of the chipped and badly stained marble floor. There were two matching leather chairs in front of Abbas's desk. Aside from a stack of files and official-looking ISIS documents, the desk showcased a small, black ISIS flag, a couple of stained coffee mugs and several pairs of worry beads.

"I apologize for making you wait, Omar, but since our return from Homs I've been swamped. Suddenly, everyone wants something from me. Just look at my calendar. It's crazy."

Abbas glanced at his watch. "I've got about fifteen minutes before my next appointment. What can I do for you?"

"It's time I found a woman. I'd like your help."

"I offered before but you refused."

"I know. I had reasons for refusing then, as you know. My life has taken on a new turn. I'm feeling more settled now."

Abbas nodded. "You've proven your loyalty to ISIS. You deserve preferential treatment. I'll see to it. Any preferences? Black, White, Asian? We have every ethnicity, every color you could want. If you're not particular, and if it's just for your sexual pleasure, we have any number of whores too."

"I don't think you understand. I'm looking for a wife who will be a good mother to my children but who is not overly religious. I told you when we met on the bus that I answered Allah's call to come kill Shiites."

"And you killed a Catholic priest instead."

"Apparently I did it worse than a goat would have."

Abbas threw his head back and laughed.

"Okay, you're not religious, but you still want to make children for the Caliphate."

"There are many ways to serve Allah. I think you agree with me."

"Yes, well put. I'm impressed but I never pegged you as—"

"As what? Not sufficiently loyal to ISIS?"

"No, it isn't that. I didn't think you were the marrying type."

"No, it's just... I'm a bit shy with women, and I've never..."

"Had sex before?"

Embarrassed, Omar closed his eyes and nodded. He had tried sleeping with a woman back in Michigan but had been unable to get an erection. The thought of failing again terrified him.

"I didn't mean to make you uncomfortable, Omar. I had no idea."

Just then, someone opened the door.

"Not now. Can't you see I'm busy?" Abbas shouted, and the man promptly shut the door.

"You've done well for us," Abbas said. "And I understand. I'll get you the woman you want."

"The men who served under me in Homs were devoted family men," said Omar. "I admired that, and I want that too. And I'd like my wife to be a widow—without children, if possible. At least she would have had some experience with a man."

"I'll get it right for you, Omar."

"An Iraqi with the same cultural connection would help too. You see, I miss my mother and my aunts and uncles, their get-togethers, their delicious cooking, and hearing Iraqi Arabic."

After committing such an abominable crime, he was grateful he still remembered love and longed for it.

"Do you have family back home… wherever that is?" he asked Abbas.

"No, I don't, and I envy you your good memories," Abbas explained. "I have none. I left home at twelve when my mother died. I've been living on my own ever since. I can barely remember her. Just as well. She wasn't a nice person."

Abbas pointed to a scar above his right eye. "See this? That's my memory of her. Hell, Omar, you know me as well as anyone here. I'm intolerable and mean-spirited most of the time and I say things I don't really mean. I know I was rough on you in Homs, but that's how we need to be with each other. It keeps us tough and battle ready. It's nothing personal."

If Abbas was trying to make amends, he was doing a stellar job, Omar thought. *And if he comes through with the right woman, I'll have no reason to cause him harm.*

"There's something else I need too," Omar said. "While you look for a woman, can you find me a place to live? Hassan has found himself a woman and wants the apartment to himself. Perfectly understandable, of course, but that leaves me homeless."

"That's easy, I can set you up in an apartment right away. It was time that you left Hassan anyway."

Had Abbas suspected all along that Hassan and I were lovers? Omar wondered.

Without further mention of Hassan, Abbas leafed through his Rolodex and pulled out a card. "This one's on the west side of town."

"I don't care where it is."

"It's a two bedroom and nicely furnished with ample room for a family and not far from the shopping district. Says here there's even a playground nearby. We reserve these special units for our favored fighters."

Abbas pulled out a set of keys from his desk drawer and selected one. "Here you go." He wrote down the address. "It's yours."

"That was easy."

"We take good care of our own, Omar. Don't forget that."

As Omar stood up to leave, Abbas said, "I may have something else for you too. A job opening just came across my desk. I think it might be a good fit, and it's a project close to the Caliph's heart. Interested?"

Anything that will get me closer to my dream job, thought Omar.

"Of course. I'm here to serve."

* * *

Omar took possession of his new apartment just as he assumed his position as Head of Indoctrination and Recruitment. He slept and showered in his new flat, grabbing clean clothes from his still unpacked carry-on and working eight to ten hours a day with no breaks. He took his meals on the go and gave no thought to stocking his pantry or refrigerator. One evening, some two weeks later, Omar heard a knock on his door. He opened it to find Abbas standing there with a woman completely covered in black. Only her eyes were showing.

Omar turned to Abbas and said, "Please, won't you come in too?"

Abbas smiled and shook his head. "You'll do just fine without me."

He said goodbye, turned and retreated down the stairs.

"Hello," the woman said as she entered the apartment. "My name is Aisha. I'm from Baghdad and I'm twenty-six years old."

As she spoke in her native Baghdadi accent, Omar was smitten in a homesick kind of way. He was also struck by her large, black, doe-like eyes. It was not until she removed her *hijab* and *abaya* that he finally saw the pretty, petite woman, with long, black hair and sculptured nose not unlike his mother's. She placed her outer garments on a nearby chair and promptly took a seat at the kitchen table.

She's quite comfortable with herself. A good sign, he thought.

"And my name is Omar. Welcome to my home."

"Where are you from?" she asked. "I don't recognize your accent."

"I was born in Baghdad but left when I was six after my father died. My mother had relatives in America, so we moved there. Is my Arabic that bad?"

"No, it just isn't native like mine, but I'm sure I don't speak English as well as you do."

"But you speak some English."

"Yes, I have a degree in education with a minor in psychology. My university required us to learn English, but I lack practice. But now I have you to help me improve."

Omar smiled. "It's a deal."

She laughed. "Is that what Americans say when they agree to something?"

"It's slang. Sorry, I'll do better and teach you proper English."

"Did you attend university?" she asked, reverting to Arabic.

"Yes, for only two years though before I answered the call to come kill infidels."

"Do you regret not having finished your studies?"

"Yes. I wanted to become an engineer like my father."

"If you could return to the States, would you?"

"Yes."

"How long have you been in Syria?"

"Three years in Homs, and I'm just completing my second year in Raqqa, two of which were in training to become an ISIS member."

He wanted to say more, but there would be time once he was sure he could trust her. "Tell me something about yourself."

"I'm a widow. I came to Raqqa with my husband four months ago. He died in battle a month after we got here, and I've just finished the required three months of mourning. It's a tradition in Islam widowed women are meant to endure, in case you aren't familiar with the custom."

"Do you have children?"

"No, we tried. He wanted a child for ISIS, but it didn't happen."

At least she knows what is supposed to happen between a man and a woman in bed, Omar thought. *That's a relief.*

"If given a choice," he said, "would you have returned to Baghdad after your husband's death?"

"Of course. I miss my family."

"I miss mine too. Every time I think of my mother and her sisters and our family reunions, I feel homesick. Do you know how to cook?"

She laughed. "What proper Iraqi woman doesn't know how to cook?"

"My mother's favorite dish is Tepsi Baytinijan. It's made with ground beef, eggplants, tomatoes, potatoes and peppers."

"I know." She nodded. "It's a favorite of *my* mother's too."

"I dream of a home-cooked meal. I haven't had one since I left the States."

Aisha smiled. "You're not like other ISIS men."

"Have you been with a lot of men?"

"No, but I hear them talk about their women, and you're different. You're respectful, and I'm grateful for that."

"Did your husband treat you well?"

"Initially yes, when we still lived in Baghdad. But when he joined ISIS, he turned into someone I didn't like."

"I'm sorry to hear that."

"Never mind. He's dead. Tell me what you do for ISIS."

"I'm in charge of the Indoctrination and Recruitment program, so I work with young children."

"Do you like what you do?"

"It's both challenging and stressful and…" He stopped in mid-sentence. "Speaking of work, it's getting late. I need to get up early. *Don't say too much, Omar,* he told himself. *You don't know this woman yet.* "Let me show you where to put your things."

He grabbed her bag and led her down the hallway to the first bedroom.

"This will be yours." *At least for now*, he wanted to add, not quite sure what else to say.

"And those will be our permanent sleeping arrangements?"

"No, I just thought we should get to know each other first, and then..."

"Yes, of course," she said, suppressing a smile.

Omar was happy with this woman and grateful to Abbas for having brought him someone both pretty and sassy.

"I'll leave you money on the kitchen table in the morning so you can go grocery shopping. I'd appreciate a good home-cooked meal."

She smiled again. "I can do that."

* * *

Omar's work primarily focused on young children who had endured multiple traumas. They were thought to be conditioned and sufficiently battle-tested to consider ISIS's brutal practices the norm. These Cubs of the Caliphate, as they were called, had already witnessed executions. Some had been repeatedly raped then discarded as trash. In some cases, they had already been forced to kill someone. Omar remembered the story told by Abbas on his first bus ride to Raqqa. Young children had been used as suicide bombers to make way for ISIS's entry and eventual control of the town. Omar had never worked with children, especially damaged ones, but he was willing to do his best if it ingratiated him into the good graces of the Caliph.

After a few unsuccessful attempts, Omar discovered recruitment of little children worked best when he was accompanied by an older boy. What youngster did not look up to an older sibling or a neighborhood kid who had already become a jihadist and earned a monthly salary, a fixed monthly stipend to help his impoverished family along with free medical care and food. While it was easy to entice the young ones with soda, sweets and toys, a soccer ball in the hands of a skilled older boy with the promise of a game at a local field attracted far more children, especially when given the opportunity to hold an ISIS flag and in some cases weapons.

When such a magic moment happened and Omar was invited to meet a child's entire family, he handed the mothers manuals on how to bring up jihadi children. These materials suggested bedtime stories about martyrdom and a trick Omar had learned from the Caliph— gradual exposure of the child to graphic content through jihadi websites. These methods subjected children to Islamic State ideology taught by those the children trusted and loved, making it more likely they would eventually trust the Caliph once they officially became his Cubs.

Omar and his team of young adults were successful recruiters, eventually enrolling 120 children into the program. From his first days, Omar put his students through a combination of rigorous physical activities and classroom visuals. He had them watch executions to break any aversion they might have to brutality, then escalated to simulated acts of violence with no pre-judgment about rightness or wrongness. The hope of ISIS was that each of these children would blindly carry out hideous acts of violence if so ordered, even the slaughter of their own parents.

The turning of already damaged children into monsters was hard to watch. Omar had to let go of his preconceived ideas of bias, of civility, of basic humanness. He had to think of his subjects as lab experiments devoid of feelings and reprogrammed to kill on order, or be disposed of, or be refitted for some lesser purpose with the goal of producing the Caliph's new army of jihadis.

There was one exception, however. Anwar had been living on the street when Omar found him. He rarely spoke, and when he did, he stuttered and broke Omar's heart, reminding him that he still had one. Omar decided to keep a close watch over Anwar, an injured soul who had undoubtedly witnessed countless atrocities.

Unlike the other children, Anwar's experiences had damaged him but had not yet turned his heart to stone. Quite the contrary. There was a gentleness about him that Omar knew would open him up to ridicule and scorn. When Anwar was bullied by the other boys for his inability to handle a gun and fire it, Omar intervened. When Anwar couldn't hold a blond-haired doll in an orange Guantanamo jump suit and behead it with a knife, Omar showed him how.

After a week, when Anwar was still unable to perform any of his assignments, Omar knew he faced two choices. He could either throw Anwar out on the street or show Anwar another way to serve Allah. Hadn't he wanted another option for himself when he had volunteered to join ISIS?

Despite what Andrew thought, Omar never wanted to be a head chopper, but he had been given three choices when his operation in Homs collapsed—agree to be transferred to an internment camp in northwestern Syria; become a fugitive to avoid capture; or join ISIS. Since he had chosen the latter—an irrevocable decision with no turning back—he was going to make the best of every opportunity.

Hassan had lacked that determination. He was not a fighter. It took moral courage to say no to the rules of ISIS, and Hassan had not been shot for insubordination, as Omar assumed he would be. Rather, as punishment for not completing his orientation, Hassan had agreed to accept a menial job.

Omar had given up too much to accept such a compromise. He had already committed unthinkable crimes and saw no way to rescind bad choices even if his initial motivation had been to avenge his father's death. Omar wanted better choices for Anwar.

Two weeks after Aisha entered his life, Omar brought the boy home to meet her. "This is Anwar," he explained. "I've adopted him. He needs a good home and loving parents."

Aisha smiled and knelt in front of Anwar.

"How old are you?"

"We're not sure," Omar said, speaking for the meek child. "From his size, I assume he is about seven or eight."

"And do you have a family?" Aisha asked Anwar.

The boy shook his head and then stuttered a bit before finally saying "No, I don't."

"Well, now you do," Aisha said, placing a kiss on the boy's cheek. "Go and wash up. Dinner is ready."

She caught hold of Omar's sleeve as he was about to walk the boy to the bathroom. "You're a kind man. It's obvious this child needs love."

After dinner, it was Aisha who put the boy to bed. When she returned to the living room, she took Omar's hand. "Now I'm going to take you to bed. It's time. It's been two long weeks."

"I'm not sure I can…"

"Listen to me. I understand your problem. I come from a long line of Iraqi women who have had lots of experience with their men warriors. My father fought in the Iran-Iraq war. He returned a traumatized man. Between the two sides, a million men died. Some Iraqi soldiers gassed Kurds in the north. Others fought in Kuwait or saw hundreds of their fellow soldiers gunned down by US troops. They had all done and seen horrific things, and they suffered varying degrees of PTSD, which left them unable to perform in bed."

"And you know how to fix that?"

Aisha nodded. "Maybe men don't talk about such problems, but women do and find solutions. If a woman can't get her man to bed, what good is she to him. Or…" she smiled seductively, "him to her."

Omar looked skeptical.

"I'm going to prepare you a tea and give you a pill to swallow, and we'll see what happens. Trust me."

Once Omar swallowed the pill, Aisha began to undress. When she stood before him naked, he was in such a state of awe that he let her undress him. When they were both naked, she led him to bed. When he was in full erection, she mounted him, and he penetrated her. He felt her riding him, slowly at first, until she knew he was ready to come, and then fireworks exploded in his head. After reaching the stars, when he finally caught his breath, he burst out laughing.

Aisha laughed, too, as she slid off and lay alongside him. "You see, it worked."

"Yes, it did."

* * *

Everything was going along nicely with Aisha and Anwar. Omar found that the happier he was at home, the less anxious he was about turning children into Cubs for the Caliphate. Two months later, though, he was asked to report to Abbas's office.

"Have there been complaints about my work?" Omar asked. "Is the Caliph unhappy with the way the program is playing out?"

"Quite the contrary, Omar. Quit being so anxious. He's actually very impressed by your work with the Cubs, but we've got an emergency on our hands. There's a big battle going on near Deir ez Zor, and the man responsible for media has been killed. You're to take his place. Caliph's orders. Head upstairs immediately. He's expecting you."

For someone who called himself a humble man of God, the Caliph's office was surprisingly well furnished with new oriental carpets, a leather couch and matching chairs.

With no courteous prelude, the Caliph addressed Omar curtly. "My elite forces have captured 120 Syrian soldiers in Deir ez Zor. You and your team are to travel there immediately. Abbas will accompany you in case you have any technical issues. I want no screw-ups. I expect sensational footage for propaganda purposes. You have the best equipment possible, so don't disappoint me, Omar."

"I won't, Caliph."

* * *

Omar introduced himself to the ten-man staff he would be leading.

"Good morning. May I have your attention, please. My name is Omar. As you know, your previous boss was killed earlier today in Deir ez Zor. The Caliph has asked me to replace him. I have some media experience but will count on all of you to get me up to speed on how this office works. For now, though, our priority is the battle in Deir ez Zor. On orders from the Caliph, we're to leave immediately to film the event, so gather up your gear immediately. We'll need transport, so who can take care of that?"

"The trucks are parked out back," one of the men said. "I'll grab the keys from the guardian."

Omar watched as his team loaded up their equipment including Nikon D850 and D5 cameras, the latest in sensor design, auto focus and image processing along with slow motion capability and video recording. Very impressive. He wished he had the use of such high-tech equipment in Homs. In three trucks, they took off for the hour-long drive to Deir ez Zor, a city like Raqqa in the Syrian desert but lucky enough to also sit on the bank of the Euphrates River.

When Omar's team arrived on the scene, the captured troops had already been divided into two groups. With cameras running, half of Omar's crew stayed with the first group of soldiers, still dressed in their Syrian Army fatigues. *This was good,* Omar thought. *There would be no mistaking who was being shot.*

The prisoners' hands were tied behind their backs, and they were directed by masked ISIS fighters at gunpoint toward an oblong hole about twenty feet deep and thirty feet long. Omar ordered some of his men to get right up to the edge and lie on the ground if necessary for a direct camera shot of the prisoners' heads as they exploded from being struck by rifle rounds. The others were directed to the opposite side of the hole to capture in slow motion the bodies tumbling over the edge and landing like rag dolls into the grave. Omar knew these kinds of images would capture the attention of the intended audience as they circulated through social media.

About thirty meters away, the other half of Omar's crew was already at the river where another group of soldiers with bound hands were being thrashed across their naked backs. With microphones in hand, the media crew captured not only the whip's hissing sound as it tore long, blood-gushing slashes the length of their backs but the agonizing howls and groans of the prisoners as they stumbled down stone steps toward the riverbank.

"Great work, Omar," Abbas shouted. "That should turn any number of stomachs upside down."

Omar ignored Abbas and continued filming the moment the bloodied prisoners were lined up along the water's edge and shot in the back
of the head. By then, Abbas was by his side and together they watched
the gentle current carry the bodies downstream, leaving a wake of blood.

Abbas left Omar abruptly to talk to the jihadist in charge. On cue,
looking directly into Omar's camera, the jihadist said, "The Shura
Council for the eastern region of Deir ez Zor has sentenced to death
these apostate soldiers who committed massacres against our brothers
and families in Syria."

As the jihadist announced the punishment, Omar filmed the other
ISIS fighters raising their black flags and chanting "God is Great."

When Omar turned his attention to the riverbank, he saw Abbas pull
one of the fighters aside. He whispered something in his ear and handed
him a knife. Omar recognized the man as one of the psychopaths who
had worked on his media team in Homs.

"Omar," Abbas shouted, "get this on film. All angles."

On cue, the fighter pulled a body out of the water and flung it onto
the ground face up. With his knife, he sliced open the soldier's chest.
While his men cheered, the fighter carved out the man's heart and liver.
Holding the organs in the air, he turned to Omar's camera and shouted,
"I swear to Allah we will eat your hearts and livers and cut your bodies
up in jagged strips and feed them to the dogs." He put the man's heart
in his mouth, then chewed and swallowed it as his fellow fighters roared
with approval.

CHAPTER FIVE

As soon as they exited their apartment's elevator, Nadia and Andrew saw the battered white Toyota Cruiser with black UN letters along the side of the vehicle. An imposing middle-aged man who stood beside the car's open back door stepped forward with his hand extended and introduced himself in Arabic.

"Good morning, Madame Khoury. My name is Antoine Saliba. I'm the UN Humanitarian Affairs Officer in Idlib, and this is Roger Nahas from our Beirut office." Saliba's companion waved hello as he loaded their luggage into the trunk.

Nadia was an international lawyer with a PhD in Human Rights from the London School of Economics. Shortly after her engagement to Dr. Andrew Sullivan, she had been appointed to the UN High Commission on Human Rights, but she never assumed her duties. After being unexpectedly caught up in the 2006 war in south Lebanon between Israel and Hezbollah, she escaped with Andrew only to be kidnapped by Hassan Jaafar, Syria's notorious intelligence czar. She spent four years as his captive. It was only after Jaafar's assassination by the American ambassador to Syria, Robert Jenkins, that she was able to escape. Now, six years later, after finally marrying her beloved Andrew, she was about to undertake a new assignment on behalf of the UN—Rapporteur for Human Rights for the Levant.

"Please call me Nadia," she said, shaking Antoine's hand. "This is my husband, Andrew Sullivan. He's on leave from his clinic in the Shatilla refugee camp to work with Doctors without Borders in Idlib."

"American?" Antoine said while shaking Andrew's hand. "I apologize, we'll switch to English."

"No need. I speak fluent Arabic," Andrew replied as he helped Nadia into the back seat. Seeing her shiver, he adjusted her jacket around her shoulders and said, "Are you going to be warm enough, darling?"

"I thought I was properly dressed, but I am a bit chilled."

Overhearing this conversation, Roger said, "And I'm afraid the heater in this car won't provide you much heat. The engine's solid, but it's otherwise an old heap, as you can see. We have time if you'd like to change into something warmer."

Andrew nodded, then looked at his wife. "Darling, you packed a parka, didn't you? I'll get it."

"Probably a good idea," Nahas said, as Andrew got out of the car. "It's 35 degrees Fahrenheit in Idlib this morning, and the forecast calls for snow, lots of it. It'll take us about five hours to get there, possibly longer if there's a flareup. It'll feel like forever if you're uncomfortable. We'll stop shortly before we get to Damascus for a snack and toilet break."

When Andrew climbed back in, he wrapped the parka across Nadia's lap. "That should help."

She took his hand and pressed it against her cheek before she turned her attention back to Nahas. "You mentioned a possible flareup. Do you anticipate a problem along the way?"

"I always expect the unexpected when I go to Syria."

She nodded. "Wise man."

"As of now, our route's reported to be quiet, but I'll be monitoring conditions along the way. If it'd been up to me, I'd have chosen the coastal route. It's much quicker, but I was advised the road around Damascus was more secure. Once we've bypassed the capital, in about two hours, we'll pick up the M5 highway, which the Syrian Army has just liberated from jihadist control."

Antoine turned in his seat to address Nadia. "I drove in from Idlib last night so I could spend this time updating you on what's happening there. It's one thing to read your policy papers but…"

Nadia smiled. "It's quite another to get a firsthand report. Thank you."

She found it difficult to look away from Antoine when he spoke because his dark, penetrating eyes were powerful and irresistible. She assumed, from his fit frame, sun-worn skin and unruly salt and pepper hair that he was probably in his late-fifties.

From her briefings, Nadia knew that Idlib province in northwest Syria along the Turkish border was both volatile and politically complex. Hayat al Tahrir al Sham, a group formerly known as al Nusra, served as al Qaeda's affiliate there. The group was headed by Muhammad Jolani who was known region-wide for his use of beheadings, rape and kidnappings to control the locals, not unlike his cohort Abu Bakr Baghdadi, the leader of ISIS in Raqqa.

"First update," Antoine said.

Nadia opened her briefcase and took out a notepad and pen.

"Our support team was due to arrive in Damascus this morning, but they missed their connection in Brussels. UN headquarters has been notified of the delay."

"Any idea when they'll arrive?"

"I assume tomorrow, same time. Could be later."

"How many?"

"Thirty, with another twenty due later in the week."

"Excellent. You and your Idlib team have been understaffed for far too long. According to my latest figures, in the last two months alone some eight hundred thousand people have fled to Idlib province. I can't imagine how you've coped."

"That's an astounding number," Andrew said, "and all of them headed to the same place. I…"

He stopped in mid-sentence, distracted by the dense fog they had driven into.

"I remember this spot. The same thing happened in 2006 when Samir was driving me to Damascus to try to find you, Nadia."

"Dear sweet Samir. How I miss him," Nadia said. She found herself tearing up from the horrible images flooding in, the roar of planes overhead, the last precious seconds of Samir's life before something sliced his upper torso away from the rest of his body.

Andrew said, "Apparently, this kind of fog happens when humidity and temperature swings collide at high altitudes. Is that right, Roger? You must drive this route often."

I wonder if Andrew didn't say this to distract me from thinking about Samir, Nadia thought. *How I love this man for his thoughtfulness.*

"Yes," Roger replied. "And as quickly as we drive into the fog, we're out of it at five thousand feet and looking out on the *Dahr al Baidar* pass, the summit of the Beirut-Damascus highway, and below, as far as the eye can see, the Bekaa Valley, which, some five thousand years ago, was the Fertile Crescent."

Distracted now from her sad memories, Nadia said, "Aren't we fortunate to live in such a special place. If only stupid men would stop trying to destroy it." She dried her eyes carefully so her mascara would not blotch.

"Can't argue with that," said Andrew. He stroked her hair.

Nadia knew Andrew had images of Samir's death in his head too. She took his hand and kissed his wrist.

"By the way," said Roger, "we'll be in Chtaura shortly. We'll stop there for our break. Once we reach the other side of Damascus, I can't predict what we'll face in the way of delays."

"Badi Massa Bini's shop is on the main road," Nadia said. "Let's stop there."

Roger nodded. "I know the place. They make great sandwiches. They'll add anything you want, no extra charge, and their toilets are clean."

Suddenly, Nadia was all business again. "Back to your briefing, Antoine. In Idlib, I'll likely have dealings with a man named Mohamed Jolani. What do you know about him?"

"His real name is Ahmed al Sharaa, born in Syria's Golan Heights. After Israel occupied the region in 1967, his family moved to Damascus. He enrolled in the Faculty of Media and Journalism at Damascus University but left Syria for Iraq in 2003 just as the US was invading and occupying the country. He was later imprisoned at the US-run Camp Bucca."

"That's where he met Baghdadi, I assume."

Antoine nodded. "That place turned a lot of people into hardened jihadists. Hardly surprising, given the torture and psychological abuse they were subjected to."

"Washington and Brussels are trying to remove Jolani and his Hayat al Tahrir al Sham from the US terrorist list. Why?"

"According to my sources," Antoine said, "they're convinced such a move will open the door to international acceptance of his de facto government in Idlib, which they view as potential leverage against Damascus given the millions of refugees languishing there."

Nadia shook her head. "How ironic—a decade after the 9/11 al Qaeda attack on American soil, the US government helps a sworn enemy that had killed Americans establish a haven in Idlib."

In fact, it was not ironic at all, Nadia thought. *It had been part of the plan all along.* As the uprising in Syria unfolded, Jake Sullivan, then national security adviser to Hilary Clinton's presidential campaign, had famously bragged, "al Qaeda is on our side in Syria."

"Eventually, a feud over strategy and finances led Jolani to split with Baghdadi," Antoine explained. "It was this break-up that enabled him to establish an iron clad grip over Idlib province, an area the size of Luxembourg and one of thirteen such districts across Syria. Jolani refers to his domain as the Government of National Salvation, probably to make it sound more legitimate. He's imposed levies and taxes on the residents across the entire Idlib province. While many Idlib locals oppose Assad, they dislike Jolani even more. Just a few weeks ago he had a nineteen-year-old shot for committing blasphemy. In cold blood... no trial. And then, last month, five men were accused of spying for the regime and killed."

"We're here," said Roger, as he pulled off the main road and parked in front of the sandwich shop. "I'll get us food while you all use the toilets."

* * *

Nadia had the spotless washroom with three stalls and a black-and-white tile floor to herself. On the otherwise white wall, in small black script just above the roll of toilet paper, someone had written the words, "Fuck ISIS." *Fair enough*, she thought. *If I lived here, I would have written the same thing.*

The shop had a dozen tables, all taken. *No surprise*, she thought. This was a Chtaura family-owned landmark on the well-traveled road to Damascus.

She spotted Andrew and the others seated alongside one of the large street-side windows. When he saw her, he called out her name. Once seated he handed her a sandwich but otherwise no one spoke. They were too busy eating. Andrew finally asked, "Shall I get you a tea?"

She shook her head and laughed. "Best not drink in case we get stuck in traffic. Right, Roger?"

He nodded. "I'm afraid there are no rest stops like this one until we get to Idlib."

A half an hour later they were back in the car, and within minutes Nadia felt Andrew's head fall onto her shoulder. She adjusted herself to better accommodate his weight, inhaling the fruity, citrus scent of verbena in his hair. *Poor darling, of course he's exhausted. He was up all night finishing a shift at the clinic so he could leave with me this morning.* She settled in and gazed out at the occasional finished house, but more often at concrete slabs with standing posts intended for an unfinished second floor. And to think that this barren part of the country had once been covered with cedar and pine forests, all the greenery long since eradicated by herds of grazing goats nibbling first on the bark and then at the trees themselves until nothing remained but a stump. She let Andrew sleep half an hour before she spoke again.

"The US is apparently grooming Jolani for future leadership in a post-Assad Syria. Any thoughts on that, Antoine?"

"I'm Lebanese, not Syrian, but we've had our share of warlords. From what I've observed firsthand, you can't turn a switch and transform someone like Jolani, or Samir Geagea—one of Lebanon's notorious warlords—into a moderate statesman. It just doesn't happen. To think otherwise is both naive and deceitful."

"I heard about Jolani from the man who kept me prisoner in Homs," Andrew said as he opened his eyes and sat up.

"You were in Homs?" asked Roger, looking in his rear mirror. "During the army siege?"

"Yes, I was captured and forced to work as al Nusra's doctor there. I had a small clinic in the Old City."

"I'm amazed you're still alive."

Andrew shuddered and said, "Me too. It was a nightmare. My captor was an Iraqi American by the name of Omar. He ran al Nusra's media center and claimed their goal was to win the hearts and minds of the local population."

Nadia grimaced and said, "Grisly suicide attacks, executions, banning non-religious music and forcing Druze and Christians to convert at gunpoint doesn't sound like an attempt to win anyone's hearts and minds."

"It's not," Andrew agreed. "According to Omar, the graver the atrocities and the greater the headline news, the greater the influx of new followers. Atrocities demonstrate not only power but arouse fear, which enables both ISIS and Jolani's group to control their local populations."

"That about sums it up, doesn't it," Antoine said.

"Afraid I can't take credit for original thought here," said Andrew. "I learned most of this from Omar."

"Andrew's right," Antoine said. "Regardless of his claim to be a moderate, Jolani needs to maintain a state of fear to hold onto his territory."

"When al Nusra fighters left Homs, did Omar go to Idlib?" asked Nadia.

"No, he fled to Raqqa and joined ISIS," Andrew replied.

"Did he actually embrace ISIS and its ideology?"

"He felt he had no choice," Andrew replied. "The US government considered him a terrorist, and he didn't want to languish in a refugee camp or be sent to a maximum-security prison in the US, so he chose ISIS. Because his father was killed by Shiite militiamen during the US occupation, he felt compelled to leave Michigan, where he lived with his mother, and come here to avenge his father's death."

Nadia shook her head sadly. "What a waste of a young man's life."

Andrew glanced out the window. "I often wonder if Omar doesn't think the same thing."

As they advanced toward Idlib, they passed towns and villages eerily deserted, just as Nadia imagined the dust towns of the American Wild West to be, with the occasional pack of dogs roaming the empty streets. Buildings were either uninhabited or piles of rubble, and those that had resisted stood strangely roofless with walls intact, the inexplicable feat that sometimes happens in indiscriminate aerial bombing raids. Normally green, fields lay barren, except in this frigid scene they were dusted with snow, the landscape looking more like frozen tundra, its biome apparently capable of surviving in a war zone. *A small miracle of nature if it did*, Nadia thought.

She shuddered. "It's getting colder."

"Time to put your parka on, darling."

Nadia leaned forward while Andrew held up the jacket from behind so she could slip her arms inside.

"I noticed your wool hat in the left pocket. Put that on, too, and you'll be toasty warm."

"Idlib City's temperature is predicted to drop well below freezing tonight," Antoine said. "At least your lodgings will be warm… unless the electricity goes out."

"Is that a possibility?" Nadia asked.

"Anything's possible, as Roger likes to say."

"How close are we?" she asked.

"Another hour. We'll hit Idlib City by mid-afternoon, and you'll see for yourselves how wacky things are."

* * *

Nadia sat erect and looked right and left at the scene around her. It had begun to snow, and the wind had picked up.

"This is how I visualize the end of the world," she said. "Masses of terrified people fleeing. The whole of humanity gone mad, everyone here trying to escape through one exit—the Turkish border."

Their UN car gave them special privileges. Roger drove on without joining the massive line of vehicles. What fascinated Nadia most were the various modes of transportation people had relied on to reach Idlib City. A fortunate few had the luxury of driving their own cars, every imaginable space filled with their personal belongings. And then there were the flat-bed trucks piled high with dozens of mattresses, carpets, bedding necessities, kitchen utensils and various other possessions salvaged from the ruins of destroyed houses. Under those layers, peering out weary-eyed, were dozens of children in the arms of their parents or grandparents, each overlayered in extra clothing meant both to ward off the cold and conserve precious space.

The most baffling were the motor bikes. Drivers with their wives and children, all huddled together, hanging on for dear life, their meager belongings precariously tied by some miracle of ingenuity to the back of the bikes. And the heart-wrenching sight of white-bearded men on foot carrying knapsacks and shivering for lack of warm clothing. All these despondent people were waiting to be assigned a place to lay their weary bodies.

"Poor people!" Andrew sighed, shaking his head.

"But in all this misery," Antoine said, "there's the occasional surprise—like the Syrian NGO by the name of Violet with its one thousand volunteers. They saw the need to evacuate families without transportation or fuel from front-line areas, so they pooled their resources and begged, borrowed and in some cases rented trucks at their own expense to help those people. It's a drop in this ocean of misery, but such a gesture goes a long way toward restoring my faith in mankind."

Andrew sighed again. "I get the occasional nice surprise in my clinic in the Shatilla refugee camp, too, but it's nothing more than a fleeting, feel-good moment. And then you look at the UN's dilemma here. How do they, or any international organization, accommodate the needs of so many desperate people? Are there even enough tents in the world to house them? Or enough food packets or medical supplies or blankets? Or enough personnel to tend to the needs of so many?"

"For the first rush of refugees, the UN sent five thousand tents," Antoine said. "In a flash, some sixty thousand more were needed, and they had to scramble to find them."

"And it still wasn't enough," Nadia added.

Antoine shook his head. "I've worked for the UN for twenty-five years. We've faced major challenges that we've always met. This crisis is beyond human capacity. I don't envy you, Nadia. You're being asked to do the impossible, and even that won't be enough."

"We do what we can," she replied. "Thankfully, we're not alone. Save the Children, World Vision, Lutheran Relief Services, Oxfam, Danish Refugee Committee, Doctors without Borders and so many others help too."

"Whatever it is, it's a pittance," Antoine offered.

"I agree," Andrew said.

Three-quarters of a million Syrians resided full-time in Idlib City, a dismal, crowded hodgepodge of drab three-and-four story buildings blackened from age or neglect, scarred by shrapnel and bullet holes, their facades cluttered with tacky, faded billboards advertising everything from dental and medical clinics to clothing, beauty salons and government service offices all under the watchful eye of HTS's security patrols.

As their UN vehicle drove through the narrow, congested streets, Nadia took note of the human traffic too—the women, despite the snow and cold, covered head to toe in black, the strict chador dress code as stipulated by HTS. They scampered along the sidewalks dragging their reluctant, wailing children behind. Male students dressed in modest school uniforms with no jackets or hats marched along the sidewalks as if they owned the space. Old women seated on the snow-covered ground begged for money to feed themselves while street vendors attempted to peddle their day-old fruit and vegetables, dragging their laden carts through slushy streets, to provide food for destitute people.

In all this mayhem, hardly visible in the swell of traffic, were young police officers, attempting to control the ebb and flow of cars and taxis discharging passengers and picking up others as motors idled and disgorged black clouds of toxic smoke. Despite the police officers' heroic efforts, horns honked impatiently and drivers in rusted and often windowless vehicles played deaf to their shrill whistles intended to hurry them on their way.

In an abandoned construction site not far from the city center, Nadia noticed scores of multi-generational refugee families crowded into one room spaces with no doors or windows and only a small fire for warmth. Many others were camped along irrigation canals or filled vacant lots next to empty apartment buildings. An abandoned soccer stadium, badly damaged by air strikes, provided some refuge in its underground level. Despite the grunginess, the certain run-in with rats and the cumulative layers of urine that permeated the walls and cement floors, people at least had a roof over their heads.

The lucky ones, according to Antoine, were living in tent camps, one of two hundred or more dotting the bleak landscape for miles. The less fortunate slept on layers of frigid cardboard in the surrounding farmland, or up on craggy hillsides among flocks of sheep or old railroad berms that would keep water and snow from wetting their belongings. For all to see, visible in the distance, was the impenetrable Turkish border, its doors sealed shut and impervious to human suffering.

"Where does Turkey fit into all this, Antoine?" Andrew asked.

"It currently hosts 3.6 million Syrian refugees on its side of the border. When the uprising began in March 2011, President Erdoğan helped the US funnel weapons into Syria by tapping into the massive arms arsenal of the newly ousted Libyan government."

"I can confirm that," Nadia said. "I was privy to a classified version of a US Senate investigation that confirmed a direct CIA role in the movement of weapons from Libya to Syria."

"Erdoğan's involvement in arms smuggling is almost an aside," Antoine said. "His more pressing priority now is how to prevent more refugees from crossing the Turkish-Syrian border. He settled on a solution. He supports Jolani because he prevents people from crossing. And any time Erdoğan feels he's not getting the cooperation he wants from the West, he threatens to open his borders and allow thousands of refugees to flow into Europe."

"How did Idlib become an insurgent stronghold?"

"It was a tactical move on Assad's part, at least initially," Antoine explained. "By transferring his opponents out of contested hot spots to a single area he was able to consolidate his control over larger and larger swaths of the country."

"Makes logistical sense," Andrew said.

"But does it?" Nadia asked. "Hasn't Assad created a no-win situation for himself? How can he defeat an insurgent group like HTS that possesses massive amounts of lethal weaponry and whose leader is backed not only by Turkey but the US? And Jolani has over two million refugees under his control. Assad can't destroy HTS without killing hundreds of thousands of his own people."

Antoine nodded with a smile. "So, Assad continues to do what he's been doing—chipping away bit by bit at the edges of Idlib province until he gets close enough to Idlib City to topple Jolani. If successful, he regains full control of his country and allows millions of refugees to return to their homes."

"And, in the meantime," Nadia added, "the US will facilitate the transfer of provisions, both military and humanitarian, to pass through the Turkish-Syrian border. They'll also allow Turkey to coordinate and cooperate with Jolani. It's a win-win situation for Turkey because Jolani is in a strong position to control territory that Turkey sees as essential to watch over the Kurdish forces that oppose his government—the same Kurdish forces who collaborate with the US forces in northeast Syria."

"What a complicated mess," Andrew said. "According to my colleagues, Idlib has more al Qaeda affiliates than anywhere else in the world. Is that possible, Antoine?"

"It is. Idlib's the end-of-the-line dumping ground for the local branches of al Qaeda, their families, foreign fighters and anyone else who supports the insurgency. The more cities that fall to the government, the more fighters are transferred here, the more the numbers grow."

"Do Jolani's men live in the tent cities alongside the fleeing refugees?" Andrew asked.

"Technically, they live apart, but they're omnipresent, always on the lookout for new recruits. And why wouldn't they be? Every man who lives in squalid conditions and is unable to feed his wife and children is a potential jihadist, especially if he's offered a substantial amount of money."

"How much are we talking about?"

"Three to four hundred a month on average."

"Quite the incentive."

They had just reached the other side of Idlib City when Nadia heard planes approaching. During Lebanon's civil war, she'd been taught that if she could hear an approaching rocket or mortar or bomb, she would have time to hide. But where was she to hide now?

A first explosion jolted the car and Roger slammed on the brakes. The abrupt motion thrust Nadia against the forward seat, leaving her stunned. Another explosion rocked the ground, then another one even closer. The car windows shattered, spraying glass everywhere.

Before Nadia could regain her senses, she felt Andrew's hands pull her back into her seat and place her head against the headrest. She turned, and as she did, she glimpsed that her three companions were mercifully unscathed. Moments later, still somewhat dazed, she looked up and saw, as if in slow motion, a five-story building collapse, each floor swallowing the one above it in a cloud of dust hiding everything except the desperate screams of people.

Nadia cranked her head upward and caught a glimpse of two planes. As she watched their lights flashing across the afternoon sky, she could not fathom how this hell could have been brought about by human beings. Every plane that dropped a bomb had a pilot or two inside. Presumably, they were young men in their twenties, terrified that a missile might collide with their plane and blow it apart. Maybe these airmen had a ring on their finger or girlfriends back home. Maybe they were reservists called up the day before their mission. Maybe they were convinced their targets were "terrorist strongholds" so it was all right to drop massive bombs over a city where they could not identify a specific target. All around her, where these bombs exploded, were ordinary people—women cradling screaming babies in their arms, old people trapped in the debris crying out for someone to rescue them, a husband frantic because he could not find his wife and children. It was complete pandemonium, and all she could do was wonder if the four of them would be the next to die.

In front of the demolished building, Nadia noticed a blackened car. The passenger door had been blown off. Inside, on the front seat, she saw a doll just before she saw the bare legs of a charred child. She turned her head and saw a bus with its top blown off, the passengers thrown helter-skelter, their remains strewn across the street. She had no way to determine how many had died in the blasts or how many lay wounded in the collapsed buildings, but what stood out was the solidarity of this neighborhood. Within minutes, people crowded around the collapsed buildings volunteering to help rescue victims from the rubble. A man, maybe a shopkeeper or an off-duty nurse, was handing out plastic gloves to protect people's hands from glass and blood. Others were rushing to give out blankets and coats to help ward off the cold. Some were just sitting next to the wounded and holding their hands until aid came to take them to the hospital.

Nadia was moved by these kind souls and the army of tireless health workers who were already at work, risking their lives, to pull bodies out of harm's way, never stopping to think about whether another explosion or another building collapse would make them victims too. And then she saw Andrew, her hero from another war, the man she was blessed to call her husband, whose first instinct was to help those in need, jump out of their car and run toward the rescue workers. "I'm a physician," she heard him say as he was led off to tend to those who had survived.

It was Antoine's voice she eventually heard calling her name and inviting her to clear the car so he and Roger could wipe it clean of glass and debris. "As soon as we're done," he said, "I'll find us a way out of this mess so we can get to the UN office. I've just spoken to my crew and explained our predicament. If we can't get out on our own, they'll come fetch us."

"And Andrew?" Nadia asked. "Are we going to leave him here?"

"Nadia, he's doing what he needs to be doing. You know that better than anyone."

She looked at him and nodded.

"He'll know where to find us when his work is done."

"Yes, of course," she replied, still reluctant to leave him. "And I can always call him later, can't I?"

* * *

By the time Nadia, Antoine and Roger reached the UN headquarters it was well after five in the afternoon. The building was conspicuous for its position on an otherwise lonely hill overlooking Idlib City and was devoid of any distinctive UN markings that might have caused it to become a Russian target during one of their indiscriminate bombing raids. The office had shut down for the day, and staff had gathered in the cafeteria for dinner. The group of twelve graciously welcomed Nadia and insisted she should join them for an evening meal. They included men and women from Ireland, Belgium, France, Norway, Algeria and Nigeria. *The cross section of nationalities one usually found with any UN foreign contingent*, Nadia thought.

"Thank you for the warm welcome," she said. "I would have wanted to announce the arrival of dozens more staff, but they missed their connection in Brussels, and after today's bombing, I'm not sure if our New York office will scrap their mission altogether. I'm terribly disappointed because I know how desperately you need additional help. I will do my best to get them here as soon as possible."

Nadia fielded questions about herself and her husband while picking at her dinner of overcooked vegetables and rice, all the while worried for Andrew's safety. She concluded the evening by saying, "I'd like to convene a meeting in the morning, if possible. I'm in need of an urgent update on what's going on here. Is there a conference room here?"

"Yes," said the man from France. "Just down the hall."

"Good. We'll meet there tomorrow morning at nine o'clock. Bring updates, questions, problems, anything that will help me better understand the situation here. Now, if you don't mind, I'm going to turn in for the night. Thanks for all you are doing. It's hard and dangerous work, but you've all demonstrated your incredible dedication to this UN mission, otherwise you wouldn't be here trying to do the impossible. Good night."

Once in her room, she anxiously called Andrew's cell number. On the sixth ring, he finally answered.

"I was worried you wouldn't pick up, darling," Nadia said. "Have things quieted down at the hospital? Would you like me to send a car so you can sleep here with me?"

"We're still tending to the wounded, Nadia. I can't leave."

"How many died today?"

"At least two dozen, maybe more. I haven't seen the official figures yet, but there are dozens wounded, many requiring surgery."

"Is the hospital adequately equipped to handle such patients?"

"The staff here does the best they can with what they have, just as I had to do in Homs. No one expects miracles. They're just grateful for any help we can give them. Sorry, Nadia—staff's calling me. I need to go. We'll talk tomorrow. Love you."

After a restless night of anxious thoughts, Nadia finally gave up on sleep. She showered, dressed and grabbed her first coffee of the day in the cafeteria. After looking at her emails, she finally forced herself to eat an egg sandwich and grabbed a second cup of coffee before joining the staff in the conference room.

"Good morning, team. Let's begin with an overview of the problem. Who wants to start?"

"I will," said the woman from Nigeria. "My name is Abeni. As the longest serving staff member here, I have a good understanding of the complex political issues that complicate our work here. The vast majority of refugees here depend on outside aid. The UN provides half of all assistance that crosses the Turkish border into Idlib province. This was made possible by a special mandate approved by a UN Security Council resolution in response to the refusal of President Assad to allow assistance into opposition-held territories. Assad claimed cross-border transfer of aid was an infringement on his state's sovereignty and insisted all aid should be routed through Damascus."

"Why?" Nadia asked.

"Damascus claims that Jolani's HTS has enriched itself by misappropriating international aid meant to help refugees in rebel-held Idlib. According to the Syrian government, as soon as aid is brought in from Turkey, those in charge seize the aid and store it in warehouses controlled by HTS. The aid then reappears on the black market and is sold for exorbitant prices.

"Bear with me, Nadia, because this part of my report gets a bit complicated. Initially, it was the Syrian government's refusal to transport aid from Damascus to Idlib that prompted the UN to open the Turkish border. When evidence surfaced that HTS was hoarding the aid, Damascus changed its mind and insisted all aid trucks be dispatched from Damascus, thus eliminating the need for any Turkish cross-border convoys. Now, it has reversed itself and given the go-ahead to the aid convoys from Damascus on condition that the Syrian Arab Red Crescent, which operates under close government supervision, handle the distribution of goods when the trucks arrive in Idlib. HTS has refused to allow aid to enter Idlib under these conditions, calling the Red Crescent an arm of Damascus.

"Critics of the Damascus route insist such aid convoys cannot replicate the size, scope or speed with which aid can be delivered through the Turkey cross-border system and have called for an end to the stalemate. Russia has given its support, despite Assad's objections, to a six-month extension of Turkish border crossing to avert a worsening humanitarian crisis. While the other three border crossings across the Syrian-Turkish border deliver mostly medicine and hospital supplies, Bab al Hawa, in the northwest corner of Idlib, is the most crucial since it allows in large amounts of food, water, sanitation and other supplies, and is the one that will remain open."

Nadia raised her hand to indicate she had a question. "Russia is Syria's ally. Why would it overrule Damascus? Concession of some kind? End of US sanctions on Syria? Recognition of the Assad regime?"

"It probably fears a resurgence of the conflict if the situation in Idlib deteriorates. I assume it also wants to preserve its good relations with Turkey, even if that country has its own working relationship with HTS. As I said earlier, the situation is complicated and not easily understood because there are so many players, each acting for their own personal gains, political or otherwise."

"An excellent point and one I agree with, Abeni." Nadia said. "Thank you. Who's next?"

"My name is Jahn, and I call Oslo home. I oversee the tent cities, and right now we have a major crisis. To date, we've had unusually brutal snowstorms hammering the region. Thousands of tents have been destroyed due to the heavy snow. My workers have been pulling people from under these collapsed tents. None of the refugees have shovels or equipment to clear the snow, so they've resorted to using their bare hands. For lack of proper shoes, children walk through the ice and snow in plastic sandals. The elderly and disabled live in ripped tents in sub-zero temperatures. My crew has been trying to clear roads, get mobile medical clinics set up to help people survive these conditions, repair or replace tents, provide blankets and winter clothing, but it isn't nearly enough. Some of these people have been living under these conditions for three years."

Clearly, Jahn was getting emotional as he described the horrible conditions. "They're understandably desperate. Some live with as many as fourteen people in one tent. Too many of these refugees arrived here with nothing. And when I say nothing, I mean nothing but the clothes on their backs. We can't even provide adequate toilets and sanitation. Open sewers run down alleyways in some camps, and when it rains, this sewage leaks into their tents. You can imagine the mess, not to mention the stink. I can't stress enough how desperate people are here. And hungry. They send their children to scavenge for bits of steel or plastic they can sell to buy extra food on the black market. And yes, the camps are full of black markets."

Suddenly, the peacefulness of the morning came to an abrupt halt. Nadia heard planes approach. Their whistling sound increased in pitch as they grew closer. Seized by panic, Nadia asked, "Where's your shelter?"

Jahn shrugged his shoulders, "This is it."

When he saw the look on Nadia's face, he said, "Sorry, it's just that we're used to these bombing raids."

"Just so you all know," Nadia said, "I'm no stranger to war situations either—Lebanon's civil war, south Lebanon in 2006 during the Israeli war with Hezbollah. I've seen family members and friends get their heads blown off, and I don't think it's ever something you get used to."

That was not an apology. *No need*, she thought. *I'm tough. Over the years I've worked through my PTSD, but as bad as the past was, this is worse.* She cleared her throat, took a deep breath and said, "Let's continue. Have you got anything else to add?"

"What's desperately needed is more money," Jahn said, "and the political will to end the conflict."

Nadia was having trouble concentrating. Bombs continued to fall. She trembled each time she heard an explosion. Yet Jahn continued unfazed, demanding her full attention. She pulled herself together and said, "I'm afraid that's not going to happen anytime soon, and it's not because UN headquarters isn't acutely aware of your needs, Jahn. We have estimated that we'll need $84 million to winterize the tent cities, but only $45 million has so far been pledged, leaving…" she made a quick calculation in her head, "a gap of some $39 million. So, because of this huge deficit, we—"

Without knocking, Antoine opened the conference room door and burst in. "Nadia, the hospital's been hit. Is Andrew still there?"

Her eyes swelled and all she could do was nod.

"I'll get the car," Antoine said.

CHAPTER SIX

As he made his way back to Raqqa from Deir ez Zor, Omar could not clear his head of Abbas's vile behavior. How could this man who compelled a crazed ISIS fighter to eat the heart and liver of another human being be the same man who intuitively knew how to choose him the perfect woman. How was that possible? Perhaps, he reluctantly reasoned, such things were inexplicable and best left unanswered. Every day with Aisha was a surprise, every day full of wonder and admiration for a woman who, descended from a long line of wise Iraqi women, knew instinctively how to handle Omar's insecurities and transform him into a humbly obedient servant of her desires. And he was helpless to resist.

But that night, after the massacre in Deir ez Zor and the appalling 126 men killed, neither the hug from Anwar nor the kiss from Aisha's mouth could shake his profound sense of disgust. After he washed up and took his place at the head of the table, though he tried to resist, he put his head in his hands and sobbed.

"Please don't cry, Baba," Anwar said.

"Whatever it is, let it go," Aisha insisted.

"I can't… the things I saw today. I can't even begin to understand."

"You'll feel better once you've eaten a good meal. I've prepared one of your favorite dishes."

In the kitchen, Aisha was as fine a chef as Omar could have hoped for. She was well versed in Iraqi cuisine and, with all due respect to his mother's fine cooking, Aisha's clever use of spices made even the most ordinary of dishes taste extraordinary.

"Thank you, Aisha. The dinner was delicious, as usual."

"And now, Anwar has a surprise for you. He's waited all day for this moment."

The boy stood tall and confident in front of his adopted father and recited the alphabet in both Arabic and English without stuttering even once. Anwar's stunning performance brought tears of joy to Omar's eyes. He put aside the horrors he had seen that day and applauded heartily before folding his arms around the boy.

"Thank you, son, for such a beautiful gift."

"While I tidy up the kitchen and put Anwar to bed, why don't you take a hot shower and change into your pajamas."

In the two months they had been together, Omar had come to appreciate everything about Aisha. He was still in awe of the things she could make him do. Given a choice, he would change none of them. When he joined her in the living room after his shower, she was lighting a nargileh, a bubble pipe.

"What are you doing? What if someone smells the tobacco and calls the ISIS police?"

"Let them." She laughed and then inhaled deeply before passing the pipe. Omar also took a long drag, holding the smoke in his lungs for some time before expelling it, making perfect circles as he did.

He giggled. "This isn't just tobacco, is it?"

She smiled and shook her head. "I added a bit of hashish."

He threw his head back and laughed some more. "Where did you find it? You know we could go to jail for this."

"Relax. I found the pipe and hash right here in the apartment. The previous owners packed away a lot of good stuff before they left. They dug out part of the walls in their closets and hid their possessions inside, then covered everything up with sliding wood panels. It was very clever of them. They must have assumed they would return some day, poor people, and that their things would stay hidden. In our bedroom,

I found a radio and a cassette player, and in Anwar's room dozens of books, which I was overjoyed to find. And now they're ours to use, and no one will ever know. Novels, many of them English classics—and math, geography, language and science books. I even found some *Tintin* and *Lucky Luke* comics in English. Do you know what this stash of books means, Omar? I'll be able to teach Anwar everything I learned at school."

"But what if someone finds out we have them? They're probably some of the only remaining ones in Raqqa. ISIS had books burned. Of course, use them, but after you're done for the day hide them back inside the closet in case ISIS decides to raid the apartment."

"Why would they do that? You're a high-ranking ISIS official."

"Okay, I'm overreacting, but you know as well as I do that ISIS is everywhere. Their men walk the streets. They question people. One slip and you're arrested and tortured. For all I know, they may even listen in on people's conversations. If we're discovered, we'll be killed, high official or not. What if Anwar mentions them by mistake, or…?"

"I'm teaching Anwar what to say and not to say when he's around other people. He's very bright. He understands much more than you give him credit for. And by the way, he's fully aware of everything ISIS is doing here."

"That settles it. I'd thought to give Anwar some small job at the media center, but now I won't. He's much better off with you. When he's a little older and more mature, maybe then we can let him do more outside the house."

"And let him get caught and turned into an ISIS Cub? No way will I let that happen."

Omar nodded. "We agree."

"If we're in agreement, why do you work for ISIS? They're monsters."

"I'm one, too, Aisha. I've cut off a man's head. I never intended it to happen, and now I'm trapped."

"Why did you join?"

"I thought I could continue doing media work, which is what I did in Homs. Little did I know I'd have to behead someone to earn my ISIS credentials, and by then it was too late to walk away. And now, here we are, both of us part of ISIS until we can find our way out."

"And we will, Omar. And Anwar will be educated so he'll fit into the world we'll find when we walk out of here."

As he inhaled the hash, his shoulders began to loosen, the knots in his gut unwound, his eyes closed and he let his worries fall away. Then, as if out of a dream, he heard Arabic music. When he opened his eyes, he saw Aisha dancing seductively in front of him as she shed her clothes. Before he could make sense of it all, he was lying naked on the floor, and she was placing another of her magic pills on his tongue. Soon he was racing to the stars again.

In bed later, he turned to face her. "That was a spectacular show you put on tonight. I liked it very much."

"The hash or the dancing?"

He laughed. "Both. But tell me what possessed you to go looking for secret panels in closets?"

"I was putting Anwar's new clothes away. That's when I noticed the wood panel along the back of his closet wall. It looked fake so I took a screwdriver I found in a kitchen drawer and removed the panel. There it was, a treasure trove."

"I can't stress enough how careful we need to be, Aisha. On my walk to work I hear what people say about ISIS. They're so terrified, they've started talking to one another in whispers. One man said his neighbor had been caught speaking to a foreign correspondent. He was beheaded. Can you imagine? And when this same man openly criticized the beheading, he was given forty lashes."

Aisha nodded knowingly, indicating that she had stories too. "There's the elderly couple who lives on the floor above us. "

"Yes, of course. I greet them whenever I see them."

"Well, Sitt Amira is either very brave or very reckless. She must think her age protects her because she's not afraid to criticize ISIS."

"That's foolish."

"I agree. Recently her husband was approached by an ISIS prayer clerk, you know,

a man who stops residents on the street and asks how often they pray. If he's not satisfied with their answer, the clerk orders them to attend compulsory Sharia classes."

"And what happened to her husband?"

"He attended the classes. As she said, 'What choice did he have?'"

"Does she know I work for ISIS?"

"She thinks we've moved here to escape battles elsewhere. I'm kind and respectful, and that's all she cares about. And she likes Anwar. He reminds her of her grandson in Aleppo who she's not allowed to visit."

"Why not?"

"ISIS doesn't let residents leave Raqqa now unless they're given special permission, which according to her is rare."

"I'm surprised she talks so freely."

"I get the impression she doesn't have many friends, or maybe they all fled when ISIS moved in. I think she's lonely and just appreciates me listening to her. You and I discuss how bad things are here. I think she feels the same way. Kindness is a rarity these days, and such simple acts of humanity have broken down mistrust between people. Best for all of us if I stay friends with her. Who knows, we may need their help someday."

"Does she ever talk about the people who lived in this building, specifically the people who lived in this apartment?"

"Only that they all fled as soon as ISIS moved in."

"I wonder why they stayed. Didn't you just say they had a son in Aleppo?"

"She didn't say, and I didn't ask. It could be a money issue, or maybe her son in Aleppo couldn't accommodate them. I'll try to find out, but in the meantime I'm learning lots of things about ISIS."

"Like what?"

"When ISIS moved into Raqqa, its men flooded the city with cash. They overpaid at restaurants. They bought up local goods like mobile phones, even trucks and cars. They reopened a flour mill just outside the city and stabilized bread prices. And then, when residents got complacent, at least according to Sitt Amira, ISIS began to replace imams at the local mosques and issue decrees demanding strict adherence to Islamic law. But they were clever. They let the local Council in Raqqa continue to operate and provide services to residents as long as they didn't challenge ISIS rule."

"I heard similar things from Abbas. Listen, but be on your guard until you're sure Amira is trustworthy."

"I understand, and I'm careful. Anwar and I usually don't leave the apartment except to go to the grocery store. I'm content to be here with him. I have fun teaching him, and it's rewarding because he enjoys learning."

"Isn't he the lucky boy!"

"He's such a sweet child, Omar. You did well to rescue him."

"I'm glad I did."

"By the way, I forgot to show you my last grocery bill. I can't believe how much food prices have soared. Lucky for us you have a good salary. Otherwise, we couldn't afford to eat as well as we do. Thank you for taking such good care of us."

Omar was haunted by what he had done to deserve such a royal paycheck and begged Allah to forgive him every day.

Aisha hesitated before she spoke again. "Please don't get angry, but I emptied your carry-on today. It was time. I've avoided it whenever I've gone into our closet, but this time I opened it. I took out all the clothes you hadn't worn in months and washed them, but I left the knife. Is that the one you used for the beheading?"

"Yes." *The day I lost my innocence and became a monster*, he thought. *Hassan was right. A loss I'll never be able to reclaim.*

"If you can't bring yourself to clean the knife, let me do it," Aisha said. "I wouldn't want Anwar to find it and wonder about the blood."

"Go ahead, and then I'll pack it away somewhere safe."

"There's something else I think we should discuss, Omar. I know it's not my place to suggest such a thing, so please forgive me, but it's time we made it official and signed the marriage papers. I'd like Anwar and any children we might have to have parents who are properly married."

"How does it work here?" asked Omar.

"I'm not sure. In Iraq, it's usually an arranged marriage."

"Even now?"

Aisha nodded. "Especially if the parents know one another and have marrying-age children. The parents arrange a meeting of the young couple-to-be. Usually, they agree to comply with their parents' wishes, even if they don't really know one other. Love is rarely part of the equation. There is a simple wedding ceremony called a *Nikah* where a marriage contract is signed, and the bride and groom each say, 'I do.'"

"That's it?"

"There are elaborate wedding ceremonies for those who can afford them, but the idea of the *Nikah* is to make marriage affordable. Not very romantic, but it's simple, efficient and official."

"It won't be like that for us, Aisha. There will be love in our marriage." *I never thought I would say that to a woman, but I have, and I mean it,* he thought. *Aisha has brought joy into my life when I thought I would never know it again.*

"I'll visit the marriage bureau tomorrow and arrange it, and as soon as the certificate is ready, we'll go together and sign it."

* * *

The news spread as quickly as raging fire across a parched landscape. At the request of the Syrian government, Russia agreed to officially enter the war to help its ally regain territory from various al Qaeda affiliated groups and reestablish stability across the country.

Omar was in the media center listening to the news when Abbas popped his head in and asked, "Have you heard? The Russians…"

Omar nodded.

"We're fucked, Omar."

"I know. We'll be their primary target."

The potential for widespread death and destruction was obvious, but how did one go about preparing for something as cataclysmic as the purposeful destruction of a city and the people in it? It was one thing to have been bombarded by the Syrian army artillery during the siege of Homs's Old City, Omar mused, but a squadron of war planes dropping bombs over Raqqa? How could he possibly protect his family from such a powerful force?

The apartment he shared with Aisha and Anwar was on the second floor of a four-story building surrounded by other buildings, so the risk of their apartment taking a direct hit was minimal, but for how long? If Russia's intent was to destroy ISIS, not a single building or site of historical importance would remain standing. Contingency plans needed to be put in place. He would prepare a shelter in the basement of their building and have Aisha stock up on food staples. He'd buy a supply of flashlights and candles should the electric grid be hit. But what if the bombing continued until winter set in? How would they heat their apartment? And if he and his family attempted an escape to the Iraqi border, what would that accomplish? ISIS was there too.

* * *

From a distance, Omar heard the planes. It was impossible to decipher the number, but the roar of multiple engines filled the night air. Aisha heard them, too, and she snuggled in closer to him. Anwar came running into the bedroom asking if he could join his parents in bed. Omar wrapped his arms around his little family and prayed to Allah. Suddenly, a loud buzzing filled the air as the jets swooped down. They came in low somewhere nearby.

Omar ordered Aisha and Anwar to run for the front door. As they made their way out, an explosion cast a blurred, red glow over the apartment. They were in the stairwell and almost to ground level when the building shook. They heard glass shatter and something heavy fall to the ground, but by then they were already in the basement. It was dark and they had no light, but they were safe. Omar listened carefully until he could tell by the sound of the planes' engines that they were arching their wings away from Raqqa.

A haunting quiet suddenly fell over the city and in that stillness he listened. When he felt certain the planes would not return that night, he led his family back up to their apartment only to discover the windows in the living and dining rooms shattered. It would be an uncomfortably chilly night.

Omar closed the doors to the other rooms and invited Anwar to join his parents in their unscathed bed where they lay in wait for the coming of dawn. At first light, Omar rose and made his way through the piles of broken glass to the balcony that faced east over Raqqa. Lingering plumes of smoke billowed up from what he thought might be a storage depot—or maybe the gas station near his old apartment. He thought of his former lover and realized, to his horror, that he might have been injured. What if…? He dared not finish his thought. As much as he feared Hassan's revenge, he did not want to think of him trapped under rubble and left to die alone. Or did he?

When he returned to the bedroom, Aisha had the transistor radio on the bed and was scanning the stations.

"What are you doing?"

"I'm trying to get some news."

"What do you expect to hear? ISIS censors everything."

"We'll find out." She turned up the volume.

A voice on the radio uttered these words: "The United States government has condemned Russian intervention and imposed economic sanctions against Russia for supporting the Syrian government. Officials at the United Nations have also condemned Russia and accused it of committing war crimes. Russian authorities have dismissed the negative stories as false and politically motivated."

Aisha tuned into another station. "Last night, the Russian Air Force targeted ISIS with eleven airstrikes over Raqqa. The primary target was the military barracks. A weapons depot was also struck. The Russian defense ministry said its planes, using precision-guided missiles, bombed a total of nine ISIS positions in and around Raqqa, reportedly killing dozens of their fighters."

So, it wasn't the gas station, Omar thought. *I had no idea Hassan and I had been living so close to a weapons depot.*

"I need to get to the office and assemble my crew," Omar announced as he climbed out of bed. "Baghdadi will want the damaged sites filmed."

"Let me fix you breakfast first."

"No time. We need to document casualties and damage and get it up on our media sites. Baghdadi will think such carnage a good recruiting tool for ISIS."

"What do you care, Omar? Let someone else do the filming today."

He was not eager to be a propagandist for ISIS, but he cared how well he did his job. A poor job performance report could lead to a menial job like Hassan's.

"I'll try to get someone here to repair the windows, but it may not be until later this afternoon. In the meantime, sweep the glass into a pile near the front door so whoever comes can haul it away. And have a look at the basement, too, Aisha. We'll need to make it livable so we can move mattresses and bedding down there. And make sure we have flashlights and candles and whatever else we need."

"I'll take care of it."

When he had dressed and was about to leave, Aisha came rushing out of the bathroom.

"Omar, wait."

She took his hand and placed it on her belly. At first, Omar didn't understand what she was doing, but then she said, "I'm carrying your child, Omar. He's not moving yet, but he will be soon enough."

"You're pregnant?" he asked, dumbfounded.

"Yes, I wasn't certain until just now. I've been calculating the days since my last menstrual cycle and as of this morning I'm 100 percent sure. I wanted the announcement to be a special occasion, but given what's happened and what could happen, this will have to do. You're going to be a father, Omar, and if it's a boy, we'll name him after your father. What was his name?"

"Walid," he replied, tears streaming down his cheeks. He pulled Aisha into his arms and kissed her forehead. "Thank you for this gift."

* * *

In the eastern part of Raqqa, the neighborhood three blocks from where Omar once lived had been reduced to uninhabitable rubble. Twelve buildings in all were destroyed, leaving well over two hundred families homeless. It was difficult for Omar to watch the helpless victims as he instructed his crew to follow a dozen or so women, some of them sobbing uncontrollably as they rummaged through the debris looking for loved ones or belongings. Scattered everywhere were the remains of wedding photos, toys, their children's textbooks, baby strollers, clothes, pages from the Quran. Wherever he looked, Omar saw gray debris, the same sad color of war he had seen in Homs—the unrecognizable streets choked with blocks of cement, twisted metal, skeletons of severely damaged cars and body parts yet to be discovered and pulled from the rubble.

And then he saw a lifeless little boy and called over his camera crew. A man in his mid-thirties pushed through the crowd that had gathered around the body. The man fell to his knees beside the boy. The child, about six or seven years old, looked like he was asleep. The man lifted the boy into his arms. Two men standing nearby helped him to his feet. He pressed the child to his chest and tenderly kissed his forehead. As the man moved away carrying the small body, the boy's head bobbed, and his thin arms dangled. The man took a few steps and stopped. He looked up, lifting the boy's body, and asked. "*Ya Allah*, why?" The crowd parted to let the man pass and Omar watched, imagining the boy could have been Anwar.

In solidarity with her grieving neighbors, a woman in the crowd let out a wail, her shrill, angry voice filling the foul, stagnant air, her message poignant and fearless. "This was once a vibrant neighborhood.

The people who live here aren't fighters. The fighters are ISIS, but we're made to pay the price for their crimes."

For such a remark, this woman would have been arrested by ISIS police and given forty lashes, but these were extraordinary times, and Omar knew she was right, as apparently everyone else in the crowd including his media team did. No one stepped forward to reprimand or report the woman. Though it gave him little comfort, Omar realized he was not the only one who disapproved of ISIS's brutal policies. And if Omar and his staff were sickened by the wanton destruction, he knew Baghdadi would be elated by the footage they had filmed and would want it prepared for social media outlets, blogs and live streaming networks as soon as possible.

Omar sent his team back to the office to prepare the footage while he walked the three blocks to his old apartment. Though he and Hassan had not parted well, he needed to know that his former lover had survived the bombing raid unscathed. Omar entered his old building, climbed the two flights of stairs and knocked on the door. As he waited for Hassan to open, he almost hoped he had already left for work.

When Hassan finally opened the door, Omar could only think to say, "Hi, I wanted to make sure you were okay… you know, after last night's bombing. It must have been terrifying, being so close. If you have a minute, I'd like to talk. Can I come in?"

"Why should I let you in?"

"Because we were friends once, Hassan, and I was concerned enough about your well-being to pay you a visit."

When Hassan stepped aside, Omar took that as an invitation and entered. At first glance, nothing had changed in the small apartment, but not wanting to give the appearance of prying, he walked directly to the kitchen and took a seat at the table. Hassan pulled out a chair and sat opposite him.

"I had hoped to meet your woman, Hassan. I mean, as long as I'm here, why not?"

"She didn't work out."

"Sorry to hear that. Since she was the reason you'd asked me to move out, I assumed it was a done deal."

"So did I. She came to the apartment, but right from the start she complained about the size of the place. She wanted to know how much money I made. I found her overbearing and sent her away."

"It's hard for people like us to find the right woman."

"That nonsense is all behind me now, Omar, and if you think that by coming here you can renew our relationship, you can leave right now. I want nothing to do with you."

"You have no worries on that score, Hassan. But I can relate to your story. I was a nervous wreck when Abbas showed up at my door with a woman. I didn't know how to talk or act around her, and here we are, almost three months into our relationship, about to sign marriage documents."

"You're lying, Omar. You don't have a—"

"No, I'm not lying. I have a wife. She's Iraqi, and she's young and beautiful and she's made me a very happy man."

Later, when Omar went over what had happened next, he realized his mistake. Carried away by his own joy, he had not paid attention to the openly hostile look on Hassan's face and, like a fool, had babbled on.

"And I have more good news I'd like to share with you, Hassan. My wife and I are expecting a baby. Can you believe it? Me, with a child on the way."

"Why would I care?" retorted Hassan.

"We've had our disagreements, and I understand your feelings, but we've each gone our own way and built new lives, so I was hoping we could end the animosity."

Later, on reflection, Omar was not sure why he had shared that news with Hassan. Part of him, he realized, was so happy about becoming a father he wanted to tell the whole world, and part of him wanted to show Hassan he had no hard feelings. But that was not how it turned out.

"You want me to believe you're no longer gay? Do you take me for a fool? Once gay, always gay. I pity any child you may have, Omar. Your wife—does she know about your sexual preference?"

Omar weighed his words carefully.

"My sexual preference, as you call it, seems to suit her quite nicely. I got her pregnant and we're both thrilled to have a child on the way."

"Maybe I should tell her who you really are, share with her some of the more intimate details about our relationship."

"Why would you want to do that, Hassan? Revenge? Why? I went my way, you went yours. Although yours doesn't seem to have brought you much satisfaction. You're unhappy here, and I know you blame me for bringing you to Raqqa. I get that, but you have plenty of cash to pay your way out if you want. Why haven't you gone? And if you've continued to hold a grudge against me because I've succeeded and you haven't, and you're stuck in some menial job, that's not my fault. That was the choice you made."

Omar paused, searching for a way to ease the tension before he spoke again.

"I admire you for that choice, Hassan. You took the moral high ground and refused to become a head chopper. It was an honorable and courageous act. I didn't, and my sin still haunts me, but as penance, I try every day to be a better person."

Hassan sneered at Omar. "A better person? Don't kid yourself. You belong in hell. Killing you is still on my to-do list, so watch your back."

"Still the same threats, Hassan? Why? I would have hoped you'd moved on. Instead, you've become petty and mean spirited. Such a pity. I came as a friend, and this is how you treat me?"

Hassan grabbed him by his shirt collar, but Omar threw him off and walked out the door.

* * *

Before rejoining his staff at the office, still shaken by his encounter with Hassan, Omar walked through his old neighborhood, worried that another Russian bombing raid would destroy it along with the innocent civilians who still lived there. He was anxious to see how those lovely green-shuttered, flat roofed houses with their herb and flower gardens had fared, as they had, at one time, provided him with an oasis of harmony with nature in the midst of spiraling chaos.

The gate to one of the houses was open, and he peered in. The windows were shuttered, the herb and flower gardens trampled, the fruit on the citrus trees left to rot on the branches. Even nature had been abandoned in Raqqa.

By the time Omar returned to the media center, his team had done a commendable job of putting all the footage together. He showed it to Baghdadi, who pronounced it of superior quality and ordered it put up on all ISIS's social media platforms.

*　*　*

When Omar returned home, he found the front door to his apartment unlocked and Aisha and Anwar gone. Panicked, he ran down the stairs and was about to scour the neighborhood when he heard their voices.

"Aisha, where are you?"

"Come and join us, Omar. We're in the basement."

When he descended the dozen or so steps that led to the lower level, he found not only his wife and Anwar but the elderly couple from the building. The man was holding a kerosene lamp.

"I was worried when I didn't find you and Anwar home," Omar said.

"Sorry," Aisha said, and turning to the neighbors, added, "I'd like you to meet Amira and Hammad. They live just above us."

"How do you do," Omar said, shaking the man's hand and nodding to his wife.

"They're going to help us build a shelter. Amira and I—and Anwar, of course…" Upon hearing his name, the boy smiled broadly as Aisha continued. "We've been down here all day trying to turn this dingy basement into what will hopefully be decent living quarters. We moved piles of debris into one corner. Hammad, whose hobby is carpentry, is going to build a wall around the driest section here…" She walked around the perimeter of the future room. "…and close it off with a door. He also knows how to tap into our power source. He'll string a wire down here so he can hang a few light bulbs. Once he's done that, we'll no longer need to use kerosene lamps for light. And Amira found a spigot on one of the back walls, so we'll also have running water."

"Well, you all have had a far more rewarding day than I have."

"Why?" Amira asked, her brows furrowed.

"I toured the neighborhood the Russians bombed last night. So many buildings are destroyed. The authorities haven't even begun to count the dead."

"All the more reason to get this shelter built as quickly as possible," Hammad said.

"I'll help in any way I can," Omar said. "I'm not a carpenter or an electrician, but I have a strong back and can carry a heavy load. In the meantime, I think it's close to dinner time, Aisha. Shall we…?"

"Yes, of course. I lost track of the time. Let's meet down here tomorrow morning, Amira."

Hammad jumped in. "And I'll buy the wood and start working on the room."

"We'll share the cost of the construction material," Omar said, and Hammad nodded. "That would be a big help. Thank you."

Later, when she had put Anwar to bed, Aisha said, "And you know the best part about today? I discovered Amira was a midwife. She'll be able to monitor my pregnancy, and when the time comes, she'll deliver baby Walid."

CHAPTER SEVEN

Andrew knew about the recent Russian bombing raids across Raqqa. Now, those same planes routinely flew over the Idlib sky. At first, he shrugged them off as annoying silver specks meant to wear down peoples' threadbare resolve. It was only when the planes' rolling thunder grew ever closer and daring that Andrew recognized the danger of a potential strike and warned the hospital staff. They refused to listen, insisting Russia had designated their hospital a protected zone.

"Meaningless words," argued Andrew, as he recounted similar guarantees he and others had received in 2006 when fleeing south Lebanon in a UN organized and Israeli approved convoy. Despite a guarantee of safe passage, midway en route to Beirut, Israeli warplanes had attacked their caravan from behind.

As he explained the details to his colleagues, Andrew relived them again. Samir had slammed on the brakes, and he had jumped out. He had craned his head upward and watched as the planes arched their wings back toward the sky only to swoop down again. Instinctively, Andrew had thrown himself to the ground and watched terrified as a missile launched a series of self-deploying blades that sliced Samir's upper torso away from the rest of his body and beheaded Tony, another friend, splattering blood, bone and sinew across Andrew's face and shirt.

He recalled these horrors and pleaded for patients to be evacuated to a nearby clinic.

Andrew was still in the hospital when the planes came in low, the sound so loud it pierced ear drums and quivered heads. At least that was how it felt as the floor beneath his feet shook his body so forcefully he could barely stay standing. Then, just as abruptly, the planes retreated. Andrew assumed they had aborted their mission, but they immediately returned. Their attack was quick and precise. The explosion created an air blast so powerful it lifted Andrew up and propelled him down the long corridor, finally tossing him like a limp doll to the floor where his head slammed into a wall, and he lost consciousness.

When he regained his senses, he tried to sit up but realized his entire torso was trapped under an undefinable heavy object. This limited his vision to the dark void above his head. He tried to give out a shout, but when he inflated his chest, something pressed against it. Whatever had fallen on him was so close to his body it limited his lung capacity. He could take shallow breaths but was otherwise at the mercy of anyone who may come looking for him.

Even as he inhaled, an earthy scent of broken ground and dirt confirmed that he was literally buried alive and would surely die alone in this desolate place if not found. He thought to pray, something he had not done since childhood when he still attended mass, but after so many years without a thought of God, why would the Almighty listen to a former Catholic pleading for his life?

Andrew got distracted and forgot about talking to God. A chill had settled over his body, made worse because his pants were now soggy. He had peed in them. It was the kind of cold that penetrated his bones, numbing his hands and feet. If left unattended, shallow breathing would follow, something he was already experiencing, then a decrease in pulse rate, and finally brain malfunction. On the off-chance God was listening, he decided to pray.

To keep his mind alert, Andrew focused on the noises around him. The groans of the battered building mingled with dangling pieces of metal clanging one against the other. Large shards of glass shattering gave way to a new sound, one he hadn't heard before. Ever-heavier chunks of mortar began to fall. They crumbled into powder once they hit something. These tiny particles began falling on Andrew's face. He blew them off so he would not suffocate, but they continued to fall until they covered his eyes, his mouth, his nose and finally his entire head. When he inhaled, they clogged his nostrils and stifled his breathing.

He had been in danger of dying when Hassan Jaafar's men had beaten him and left him unconscious, but this was far worse. This time his mental faculties were on full alert to register his slow, agonizing death. He closed his eyes and thought of Nadia, the woman he had loved from the moment he had first seen her. After years of unpredictable tragedies, they had finally begun a life together, and he gave thanks for that joy.

He then begged God, if it was to be his fate to die in this way, to take him quickly. As he prayed, he heard someone call out his name. The sound of that voice echoed and reverberated just as Andrew imagined God's voice would if He were calling out to him. He heard the voice again. Surely, this must be God. Who else would know his name or where to find him? And then he heard a sound completely unlike the first—the crackling of a walkie talkie and another voice asking, "Any sign of Dr. Sullivan?"

The man close by pressed a button and responded, "Not yet."

Andrew let out a long, desperate moan but his cry went unheard over the noise of the walkie talkie.

The man on the walkie-talkie instructed, "Keep looking. He must be here somewhere."

Before Andrew could gather the strength to make another sound, the man walked off. He knew he had but minutes before his lungs shut down. As he again pleaded for God's help, two men returned. When he knew they were close enough, Andrew let out a desperate moan.

"Did you hear that?" one of the men asked.

Ever weaker, Andrew tried one last time.

"I hear him!" someone said. "He's around here somewhere. Let's start digging."

The men used picks and shovels and finally bare hands to lift the solid block of concrete and free Andrew. He sputtered and gasped for air while one of the men dusted off his face before slipping an oxygen mask over his nose and mouth. As he breathed in, Andrew looked up at his rescuers and nodded thanks.

"You're going to be just fine. Just keep taking slow, long breaths."

He recognized an accent, likely English. How extraordinary. God did indeed work in mysterious ways. Andrew closed his eyes and thanked Him again.

"My name's Tom," the man said. "I'm a physician." The doctor turned to his co-rescue worker and introduced Salim. "He's with the Syrian Civil Defense. We'll get you out of here as quickly as we can. Now let me check you for injuries."

"Any pain anywhere?" Tom asked as he bent Andrew's legs and arms for signs of fractures.

Andrew shook his head. "Just a bit weak and… as you can see, I've peed in my pants."

Tom laughed out loud. "I'd have shit myself if I'd been in your place."

Before Andrew could think of an equally cheeky reply, the walkie talkie went off again. "Have you found him yet?"

"We have," Tom replied. "He's all right. We're on our way out."

"Well done! His wife will be very happy to hear the good news. She's been here the entire time."

Andrew teared up when he heard Nadia mentioned.

"How long have I been here?" he asked.

"A few hours," Salim said. "It took us a while to clear a path in the rubble to come look for you."

"It felt like forever. I was on my last breath when..."

"I know. I saw you struggling. It couldn't have been easy. We'd normally place you on a stretcher," Salim continued, "but that's not possible with all the debris. I'm afraid you'll have to try to walk out."

Just as Andrew was being helped to his feet, an explosion inside the building blinded them with a cloud of dust. Unable to see, Andrew stumbled but Salim swiftly picked him up and bundled him in his arms. As Tom attempted to shelter them from flying debris, they fumbled toward the light just as a second blast reduced the inside of the hospital to rubble.

Once outside, Nadia ran to Andrew as he was being placed on a stretcher. Crying, she kissed his face and thanked the men for saving his life. A medic rolled him into a large triage tent and placed him alongside other patients. A volunteer covered him with a heavy blanket and wished him a speedy recovery while a nurse administered a warm IV. Grateful to be alive, Andrew offered up thanks again before he closed his eyes and fell asleep.

* * *

When he woke up, Nadia was gazing down at him.

"Good morning, my darling," she said, caressing his face. "You've had a good long rest. You probably don't remember much, but you were transferred to this hospital from the triage center. You've been thoroughly examined and deemed miraculously intact," she added with a smile.

As Nadia spoke, Andrew heard someone from the other side of the room clear his voice. He turned to see his friend Fouad.

"Please don't make this a habit," Fouad said. "I don't like seeing you in hospital beds. It brings back too many bad memories." Andrew knew Fouad was referring to the attack by Hassan Jaafar's thugs that had left him close to death. It had taken a full year, but he had made a full recovery thanks to Fouad's care.

"I thought I'd die." Andrew's voice fell, his eyes moist.

"We feared you had. Thankfully, I was in Damascus when Nadia notified me and I made it here quickly."

Andrew closed his eyes. Nadia wiped his eyes with a tissue.

"Were there many deaths?" Andrew asked

"Very few, thanks to you. Staff said it was you who insisted they evacuate patients and—"

Someone knocked on the door, then peered in.

"May I come in," a man asked in a lively, pleasant voice.

Andrew immediately recognized that voice. He opened his arms wide and, sobbing, called Tom to his bedside and hugged him. "Thank you."

"Please," Tom said, pulling back. "I didn't mean to intrude, but staff told me you were awake, so I thought I'd pop in to see how you were doing. It wasn't the right time yesterday for formal intros, but I'm Tom Cooke. I'm on staff with the Doctors without Borders clinic here."

Nadia said, "As soon as Tom heard that the new staff member was in danger, he insisted on joining the search team."

"Enough of that," Tom said. "How are you feeling?"

"A bit too emotional as you can see."

"Nah, it'd be odd if you weren't. Don't think anything of it."

"Tom, I'd like you to meet my wife, Nadia Khoury. She heads the UN mission here, and this is my dear friend Fouad Nasr from Beirut."

"Welcome to Idlib," Tom said. "All of you, even though your arrival was more than you bargained for."

"Hey, I was the one who jumped into the fray," said Andrew. "You're from England. What part?"

"From London," Tom answered. "I did my training at St. Andrew's Hospital, then stayed on to specialize. I retired early after my wife died five years ago, but then I got bored and joined Doctors without Borders."

"I wonder if we were in London at the same time," Andrew said. "I did an internal medicine residency at St. Thomas Hospital as a visiting scholar."

"I doubt it. I'm quite a few years older than you," Tom said, laughing. "But thanks for thinking I was still young."

"I know your clinic is short staffed," Andrew said. "That's why I came. I'd like to start work as soon as possible."

"That's out of the question," Nadia insisted. "You've had a bad time of it. You need to rest."

"I agree," Tom said. "I just had a chat with your doctor. He plans to keep you here a few more days. But depending on your recovery, he didn't exclude you gradually seeing patients at the clinic. Sound reasonable?"

"As long as it's not more than a few days. Otherwise, I'll go crazy."

"We won't let that happen, I promise," Tom said as he fished in his pocket and pulled out a card. "Here's my mobile number. Call when you're ready. To be honest, we need your expertise as soon as you can give it. We've got a cholera outbreak on our hands. One of your colleagues told us how you stopped its spread in Shatilla. We're hoping you can do the same here."

"You'll hear from me very soon."

As soon as Tom left the room, Nadia reverted to Arabic, the language all three of them often spoke when together. "He certainly speaks a beautiful English."

"Yes, he does. And such a likable man," Andrew said. "I look forward to working with him."

"But I insist you give yourself time to make a full recovery before that happens," Nadia said. "You've only been out of Homs two months, and you're still underweight and—"

Andrew took Nadia's hand and kissed it. "Darling, you came here to do important work, and so did I. We've no time to waste. Tell me, did your additional staff finally arrive? There was some problem with delayed flights if I recall. Did everything resolve itself?"

"Yes, my darling, but don't worry yourself with such things. You…"

Andrew stared at his wife and saw her eyes tear up. "You were afraid for me, weren't you."

"Terrified," she confessed, bursting into tears as Andrew pulled her down into his chest. "I've only just gotten you back after all those years we were apart. I couldn't bear to have anything else happen to you."

"Nothing will, Nadia," he said, lifting up her chin and wiping away her tears.

"But there are risks. You'll be out in the field."

"You face risks too," replied Andrew.

"Not like you," Nadia laughed. "I sit at a desk and order others to take the risks."

"Nadia," said Fouad, "you're overwrought. I sympathize. Yesterday was a nightmare. The injuries he sustained from Jaafar's men were meant to kill him. But you know why you should stop fretting? He's already come back once from the dead. It took him a year to recover, but he made it and went on to work in a refugee camp and then survive captivity in Homs. He's a goddamn superman—let him go to work."

Nadia laughed and looked at Andrew.

"I love you, Andrew Sullivan. I hope Fouad's right."

* * *

The Shatilla refugee camp in Beirut was one square kilometer in size with a population of some 25,000. The challenge of preventing a cholera outbreak there had been straightforward and relatively easy to accomplish. Throughout the camp, Andrew had posted a list of the symptoms—diarrhea, nausea and vomiting, severe dehydration, rapid heart rate, thirst and muscle cramps. Anyone exhibiting any of the above was instructed to visit his clinic. Treatment included readily available oral hydration kits. For severe cases, he administered IV fluids and prescribed antibiotics and zinc supplements. The mounds of garbage were no longer allowed to accumulate. Teams of volunteers placed bins throughout the camp, and the garbage was collected on set days and disposed of in a landfill outside the camp, where it became the responsibility of the municipality of Beirut. This was not an ideal arrangement, as Andrew recalled, but at least garbage no longer piled up and spread disease within the confines of the camp. A group of volunteers helped install clean water facilities while another team constructed sewage drainage networks where none had existed.

By contrast, in Idlib, Andrew faced a perfect storm. The recent cholera outbreak here, if left untreated, would ultimately affect close to three million refugees, many of whom were elderly or widowed women with malnourished children. They lived among some twenty thousand known Salafi-jihadists, all clustered in a thousand-square-kilometer strip along the sealed Turkish border. Andrew wondered what he could possibly accomplish against such odds when the UN and other aid agencies had failed. He wasn't sure, but he was ready to try. When he got the clearance from his doctor, he called Tom.

"I'd like to start working."

"Excellent news. How do you feel?"

"Physically better, but sleep's a problem, along with occasional nightmares."

"Understandable. The hazards of idleness. It allows the mind to wander into dark corners. You most definitely need to get back to work. I'll fetch you in the morning at nine o'clock and we'll begin with a tour of some of the camps. Dress warmly, the weather's turned nasty."

"No worries, I came prepared."

* * *

It was hard to mistake Tom Cooke in his bright red parka with the Doctors without Borders emblem down both arms. Even his red stocking cap had the logo prominently displayed across the front. His beat-up Land Cruiser sported the same logo along its sides and across the roof.

"We won't be hard to find," Andrew joked.

"If Russian planes fly overhead again, you'll be glad they can tell who we are."

Andrew nodded. "You're right."

He had no sooner buckled up and closed his door when Tom started in with his questions.

"You know practically everything there is to know about me. Now, it's your turn to reveal *your* life story."

"Well, by my name, you know I'm American of Irish descent. My grandparents hailed from County Kerry. I left a cardiology practice in Washington, DC, to come to Beirut in 2006 to become officially engaged to Nadia, and for some convoluted reasons too numerous to mention, we ended up in south Lebanon in 2006 just as Israel and Hezbollah began their war. After we escaped, Nadia was kidnapped by a Syrian intelligence czar named Hassan Jaafar and held captive for four years until his assassination freed her. During that time, Jaafar's goons almost killed me. While I recovered, I studied Arabic, and when fluent started working at Shatilla. Fast forward to two years ago when I was kidnapped by al Nusra and forced to run their medical clinic in Homs during the Syrian army siege." Laughing, Andrew added, "Anything else you want to know?"

"My God, you're more familiar with armed conflict than I am. Your impressive list of challenges will serve you well here. The work's difficult with few rewards, but I wouldn't want to be doing anything else."

"I feel the same way about the work I do in the Shatilla camp, but mine is small scale misery compared to the sheer number of people here. In Homs, I didn't have the proper equipment or the drugs to do much of anything except keep the wounded comfortable until they died. Is it any different here?"

"There's a different set of circumstances here. I do what I can to help patients and leave the politics to the other players. That's important to remember. There aren't a lot of nice people here."

"Thanks for the heads up. So, who are these people? What do they hope to accomplish?

"Let's start with the head of Hayat Tahrir al Sham, or HTS as it's called here. He's a ruthless bastard by the name of Mahmoud Jolani."

"I've heard of him."

"Well, I've clashed with him on multiple occasions over camp policies. He controls not only Idlib with an iron fist but every local committee that benefits from international aid. His aim is to see the area he controls remain a Turkish-protected buffer zone so his Islamic emirate can flourish. Turkey's Erdoğan, on the other hand, tolerates Jolani because he keeps the Turkish-Syrian border quiet and prevents refugees from crossing over. Turkey has two problems along its border with Syria. The

Kurdish PKK and YPG are both sworn enemies of the Turkish State and have been designated as terrorist groups by Turkey, the US and the EU. Yet the YPG dominates the Kurdish ranks of the Syrian Defense Forces, which the US uses as its coalition partner to supposedly deter ISIS activities along the Turkish-Syrian border. But the irony is that we all know the US gives ISIS free rein to operate here when it suits them, and that irritates the hell out of Erdoğan."

"What a complicated mess."

"Everything's complicated here. Look at the Kurds. They still believe the US will hold true to its promise to give them a state of their own in northeast Syria. The US made similar promises to the Kurds in Iraq, as you may recall, and we all know how that went. But I digress. Back to the chessboard. Assad's goal is to reclaim as much Syrian territory as possible and free it from Western intervention. A worthy goal if you ask me. What leader wouldn't want to regain full control of his country."

"And what about the Russians?"

"Since the time of Bashar Assad's father, the Russians and the Syrians have maintained a military pact. Bashar knew he couldn't defeat the West's regime change agenda alone, so he asked the Russians for help. So far, they've been very effective in helping him regain control of his country."

"Except when they bomb hospitals."

Tom shook his head and raised his eyebrows. "As despicable as such acts are, the Russians claim they had intel that Jolani's HTS men were using the hospital to store weapons. Sadly, it's not as far-fetched as it sounds. It's well known that HTS has weapon depots all over Idlib. With the military situation on the ground, and Washington's apparent lack of interest in confronting Russia over Idlib, this rebel-held pocket will likely be reduced over time to a small, overpopulated border strip like Gaza with HTS in control. This would essentially force the international community to work with them because they'll be the de facto authority here... at least that's what Jolani hopes."

"Pretty bleak assessment."

"If you're looking for some uplifting news, I'll give you some." Tom added. "Jolani's terrorists now control only three thousand square kilometers in Idlib, down from seven thousand last year, and down from nine thousand the previous year. In the last year, approximately a half-million refugees have fled Idlib for Aleppo and other regions of the country where the Syrian government has regained control. If that trend holds, and if HTS doesn't forcibly detain those refugees trying to flee his enclave, Jolani and his men will be the only ones left in Idlib. That's when Syria and Russia will launch a military offensive and crush them, ending the war."

"Assuming the US will let that happen."

Tom nodded. "It's unlikely they will. The US is leveraging ISIS's power to impose regime change on Bashar Assad."

"What's our role in all of this?"

"It's mission impossible. Learn that right off, so you won't get discouraged and leave. Idlib is Shatilla multiplied by several million patients, Andrew."

"I get that."

"No, you don't. Unlike Shatilla, your successes here will be few and far between. You and I, all of us working here, we desperately want to do more, but we're mere humans, not gods. If you've managed to comfort a few in their misery each day, and maybe found them warmer clothes or accommodations inside a flimsy tent, you'll leave at night thinking you've had a pretty good day."

"And what about the cholera outbreak?"

"I'll get to that soon," Tom said as he parked his car alongside a camp. "Before you get out, put on this jacket and hat."

When Andrew had changed, Tom beamed, "Now you look like one of us. Let's go."

A bare metal frame caught Andrew's attention as he walked toward the encampment. The tent was gone. A man stood alongside the charred debris scattered across the trampled snow. The previous night he had lost not only his home but his wife and five of his children when he tried to light the heater, something he routinely did every night. It had malfunctioned and caught fire. The flames spread to a motorcycle parked alongside the tent. Its gas tank exploded and set the tent on fire. The man's youngest daughter, who had managed to escape the tent, suffered severe burns. She was transported to Turkey for treatment, but her father was not allowed to accompany her.

"Such things happen here every day," Tom said as they walked toward another tent. "They're tragic stories, but you mustn't take any of them on, Andrew. The burden's too heavy."

Before Andrew could respond, a man rushed up to them. "I wish to file a complaint."

"What's the problem," Andrew asked, impressed by the man's formality.

"My family and I set up camp in this field a year ago. At the time, we were the only ones here. We chose it because it was remote from all the other sites. And now, we're a hundred families, maybe more. I can't keep track.

"This morning, aid workers came by—in fact you just missed them—to tell us about the cholera outbreak. We were instructed to always wash our hands and vegetables before we eat. Tell me how we're supposed to do that! What precious little water we're able to find we haul here in buckets or jerrycans from a quarter mile away. With that we're barely able to keep our bodies clean, much less our food. As for our portable toilets, they're filthy and the stench is so bad we gag whenever we get anywhere near them. And we've only been allocated five toilets for approximately one thousand people. If you factor in ten or more per tent, that translates into long lines anytime we want to use them.

"All of this is to say it's impossible to practice proper hygiene. During the cholera outbreak fifteen years ago, I lost both my parents. I don't want to see my wife and children die this time. I'm a simple man, a schoolteacher by training. I feel like I should be doing something about the situation, but I feel helpless. Please tell me what I can do."

"What's your name?" Andrew asked.

"Bulos."

"That's Arabic for Paul, isn't it."

The man smiled broadly. "Yes, that's right."

"Well. Bulos, as a matter of fact I do have an idea that involves using people onsite here. And I'll need someone to be in charge. Would you be interested?"

"Of course!"

"Great! I will be in touch with you before too long. We'll do our best to make things better here, Bulos."

"Thank you."

As Bulos walked away, Tom asked, "Do you really have a plan?"

Andrew smiled. "Yes, I do. I'll explain it to you when we're done here."

When they were a safe distance away, Andrew said, "What the fuck, Tom? Can't we at least bring in more toilets for these people? We're dealing with a cholera outbreak, and its eradication begins with sanitation."

"Look, it's not as if we aren't doing anything. Since the outbreak we've added three emergency mobile clinics. We need a hundred more. We've set up oral rehydration points for first level treatment. We need thousands more. We've distributed hygiene kits that include jerrycans, soap and chlorine tablets, but as you know, extreme cholera cases are caused by ingesting bacteria of fecal origin, which is found in water, most of which is trucked in and stored in containers. We're working with other aid organizations to chlorinate those storage facilities to try to reduce contamination, but that costs money. Water sanitation and hygiene projects represent 4 percent of the entire humanitarian response budget for the whole country. What can I say? This outbreak is beyond our control."

"And clearly beyond anything I ever had to deal with in Shatilla."

"And there's another problem. Syria is suffering from a severe drought, which means we face critical water shortages. If prolonged, the shortages will lead to a low wheat harvest, which will lead to higher prices for the scarcity of available food. These are facts I can't alter. It's one thing for the WHO and other agencies to insist we need to scale up surveillance and testing capacity and truck clean water into the communities most affected. How are we going to do that when the Western nations most responsible for this crisis refuse to help? HTS steals aid when it comes through the Turkish border. How do we stop them? Tell me what more we can do that we're not already doing?"

"Aren't there other ways we can alleviate some of the hardship, like making sure everyone here has warm clothes and proper boots so they're less likely to fall ill?"

Tom threw up his hands as if tired of describing the numerous difficulties. "Here's the thing. Before winter set in, aid workers distributed whatever warm clothing they had collected. We're ten years into this war, Andrew. Funding fatigue's set in. Only 40 percent of the four billion dollars pledged has come in. Countries are reluctant to donate to a conflict zone run by terrorists, and if it isn't in their interest, our politicians aren't willing to find a peaceful solution. It apparently means nothing to them that an elderly or disabled person is sheltering in a flimsy tent that'll collapse in a snowstorm or will freeze to death for lack of warm clothes or starve from an inadequate food supply. And I haven't even mentioned the children, the most vulnerable of all. Of course, they shouldn't be made to walk in the snow in flip flops or freeze to death or shiver all night when the temperature barely rises above twenty degrees, but they do. That's the ugliest of realities."

Tom went on. "Being scared and feeling powerless is a permanent state of mind here, Andrew, so get used to it. I'm always scared because I can't be at my best. I'm scared because we don't have the medicine, or the equipment needed to treat our patients. And what'll happen in spring when the snow melts and the soil turns to mush and the soggy earth begins to permeate the tents and cause respiratory illnesses? I'm scared for the children in these camps who've seen bodies without heads or arms and legs, or seen their parents or siblings killed, and haven't been inside a classroom for years. Who among them will be sufficiently sane or properly educated to contribute to rebuilding this country once this dirty war ends?"

"Are you a religious man, Tom?"

"If you're asking me if I practice the religion I was brought up in, the answer's no. When I lost my wife to cancer, her death shook any notion of God right out of me. Now my wife's the spiritual presence in my life. I can't see her. I can't touch her. But I know she's there, and it brings me comfort. That same hard-to-define spiritual presence helps me do the work I do without the sacred rites and observances associated with religion. Does that define me as a religious man? I don't know."

"Like you, I grew up Catholic," Andrew said. "I was even an altar boy, but I haven't been inside a church in years. And after living in this place for so long, any sensitivities I may still have had about religion were shaken out of me. And yet, when I thought I was about to die in that bombed-out hospital, I reached out to God and asked for his help. Was it luck that I was rescued, or did God answer my prayer. And if so, why?"

"I've come to realize that even if we abandon God," Tom replied, "He never abandons us."

Andrew looked at Tom and nodded. "I'm only just discovering that. Maybe I should talk to Him more often, especially on those down days when my emotions overwhelm me."

"Well, look at the two of us discussing the mysteries of God. How about that?" Tom put his arm around Andrew's shoulders and gave him a squeeze.

"I'd like to explain my idea," Andrew said. "May I run it by you?"

"By all means. Tell me something hopeful."

"I'd like to take the camp we just visited and turn it into an incubator, treat it like a start-up business and teach everyone to work collaboratively for the good of all. I'd divide the camp into small work units and give each team a duty with regular shifts. One team cleans the toilets for a week, the following week it's another team, and so on. In the meantime, that first team is doing something else. Those who are able-bodied could gather firewood from the nearby forest while women, divided into teams throughout the camp, could divvy up extra clothing and share with those who have none, or find material or discarded clothes and convert them into something useful.

"Given the number of people, multiple teams would clean vegetables properly then distribute them for cooking. Those with plumbing skills could try to find a way to transport water, maybe via a pumping system that would bring water directly into the camp. One team could put together the hydration kits and distribute them, the idea being to teach everyone in the camp a skill or two. I'm just throwing ideas out as they come to me but…"

"No, keep going. I like what I'm hearing. I think you're onto something. It'll need some fine-tuning depending on the conditions in each camp, but it's the spark of an idea that just might work. This excites me."

"And I'd like to put Bulos in charge of the project."

"Good. He'd be my choice, too. Let's visit one more camp before I take you back to your quarters."

* * *

Over the horizon and possibly beyond, Andrew saw nothing but the whites of tents, thousands of them, blindingly incandescent in the snow-covered landscape.

"Impressive, isn't it," Tom said as they stood alongside their car.

"We caught a glimpse of these tent cities as we drove in from Beirut," Andrew replied. He shielded his eyes with his hand and gawked. "But up close, its scope is not only staggering, it's terrifying."

"Welcome to the Atmeh refugee camp, population one hundred seventy thousand. It sits next to the Bab al Hawa transit zone where international aid arrives. Come on, I'll show you around."

They had barely set foot inside the camp when they heard men angrily shouting and women wailing. Within seconds, this choir of voices spread as fast as a hail of bullets throughout the camp.

"What are they chanting?" Andrew asked.

"I can't make it out. Let's get a little closer."

An aid worker Tom knew stopped them. "You don't want to go in there, Doctor. HTS just shot a woman in the head for smuggling fuel into the camp. The residents were so outraged they attacked an HTS security checkpoint and set fire to one of their buildings. No telling what HTS will do in response."

Tom asked. "Who was the woman, do you know?"

"Her name was Fatima. She was from a village just south of here, a widow with four young children. Poor woman, she only wanted to keep her little ones warm, like everyone else here."

"Why was that a crime?" Andrew asked.

"You must be new here, Doctor."

"Yes, first day."

"Best you learn HTS's rules straight off. The transport of fuel from Syrian-held areas into Idlib is forbidden. HTS has a monopoly over all commodities brought into Idlib, and that includes foodstuff and fuel. HTS also controls the prices and imposes royalties and taxes on businesses."

Andrew nodded his understanding. "If people can't find fuel to heat their tents, it's only normal they resort to desperate acts."

"Many of them burn dried sheep manure they begin piling up in the summer. It's economical and it keeps them warm. And then you have people like that poor lady who braved the elements to smuggle in fuel. I know a woman who was attempting to bring in fuel one night with the help of one of her daughters. The girl was trying to balance five liters of diesel as she slid between the barbed wire. She slipped on the snow and fell. HTS watched this happen and forced the woman to pour the diesel on the road, and then made her and her daughter watch while they burned it."

Andrew furrowed his brows and grimaced in disgust.

"Before you go off on a tangent," Tom said, "let me explain a few things. Doctors without Borders has worked out a modus operandi with HTS. They give us permission to work in the camps. In return, we don't interfere with their activities."

"No matter how egregious?"

Tom nodded. "Pretty much."

"That's outrageous."

Andrew recalled that al Nusra had similar rules in Homs, but that didn't keep him from voicing his discontent and taking direct action when he deemed it necessary.

"I suggest you leave the camp while you can," said the man. "HTS is going to come down hard on anyone they find, no exceptions."

As they walked back toward the car, Andrew asked, "Where's Jolani's office?"

"Why?"

"I want you to take me there."

"Why? Do you know him?" asked Tom.

"No, but we're about to become acquainted."

"I don't advise it, not today. Besides, he's probably not even there, not on a day like this."

Andrew spun around and asked, "You're afraid of him?"

"And you're not?"

"I dealt with men like him in Homs, so no, I'm not afraid of him."

"You realize you could jeopardize our work here."

"Trust me. I know not to go in guns blaring. I can be both firm and diplomatic."

"Do I have a choice? You seem determined no matter what I say."

"Trust me."

Tom parked the car across from Jolani's office. "I'll wait here," he said.

"No, you won't. Let's go."

As soon as they neared the building, two men stopped them. They slipped their guns off their shoulders and pointed them menacingly. One of them said, "Where do you think you're going?"

"To see Mr. Jolani," Andrew responded in Arabic.

"Is he expecting you?"

"I'm a friend of one of his former al Nusra colleagues."

"And who's he?" The guard pointed at Tom.

"My colleague."

One of the two spoke into a walkie talkie. Within minutes, a man opened the front door of the building and motioned to Andrew and Tom to advance. They were frisked for weapons, then told, "Follow me."

They were led up a flight of stairs. With a raised hand, they were signaled to wait while the man knocked on a door.

"Enter."

The man swung the door open and stood aside. With a tilt of his head, he directed them to enter. Andrew went in ahead of Tom. He advanced a few feet then stopped abruptly. A halo of smoke hung over the room. The acrid smell of body sweat and the competing scent of Febreze air freshener, combined with the stench of an overflowing ashtray jolted Andrew's senses.

He was expecting Jolani to be a tall, imposing figure proportionate to his notoriety. Instead, he found himself staring at an unremarkable man in his early forties dressed in the ubiquitous black T-shirt and stocking cap, with a narrow, pointed nose, a pair of angry, dark eyes, his face framed by black hair and a long beard.

When Jolani, seated behind his desk, saw Andrew, he barked out, "I'm supposed to know you?"

"No, but we have a mutual acquaintance. His name's Omar. I worked under him in Homs. My name is Andrew Sullivan, and this is my colleague, Dr. Collins who—"

"I know who he is."

Just then a figure seated in a chair across from Jolani turned. Andrew recognized him immediately. Ambassador Robert Jenkins had lauded him as his loyal aid and future campaign manager at Nadia's luncheon just minutes before the ambassador was assassinated.

"Hello John," Andrew said in English. "What are you doing here?"

John nodded back uneasily.

Still staring at Andrew, Jolani shouted, "Omar? Homs? I know no such man. Get out, both of you!" Jolani called his guard. "Throw these intruders out!"

"Just a minute," John said as he leaned in toward Jolani and whispered something. Jolani turned to Andrew with a milder expression and dismissed his guard with a wave of his hand.

"Have a seat, Dr. Sullivan," Jolani said. "You, too, Collins."

Andrew's plan was simple and straightforward, and with Jolani's cooperation, easy enough to execute. John's unexpected presence was an extra bonus. It gave Andrew an even better hand to play.

"This was my first day on the job as a member of Doctors without Borders staff here in Idlib. I'd have started days ago if it hadn't been for the hospital bombing and—"

"Yes, I heard," Jolani said. "You're to be commended for saving many lives, Dr. Sullivan."

"Thanks, but I didn't come here for praise. I have something far more important to discuss with you."

"Coffee, water?" Jolani asked.

Andrew shook his head.

"This morning Dr. Collins gave me a tour of some of the camps. As you well know, the appalling conditions are almost too numerous to mention. On top of that, there's a cholera outbreak, which I assume you're aware of."

"That's the UN's problem, not mine."

"Quite the contrary! The UN is already doing what it can on an international level to raise awareness and bring in aid, but this cholera outbreak is local, which makes it your problem."

"How so?"

"Cholera is an acute diarrheal disease that can kill within hours if left untreated. It's caused by a specific kind of bacteria in the intestines and is spread through contaminated water. Safe water and sanitation are critical to preventing and controlling."

"Don't waste your breath, Sullivan. I know all this."

"Perhaps, but you and your men are just as susceptible to cholera as the refugees in these camps, and I think I have a solution that could prevent *anyone* from getting sick."

Jolani's gaze at Andrew seemed to grow in intensity. "Continue."

"Dr. Collins and I just visited one small camp. What was its name?" Andrew asked, turning to Tom.

"Atmeh."

"I know it," Jolani said. "Get to the point."

"I'd like to turn this camp into a prototype."

Andrew explained the idea he had already shared with Tom, closing with, "But to do this, I'd need piping and other building material to deliver clean water directly into the camps."

"Those items are forbidden in the camps."

"Forbidden by you, Mr. Jolani, which means you have the power to reverse that decision."

"Why would I do such a thing?"

"My sources tell me you control all international aid that comes through Idlib from outside. I also understand that you make a handsome profit off each shipment of goods."

Suddenly, Jolani grew agitated. "You dare sit there and accuse me of..."

"Stealing? You're in no position to deny it." Andrew knew he was taking a big chance by provoking Jolani's wrath, but he was in too deep to back out, so he continued. "There's ample proof, so let's not kid each other. You're trying to shed your extremist roots to please your Western backers, and what better way than to allow equipment in that will improve the lives of the refugees who've sought shelter here."

Andrew watched Jolani turn his head slightly to catch John's eye. Without a word, John gave Jolani a slight nod.

"Your project's got merit, Dr. Sullivan," Jolani said as he stood. "I'll study your proposal and get back to you."

"Quickly, I hope."

Andrew and Tom stood. "Good day," Andrew said.

On their way back to the car, Tom patted Andrew on the shoulder, "That was brilliant, and it wasn't what I expected."

"It's much too early to declare victory."

"But you did make a compelling case," answered Tom.

"Never underestimate the likes of Jolani. He has friends in high places. One phone call and I could be told to back off."

"If that happens, we'll call a press conference. I know journalists who'd be happy to take this story on, at least in the European press. I assume you know a few state-side."

Mary and Sonia came to mind. "Even if I did, who'd publish such a story? To catch the West's attention it would have to be Assad depicted as the bad guy obstructing a cholera-prevention program. Let's wait and see what Jolani does. In the meantime, I'm ready to call it a day. Why don't you take me back to UN headquarters and stay for a beer or two."

"Don't mind if I do."

CHAPTER EIGHT

Omar arrived home late afternoon. He opened the door to the basement and was about to descend the stairs when he heard an unfamiliar voice. Hesitant, he peered over the railing only to discover Aisha, Anwar and his neighbors seated around the radio Aisha had found in their apartment. When she saw Omar, she motioned him down the stairs.

"Come listen," she said.

"In phase one of Operation Wrath of Euphrates, the coalition of US-backed and YPG Kurdish-led Syrian Democratic Forces have liberated a seven-hundred-square-kilometer region north of Raqqa. The remaining phases of this operation will conclude with the encirclement of Raqqa and the collapse of ISIS. Ground troops, aircraft with rapid reach capability, along with armed surveillance drones will remain positioned outside the city limits until the mission is completed."

Aisha looked up at Omar. "Such dreadful news. I'm relieved you're home. I don't like being separated with the baby due any day. Thankfully we have the radio to give us updates."

"And what a gem it is," Hammad said. "A four-band radio with multi-frequency short wave AM-FM capacity. Vintage 1970s. I didn't know anyone still had one of these."

"What a relief to know I don't have to worry about your safety," Omar said.

Designed and executed by Hammad with some help from Omar, the two had fashioned a suitable shelter. Hammad had partitioned off a sec-

tion of the basement to create a space that included two bedrooms separated by plywood, a bathroom and a kitchen-dining-sitting area. The
Russian bombing raids had stopped, but the two families had decided
to err on the side of caution and spend most of their time in the shelter.

"Did Aisha tell you where she found the radio?" asked Omar.

"She did, and I laughed, because I did the same thing to hide my
computer."

"But you need internet access for a computer."

"I have it."

"But how?"

"It's issued on a need to have basis. In my case, it's for any emergency I might have at the Tabqa dam. I'm the head engineer there."

"Isn't that outside ISIS control?" asked Omar.

"That's right."

"Which means we're not only privy to news from reliable sources,"
Omar said, "we've also got an important man in our presence."

Aisha patted her belly and said, "And if I have a complication giving
birth, and need to reach a hospital, we'll get the help we need."

Hammad laughed nervously. "I'm not able to call up that kind of help."

"She wasn't serious," Omar said.

"Yes, I was!"

"Aisha, you'll give me an ulcer with all your fretting," Amira said.
"You've had a normal pregnancy. I anticipate no problems. Now go
finish preparing dinner while I set the table. Omar, luckily, I went to the
market early today, before the news broke. Otherwise, I would have had
to fight off a rush of panicked women for the fresh eggplants, tomatoes
and lamb I miraculously found. Aisha was so excited she prepared your
favorite dish, Tepsi Baytinijan."

When Aisha set the bubbling casserole on the table, Omar leaned in
to inhale the bouquet of silky, fried eggplants set in a bed of sautéed onions, garlic, sliced potatoes and meatballs, all smothered in a well-sea-
soned tomato sauce, then slowly braised.

"It's nothing fancy," Aisha insisted, "but it's full of soul comfort."

"Praise Allah," said Omar as he put a spoonful in his mouth, chewed it slowly and savored the rich flavors of his ancestral homeland. He knew this might be the last good meal he would have for a long time.

After they had cleared the table, Amira and Aisha retreated to the kitchen while Omar watched Hammad scan the AM and FM stations.

"Do you have a favorite?" he asked.

"I listen to all sides, whether I agree or not," Hammad said. "I know enough to be able to discern misinformation from disinformation." He checked his watch. "It's the top of the hour. Let's see what BBC Arabic has to say."

When they tuned in, the host and his guest were discussing Raqqa. The host said, "The goal of Operation Wrath of Euphrates is to isolate the so-called Islamic State's de facto capital and recapture Raqqa, but as the Syrian Defense Forces advance, they'll face considerable resistance from the ISIS fighters."

The guest added, "That's probably the reason why US Defense Secretary James Mattis decided to switch from attrition to annihilation tactics, the objective being the elimination of ISIS."

"The coalition estimates there are three to four thousand fighters holed up inside Raqqa," the host replied. "It's unclear how many civilians are trapped there, but the International Rescue Committee has put the figure at two hundred thousand. These civilians are at risk of either being killed if they attempt to flee, or used by ISIS as human shields if they remain. General Mattis has recognized these concerns, saying, and I quote, 'The US forces will do everything humanly possible to prevent civilian casualties. However, in certain circumstances, that's not always possible.'"

"That's not something I want to hear," Aisha shouted from the kitchen. "He makes it sound like we're expendable."

"He's referring to extreme situations," Omar said. "Such decisions aren't hastily made without some rationale behind them."

"If there's a risk of collateral damage, such operations shouldn't be undertaken," Amira said. "I don't want to end up on a list of unidentified victims."

"None of us do, but it's the cost of war," Hammad said as he turned the dial to find a different station. Suddenly, the radio emitted a brittle voice. "This is Radio Monte Carlo *Doualiya*."

Aisha said, "I never realized there were so many western stations delivering news in Arabic."

Hammad answered, "They're a godsend for people like me who know very little English. Have a listen."

The radio voice continued. "It's not the first time in history that Raqqa has been on the map. In the late eighth century, Haroun al Rashid made Raqqa the capital of his Caliphate, which encompassed much of North Africa as well as Iraq and Syria. Sitting on the banks of the Euphrates, Raqqa was rivaled only by Baghdad in size and became a center of scientific and cultural achievement until it was destroyed by the Mongols in 1265.

"The Syrian army recently boasted that recapturing Palmyra from ISIS would be a launch-pad to expand military operations into Raqqa. However, the Syrian units are so depleted after five years of combat they are in no condition to launch a frontal assault on the ISIS Caliphate. This suits the US. They do not want to see the Syrian regime and its Russian allies win the race to Raqqa."

Omar nodded. "So, that's why the US decided to attack Raqqa now."

"It hasn't always been so obvious when they'd fight ISIS," Hammad said. "Their response so far has been spotty."

"Why is that?"

"Their goal is regime change. They simply use ISIS as leverage. Like most Syrians, I know the CIA's been at it here for the last seventy years attempting coups and assassinations. Their strategy changes depending on the circumstances, but they generally use a familiar cast of characters. In Afghanistan they were called mujahadeen."

Omar nodded. "In Iraq, they were al Qaeda, and now they're ISIS."

And the most devious of all iterations, thought Omar, as he recalled both the propaganda he received from his minders while in training and the barbaric videos he produced to attract new followers.

Hammad then switched on his computer and winked. "For personal use, on occasion."

"Of course," Omar said as he watched Hammad peruse a few sites.

"Listen to this," Hammad said, reading from an article translated into Arabic from the *LA Times*. "It's a quote from Mark Toner, US State Department spokesperson. 'We refuse to laud the Syrians for their defeat of ISIS in Palmyra. While our priority is to defeat ISIS, replacing ISIS with Assad's tyranny is not a solution. ISIS is in Syria because Assad allows it to flourish. The fact that he's taken on ISIS in Palmyra doesn't exonerate him from the atrocities he has committed against his own people. With ISIS in decline, the US has decided to take over large swaths of northeastern Syria from the terror group, including the country's major energy and grain producing regions. This will provide Washington with new leverage against Damascus, depriving Assad of resources he needs to successfully govern and rebuild his country.'"

"So, the US and its coalition will take Raqqa," Omar said, "and we'll likely die. What about Baghdadi and ISIS?"

Hammad shook his head. "Against US fire and air power? Not a chance in hell."

"Amira, you mentioned a while back that you and Hammad had a son in Aleppo. Why didn't you move there when ISIS took over Raqqa?" asked Aisha.

"Rami runs his own pharmacy," Amira explained. "He faced enormous challenges when Aleppo fell under ISIS control. Thankfully, the Syrian Army liberated the city and he and his family are safe, but he's busy rebuilding his business. He doesn't need us there to fuss over. When ISIS moved into Raqqa, they left Hammad and his colleagues alone because their work at the Tabqa dam was so vital. That's also why we stayed."

"Why is this dam so important?" Omar asked.

"To begin with, it generates 880 megawatts of electricity not just for Raqqa but for all of northern Syria. It provides drinking water and irrigation for more than 1.5 million acres of land. It's crucial for the dam to remain functional because it sits upstream from Raqqa. If it ever overflowed or got damaged, water would rush over the dam with such a force that people living in this entire area would be swept away."

Omar thought for a moment, then asked, "ISIS controls the dam—so does that mean you work for ISIS?"

"Let me put it this way. When ISIS moved in, we were ordered to remain on the job. If we hadn't, there would be no drinking water or electricity because those crazies know nothing about running anything except their organization. The irony is that they needed us, but they didn't trust us, so they put in their loyalists as our supervisors to make sure we did our work properly. So yes, strictly speaking, I work for ISIS."

"Aside from possible death, what can we expect?" Amira asked.

Hammad replied, "Probable military conscription for men and boys."

"What?"

"According to ISIS," Hammad explained, "boys should no longer stay at home like the women. They must join the jihad. It starts with boys over fourteen. Some of my fellow workers who have sons that age or older are terrified ISIS will force them to join the fight. Eventually, ISIS will need to replenish their fighters. That's when they'll come for us, Omar."

"Thank God our Anwar is still young," Aisha said.

"ISIS tries to recruit young boys too," Hammad said.

Aisha looked troubled. "I don't want ISIS eyes to ever fall on our son."

"Of course," Amira said.

"Some of my colleagues at the dam have mentioned secret smuggling routes to Turkey," Hammad said. "Apparently, the smugglers supply people with false IDs and accompany them across the border."

"I'd need a false ID if I chose to hire a smuggler," Omar said. "ISIS confiscated mine. Did the same with everyone in my office."

Omar had often thought about this method of escape but had not discussed it with Aisha. It was the only logical thing to do once the baby was born. Aisha still had family in Iraq. Surely, her family would take good care of Aisha and the children.

"Any idea what they charge per family?"

Hammad shrugged his shoulders. "No idea, but it's probably a sum I can't afford."

* * *

Omar woke one morning in early June with the intention to accompany Hammad to the dam. Over breakfast, he set about asking Hammad for permission.

"Why do you want to visit the dam?" Hammad asked.

"I have a vision in my head of this towering structure on the Euphrates, and I'd like to see it for myself, if possible."

"Why not?" Hammad answered enthusiastically. "I'm on friendly terms with the guard who works mornings. He won't say anything. If he does, I'll say you're a fellow engineer." He looked at his watch. "I'll be leaving in fifteen minutes. Can you be ready?"

"Of course."

* * *

The Tabqa dam was located twenty miles west of Raqqa. To avoid the coalition forces positioned to the north of Raqqa, Hammad drove south from their northeast neighborhood through the city center. From there he picked up Highway 4.

As they drove through the city, Omar remarked on the hordes of people in the streets. "ISIS hasn't been very successful in preventing the flow of information, has it. People know what's coming. They're terrified and they're out buying provisions."

Hammad nodded and said, "ISIS can ban home internet service and satellite dishes and shut down the cafés and arrest and kill journalists, but when people want information, they always find a way to get it. As in any crisis, news comes from an underground network of internet hackers, NGOs and human rights groups who make it their business to inform the public."

"Look at the long line for bread outside al-Rayan Bakery," Omar said. "It must extend a full city block."

"There's probably the same long line over on Mansour Street at the Nadeer bakery," Hammad said. "I'm not sure there's enough flour to meet everyone's needs."

"Slow down a bit. Look to your left. There's a fistfight outside that green grocer's. Looks like two women fighting over onions and potatoes and whatever else is left. Amazing!"

"Fear is a powerful force," Hammad mused aloud as he brought his car to a full stop, allowing pedestrians to cross in front of the car. "Look at those men carrying cartons of bottled water on their shoulders. They must think the dam will be struck. I hope they're wrong."

"And those women," Omar said, pointing to his right. "They've put their groceries in baby carriages and strollers for easy transport. One is using her child's go cart."

"The people of Raqqa have heard enough stories of displaced persons from places like Homs and Aleppo. They know they're about to face the same horrors."

As Hammad drove on though the underpass that connected one part of the city to another, Omar noticed men parking their cars along the sides of the tunnel. "How futile!" he declared. "They think these walls will protect their cars from damage?"

"I'd do the same. I wish I had somewhere safe to park mine."

* * *

Once Hammad left the city and caught Highway 4, they encountered no traffic. Even from afar it was impossible to miss the twenty-five-mile-long dam on the southern bank of the Euphrates River with its eight floodgates along the upper section.

"How do those floodgates work?" asked Omar.

"Each one is capable of releasing 1,800 cubic meters of water per second when fully open. If the flow was to increase to 2,500 cubic meters per second, it would cause a major flood and submerge Raqqa within an hour. If the dam were ever damaged or bombed, we'd face a humanitarian crisis of historic proportions in all areas downstream."

"*Ya Allah,* protect us from such a fate."

"The staff works round the clock to prevent such scenarios. If the dam were to go out of service for even three hours, such a slowdown would lead to a catastrophe that would be impossible to stop."

Hammad drove up to the dam's only entrance. When the guard saw him, he waved them through.

As Hammad pulled into the space reserved for the manager and parked his car, he said, "That was easy enough. Follow me." He grabbed his briefcase, and they walked up several flights of stairs along the outside of the building until they reached Hammad's office.

"The view's stunning," Omar said, glancing out at the still body of water. "It looks like a sheet of glass."

As Omar would later recall, they had not been in Hammad's office more than fifteen minutes when they heard a plane overhead. Within seconds, a powerful force hit the structure. Omar and Hammad were thrown off their feet, then tossed back on the ground.

"Did that plane just drop a bomb on the dam?" Omar asked frantically.

"If it had been a bomb, it would have exploded."

"Unless it was a dud."

Confused, Hammad opened a side door to his office and stepped onto the steel deck to see what had happened.

A second later, he was back inside. "There's a plane circling overhead. I don't know why it's still there or what it might do, but I need to get down to the operations room."

"You sure it's safe?" Omar asked.

"How the hell would I know? Let's go."

Omar followed Hammad as they ran down the stairs. As they entered the operations room, Omar's hair stood on end when he saw the twenty-foot bomb that had penetrated the first five stories of the eighteen-story structure before landing in the center of the room. It hadn't exploded but the staff was frantic, terrified it still could.

"How much do you think it weighs?" Omar asked.

"I'd say at least two thousand pounds."

"Damage report!" shouted Hammad.

"The impact has damaged the electrical circuits that control the water pumps. The flooding's begun, and the electrical equipment is short-circuiting boss. There's no power to run any of the crucial machinery, including the manual crane," replied a panicked engineer.

"Hammad," said the technician at the control panel, "the reservoir's risen more than 1,500 cubic meters. What should I do?"

"Omar," shouted Hammad, "in my office, inside my briefcase, there's a satellite phone. Get it, please."

Omar sped up the dozens of steps knowing that countless lives depended on him. Minutes later, he was back in the control room. Hammad grabbed the phone, dialed a number he knew by heart and entered a code. He was greeted by a voice that said, "Office of the President."

Omar listened as Hammad explained the situation and then he heard Hammad say, "Hold on while I pass your through to General Dvornikou." Hammad urgently explained the imminence of the major catastrophe at hand to the Commander of the Russian Armed Forces in Syria.

General Dvornikou promptly responded, "I'll notify General Kurilla at US Central Command Headquarters in Qatar. I'm confident they'll understand the potential for a major disaster and order all parties under their command to agree to a temporary ceasefire. Meanwhile, I'll dispatch two of our engineers. They have the know-how to repair the crane so you can save the dam."

"Thank you, sir," Hammad said as he hung up.

"Incredible!" Omar said. "Two generals on opposite sides of the conflict talking to one another. How is that possible?"

"Most politicians have never fought in a war. Generals have. They know the risks, and they talk to their adversaries so they can better advise their respective leaders on decisions they may have to make in haste."

A half hour later, the engineer monitoring the control panel shouted out, "The level's risen to 2,000 square meters. If it continues to rise, I won't be able to reverse it. What—"

Suddenly, the door to the control room opened and two men rushed in. One of them asked in Arabic, "The damaged manual crane—where is it?"

Hammad showed him.

The other man saw the bomb on the floor. Without a word, after examining it, he opened his satchel and pulled out some tools.

"Shouldn't we clear the room?" Omar asked in Arabic.

When the man looked up confused, Omar repeated the question in English.

"Not necessary," the technician replied in broken English. "I know what to do." The man calmly opened a steel panel at the tail end of the bomb.

"What are you doing?" Omar asked anxiously. "Couldn't it explode?"

"Here," the man said, pointing. "Action tail fuse. I dismantle. No explode."

When Omar explained this to the others in the room, they spontaneously applauded.

Just then, Hammad returned to the control room and said, "The manual crane has been repaired. We're back in operation."

There was another round of applause.

Weary, Omar and Hammad walked the two volunteers to their van. As they waved to the volunteers, they heard a plane overhead. Suddenly, the van was hit by a missile and burst into flames.

They were thrown to the ground by the force of the impact. "Oh my God," Omar said. "Those men just saved us… and now they're dead. Do you know if they were Russian?"

"They could have been ISIS for all I know. Whoever they were, they helped us save the dam. May they rest in peace."

Back in his office, Hammad fell silent until Omar asked, "Why do you think the dam was hit?"

"I have no idea," Hammad replied, his voice somber.

"Hammad, you were a hero today."

"No, Omar. My staff and those two volunteers were the heroes."

* * *

It was late afternoon when Omar and Hammad returned to the shelter. At the sound of their shoes on the wooden stairs, Amira rushed to greet them, saying, "*Alhamdulillah!* We've been worried sick."

"Where's Aisha?" Omar asked when he didn't see his wife.

"In labor. And a perfect wreck she's been all day. She's in bed."

Omar anxiously rushed to his wife.

As soon as she saw him, she burst into tears. She took his hand and kissed it. "*Mnishkurallah.*"

"How do you feel? Is there anything I can do to help?"

"Stay by the radio and keep Hammad company."

He kissed her forehead tenderly. "Let me know if you need anything."

"Thank you."

"Omar!" Amira yelled from the kitchen. "I've put out some food. Come join Hammad."

When Omar saw little Anwar seated at the table, he scooped him off his chair and lifted him in the air. "You're going to have a little sister or brother soon," he said. "Which would you prefer, my son?"

"A brother so I'll have a playmate."

"We'll know very soon," Amira smiled.

Omar still found it hard to grasp that he was about to become a father, and that he would be sitting on the opposite side of a thin wall listening to this miracle happen. He sighed when he heard Amira say, "Bless you, Aisha. You waited until our men got home safely. You now have my undivided attention. Let's get to work."

* * *

At one o'clock in the morning, a voice delivered by Radio Monte Carlo said, "The US coalition dismissed reports of serious damage at the dam near Raqqa today as Syrian propaganda. A military spokesperson said the coalition hit the dam with only light weapons so as not to cause damage."An hour later, the same voice on Radio Monte Carlo reported that members of a top-secret US Special Operations strike force called Talon Anvil had carried out the mission despite orders not to bomb the dam because the damage would cause a major flood and kill tens of thousands of civilians. According to military intelligence sources, the same US strike force has launched tens of thousands of missile attacks across Syria, resulting in the deaths of thousands of civilians.""*Ya Ikhwat al Sharmoota*," (you sons of whores) shouted Omar angrily. "*Ya...*"

Omar stopped in mid-sentence. *Why waste my energy cursing an unseen enemy when I could be listening to Amira's voice*, he thought. *She was about to help Aisha bring his child into the world.*

"You're doing great, Aisha," Amira said. "I'm told Iraqi women are warriors. Prove it. Show me how hard you can push."

Aisha let out a loud cry.

Amira continued to encourage her. "Push, Aisha. I can see the head. Yes, keep pushing. You can do it. Good, take a few short breaths. Now push again. Again. Push! Good! Blow out through your mouth, just like we practiced. We want the baby's head to exit slowly and gently so you won't tear the skin or muscles around your vagina. Do as I say, and you'll thank me later."

Aisha nodded, sweat running down her forehead.

"You're doing a great job. The head's out. Keep pushing," urged Amira.

Suddenly, she cried out in excitement. "I've never seen so much hair on a newborn! Now bring your knees back as far as they'll go. Hold them there while I massage your tummy and free the shoulders. One side's out, Aisha. Now, the other shoulder. Push gently."

When Omar heard Amira say, "*Mabrouk,* you've delivered a healthy baby boy," he wept. *And he will be called Walid, after my father,* Omar thought proudly.

Amira placed the baby on Aisha's chest and guided his mouth to her nipple. "Leave him there for a while. His sucking will help produce the hormone that'll induce contractions." When Amira saw the look on Aisha's face, she said, "They'll be mild, I promise, but we need them if we're to flush out the placenta."

Aisha did as she was told, and Amira wrapped the placenta in a clean diaper and showed it to her.

Aisha grimaced, "It's ugly and full of blood."

Amira laughed, "Yes, but it's one of the most important organs in your body. It deserves respect. It's what kept your baby alive and well during your pregnancy. I don't know if traditions are different in Iraq, but here we bury the placenta in the courtyard of a mosque. We're encouraged to bury any separated part of the body out of respect, just as we'd do with a dead human body. We could bury it now if you'd like."

"But there's sure to be more bombing."

"Then we'll wait and bury it later. For now, I'll wash it and place it in a container."

Once the afterbirth ritual was completed, Aisha called out to Omar. "My husband, come see your son."

When Omar entered, he found the baby nursing on his wife's breast. Tears streamed down his cheeks as he leaned in and kissed Aisha on her forehead. "Thank you, my wife, for this gift," he said gently. "May I bring in Anwar?"

"Of course."

He returned with the boy by his side. "Anwar, meet your brother, Walid," Omar said.

Anwar smiled and placed a kiss on the baby's forehead.

* * *

The bombs arrived, loud and angry, breaking into the former stillness of their night. Omar tried to convince himself the bombing was some distant thing on the other side of Raqqa, or in his old neighborhood, or maybe not bombs at all, but someone who had accidentally stepped on a mine or IED. In a matter of minutes—or had it only been seconds—the earth under him erupted. The building shook and nearby glass shattered. The deafening shrill and the vibrations from each thud seemed to erupt inside his head.

With a suffocating gasp, Omar sat up. His panic caused an outbreak of fear in Anwar, who plugged his ears and buried his head in his father's lap. Walid, sucking at Aisha's breast, sensed his mother's fright and let out a cry. Then it was Hammad and Amira's turn. Their collective angst and pleas to Allah gave rise to a frenzy of chanting. When morning finally came and everything around them went quiet, they were left stunned and confused by the abrupt stillness after such chaos.

According to Hammad, local activists had funneled news to exiled Syrians running media outlets. The best known of these groups, Raqqa is Being Slaughtered Silently, which Hammad accessed on his computer, reported that in its first night of bombing the US-led coalition had hit a school, a train station, the immigration and passport building, a mosque and multiple residential neighborhoods, killing sixteen civilians.

Days passed and the shelling continued. When a semblance of calm finally settled over the city, residents, still unfamiliar with the unpredictability of living in a war zone, dared to hope. Thinking the coalition forces might have come to some sort of ceasefire arrangement with ISIS, they risked venturing out.

It was market day, and everyone needed their provisions replenished. Omar had offered to go, insisting it was his turn to run errands, but Hammad and Amira convinced him to stay and enjoy some intimate time with his family. The couple had only been gone about fifteen minutes when a sudden, thunderous bombing raid struck nearby. It was close enough to shake the building and rattle glass windows and doors.

Omar huddled quietly with Aisha and his children until he was distracted by the sound of a thump, as if someone had fallen or dropped something above them. He cautiously made his way up the stairs and opened the door where he found Hammad on his knees, shoulders slouched, sobbing.

When Omar knelt beside him and saw blood on his friend's hands and shirt, he asked, "What happened?"

Hammad's chest heaved as he gasped convulsively for air.

"Hammad, tell me. Where's Amira?"

When Hammad tried to speak, his face contorted. He lifted a trembling hand and sobbed desperately.

"I tried to save her, but I couldn't."

Unable to control his own emotions, Omar pulled Hammad to his feet. Calling Aisha for help, he guided Hammad down the stairs and into a chair. In tears, Omar and Aisha fell to their knees in front of Hammad and waited as he tried to speak.

"Take a deep breath, Hammad," Aisha said.

Hammad breathed in, then sighed and said, "I heard a terrifying noise, and then everything turned black. A powerful force picked me up. It slammed me against a nearby wall and left me stunned. My ears rang and I couldn't hear anything. I assumed Amira was right beside me. We'd been walking side by side when the bomb exploded, and before I could even look around a second bomb struck."

Aisha covered her mouth with her hands and wept.

"Then I heard Amira screaming. She was lying on the ground nearby. Her legs were sliced open to the bone." He sobbed uncontrollably. "She kept screaming 'Hammad, make the pain go away.' I felt so helpless."

In shock, Hammad grabbed hold of Omar's shirt and pulled him closer. "I couldn't do anything... I couldn't help her."

"There was nothing you could have done, my friend."

"I couldn't just leave her there, so I tried to lift her. That's when I saw the blood on the back of her head and down her back. My poor Amira."

"I'm so, so sorry, Hammad," Aisha cried, barely able to utter the words through her tears.

"Finally, I ignored her screams," Hammad said. "I lifted her in my arms and walked as fast as I could to the hospital. When I got there, the ISIS guard at the door said she wasn't eligible for treatment and ordered me to leave. 'But she is,' I insisted. 'I'm the manager at the dam. ISIS employs me.' He saw how badly Amira was injured, but he didn't care. I didn't know what to do, so I kept walking, trying to find another hospital, but she died in my arms."

Hammad buried his face in his hands and let out a long, sorrowful moan. "My poor Amira."

Omar wrapped his arms around Hammad and wept with him while Aisha, still on her knees, crumbled to the floor.

Finally, Omar pulled away and asked, "Where is Amira's body now?"

"At the city morgue. When the bombing stops, I'll go and prepare her for burial."

"I won't let you do that alone," Omar said. "I'll go with you."

"If I had someone to take care of the children," Aisha said, "I'd bathe and prepare her myself."

Hammad nodded. "I know."

In that moment, Omar made a promise to himself. He would dig into his stash of cash and hire a smuggler to take Hammad to his son in Aleppo. It was the least he could do.

If Omar could find him, he might be able to convince Abbas to help him find a reliable smuggler who would also take Aisha and the children to Iraq. He had not yet broached the idea with Aisha, and he knew it might take some persuading, but he was certain she would eventually acquiesce. This might be his last noble gesture ever. He was ISIS, and he did not know what awaited him once the siege ended.

* * *

Two days passed before it was calm enough for Omar to accompany Hammad to the city morgue. When Omar pulled open the heavy door, he and Hammad were thrust into a crowd of mourners crammed into the vestibule. He and Hammad nudged their way forward until they reached the information desk.

"I'm here to prepare my wife for burial," Hammad said.

When the attendant looked up, he recognized Hammad and asked, concerned, "What are you doing here?" When Hammad didn't respond, the attendant realized what had happened and said, "Oh my God, it's Amira, isn't it?" He scurried from behind his desk and hugged Hammad. "I'm so, so sorry."

Hammad nodded and turned to Omar, gesturing toward the attendant.

"Omar, this is my friend, Michel. We've known each other since childhood."

Michel hugged Hammad again before he returned to his desk. "Give me a minute, Hammad. Let me find Amira." He ran his finger down one page, then another and another until he finally found her name and corresponding number.

"It isn't pleasant in there," he said. "Are you sure you want to go inside? I can have one of the women prepare her for burial."

"No," Hammad said. "I want to do it."

"I understand, my friend," said Michel. "I'll take you to her, and if you need anything, please let me know."

The stench of decomposing bodies in the hot, windowless room was unbearable. Omar felt the urge to vomit and swallowed hard to stop the convulsion. He and Hammad followed Michel down row after row of what looked like a slaughterhouse of bloodied carcasses, some missing limbs, others with open abdomens. Suddenly, they stopped. When Michel pulled a sheet down to reveal Amira's face, Hammad burst into tears.

"My deepest condolences, my friend," Michel said quietly. "You have thirty minutes to prepare her for burial. You're welcome to stay for the joint funeral rites. Given the circumstances, both a priest and an imam will perform the funeral service for all of the deceased."

Within a few minutes, a woman brought Hammad a sponge, fresh water, three sheets and three pieces of rope. Hammad worked under the sheet to undress his wife and wash what was left of her body. The only time Omar saw any nakedness was when Hammad lifted her upper torso to clean her back. When Hammad had finished, he bent down and lovingly kissed his wife for the last time. Omar helped him wrap her in the three sheets, tying them at the top, the middle and the base of her feet.

He then led Hammad back to the foyer to join the other mourners. The bodies were carried out and placed on the ground in a courtyard behind the morgue. During the service, Omar and Hammad repeated the prayers with the other mourners as the bodies were lifted down one by one to the grave diggers who laid them next to each other in one of a dozen similar graves. Quicklime was spread over the remains before each gravesite was filled with dirt. Given the circumstances, and the number of bodies buried together, there were no individual grave markers.

Omar wrapped his arm around Hammad, then softly said, "May she rest in peace." He then led Hammad away.

* * *

From the morgue, Omar walked Hammad through Rashid Park. They were close to the open-air market when another bevy of bombs fell nearby, causing mass confusion and igniting a fire in a nearby building. People frantically ran out screaming for volunteers to search for survivors.

Omar rushed inside the building with Hammad close behind. Dozens of bodies lay scattered across the blood-soaked lobby floor. Omar spotted Hassan's mangled body lying in a corner and rushed to his side. He fell to his knees beside the dying man.

"Hassan! It's me, Omar. I'm so sorry," he said, shaking in shock. He leaned in close and spoke quietly in English, the only language the two had ever spoken together. "Please forgive me."

Hassan struggled to speak until he finally let out a long, mournful cry. "No, you're a head chopper." He repeated the word again until Omar put his hand over Hassan's mouth and left it there. He stared into Hassan's eyes until the Somalian stopped convulsing and his body went limp. Omar stood up and somberly walked away.

As they made their way back home, Hammad asked Omar, "Who was that man? He kept yelling something I couldn't understand."

"A friend I knew a long time ago."

CHAPTER NINE

Tom parked his Cruiser beside the other vehicles at the UN headquarters and followed Andrew through the front door while still talking about the prototype project.

"You realize that if you succeed here, you'll be asked to travel to other camps."

"Let's take care of Idlib first, and then we'll see," Andrew said before walking on.

"Hold on," Tom said, poking his head into a room on his left. "Conference room?"

"Yes, and offices across the hall."

"Not bad."

"I agree. Staff's comfortably set up here, with a cafeteria at the end of the hall."

"Bedrooms?"

"Plenty of them upstairs with a shared bathroom at the end of the corridor."

"Does the toilet flush?" Tom asked.

Andrew laughed. "It does."

"And do you have running water and heat?"

Andrew nodded.

"Then you've got it pretty nice here."

"Don't think that I'm not grateful for these luxuries, my friend, and for the food we're served, while outside these walls people are living in tents and starving. Come on, the cafeteria's just down the hall."

Before they went in, Andrew heard the voice of a woman he hated for the self-serving crimes she had committed. This woman and Nadia were going hell for leather at each other in Lebanese Arabic, punctuated by the occasional English or French phrases.

"Sounds like a firestorm in there," Tom said, concerned.

Andrew peeked in the room and nodded.

"See that woman with the eye patch? That's Sonia Rizk, a real piece of work. She orchestrated Nadia's kidnapping. Made a pact with Hassan Jaafar—Nadia in exchange for information about the Harari assassination."

"You mentioned Jaafar earlier. Wasn't he Syria's intelligence chief?"

"The same."

"So, what's this Sonia woman doing here?"

"I guess we're about to find out."

Tom asked, "What about the attractive lady sitting opposite your wife. Who is she?"

"Mary O'Brien, an American journalist."

"She could warm an old man's heart."

"She's been through a lot. Leave her alone."

"She's beautiful, why would I do that?"

"Because you're a gentleman."

Tom laughed. "Don't be so sure."

Andrew rolled his eyes. "Come on, lover boy, let's discover the worst."

Andrew knew that Nadia and Sonia had not met since the kidnapping, so Nadia was rightfully venting her fury, but this was not the appropriate setting. As head of the UN operations in Idlib, Nadia could not be seen as irate, but that was exactly how she appeared.

"You waltz in here unannounced with your clueless sidekick," Nadia was screaming at Sonia, "and unashamedly ask for forgiveness while you should be groveling on the floor like a supplicant. I should dig your other eye out with a plastic fork! *Ya Sharmoota!* (female whole)."

"*Kiss emik*" (your mother's vagina)," Sonia screamed back.

Andrew heard the alarming fury in Nadia's voice and knew he had to intervene before the situation further degenerated.

"Hello ladies!" Andrew said brightly in English as he and Tom approached the table. "Lively discussion going on here, I see. Let's move away from any sharp objects."

Nadia glared at Andrew, still panting with rage.

He came closer and whispered, "Had I known she was here, I'd have come sooner."

Nadia nodded and, recomposing herself said, "You must be exhausted after such a long day."

"Actually, I'm not. We had a very productive day."

Andrew and Tom pulled up two chairs and joined the women at the table.

"Well, Tom, you must have had something to do with it since you two spent the day together," Nadia said.

Tom graciously bowed his head.

"As to my day," Nadia said, "imagine my surprise when Sonia showed up in my office with her friend."

"I apologize," Mary said. "We should have called ahead."

Nadia turned to her and said, "*You're* welcome, Mary. What brings you here with this parasite?"

They all looked at each other awkwardly, and Tom broke out laughing. Mary, clearly trying to defuse the tension, said, "We were in Damascus, attending a conference on Assad's alleged use of chemical weapons. For some unknown reason, so was Mohammad Jolani. We couldn't figure out what the head of the largest jihadist stronghold in Syria was doing there, so we decided to come to Idlib to find out. We knew you two were working here—another incentive, for me at least—so we hired a driver and here we are. I was unaware our arrival would cause such a ruckus. I'm so sorry."

Nadia ignored her apology and turned her attention to Tom.

"Tom, I'd like you to meet Sonia Rizk, an Arab analysist, and Mary O'Brian, a journalist from the US."

Turning to the two women, she continued her introductions. "Tom is a British staff physician with Doctors without Borders here in Idlib City. Andrew will be working in their clinic while I'm on assignment here."

After shaking the ladies' hands, Tom wrapped his arm around Andrew's shoulder and said, "You all need to know what this boy's just done. Not only will he be seeing patients in our clinic, but he has just proposed a major project to Jolani. If approved, it will revolutionize the way we treat a cholera outbreak." He went on to explain Andrew's ideas.

"Bravo, Andrew," Nadia said, kissing his cheek. "No wonder you're so happy."

"No accolades yet, please. First, Jolani must approve the plan. Then, if he does, the hard work begins."

"Kids, I'm desperate for a beer right now," Tom said. "Anyone else?"

"Absolutely!" Mary chimed in.

Tom and Andrew left for the kitchen and returned with beer-laden arms. Tom then asked the two newcomers, "And where will you be lodging?"

"Sonia booked us a room at the Tughra Hotel."

"Poppycock! It's miles out of town and you're carless," Tom said. "What were you thinking? I live in a house much closer to town with plenty of room. You're welcome to stay there. And I can help you with your Jolani inquiries. I know just about everything there is to know about that slimy bastard."

"That's very kind of you," Mary said as she glanced at Sonia for her approval. "We gladly accept your invitation."

"Then it's settled."

"Glad that worked out," Andrew said with a smile.

"I'll notify the kitchen that we have guests for dinner," Nadia said.

Tom quickly changed chairs and set himself next to Mary. Grinning at her, he said, "Morning, my dear."

"It isn't morning," Mary replied.

Tom guffawed and said, "Hark at this one! She's sharp as a tack."

Mary laughed and punched his shoulder. "Ouch!" he cried. "And she's got a sharp right hook as well."

Andrew was telling Mary and Sonia about his encounter with John in Jolani's office when Nadia returned.

"I saw them talking to one another in Damascus," Mary said. "How do John and Jolani even know one another?"

"Here's my theory," Andrew said. "It's the only thing that makes any sense. John was Jenkins's security officer. Jenkins was CIA. John probably is, too, and if so, he takes his orders from the same higher-ups the ambassador did—likely the same people who support Jolani's make-over in Washington from jihadist to influential counterbalance to Bashar Assad. Antoine, our UN Coordinator, confirmed a lot of this on our trip up here, didn't he?" Andrew asked Nadia.

"Yes, he did," she replied.

"I've suspected all along that John had something to do with Jenkins's assassination," Sonia said.

"After our encounter with him in Damascus, I agree," Mary said.

Andrew saw the confusion on Tom's face.

"Robert Jenkins was the US Ambassador to Syria. He was charged with carrying out his government's regime change policy here. Thanks to Nadia's influence, he resigned his post and intended to write a book about his role here, but he was assassinated at a luncheon we all attended. We saw the whole thing happen, from his head falling onto the table to the blood on the white tablecloth."

"There you have it," Tom said. "The motive for his assassination. Whether John was the culprit or not, no intelligence agency tolerates a traitor. Was John at the luncheon?"

"Yes," Nadia said. "He was seated right next to Jenkins."

"John and I spent quite a bit of time together in Boston preparing for Robert's funeral," Nadia said. "He appeared devastated by the ambassador's death. In fact, he was very convincing. Had me fooled, if he was lying. He had planned to resign, too, as you may recall, to run Robert's senatorial campaign, but the meeting he had with Jolani now calls everything he said into question."

"His standoffish behavior in Damascus, especially when he didn't like what we were saying, only confirms this," Mary said.

"If he was so upset about Robert's murder and had planned to retire, why did he choose to stay in Damascus?" Tom asked.

"He claimed the embassy was short staffed and needed his help," replied Sonia.

"Made sense when we heard him say that," Mary said, "but then he showed up at the chemical weapons conference when he had told us he had a prior commitment at the embassy that day."

"What if he never intended to retire or leave Damascus?" Nadia asked. "What if he's Washington's conduit to Jolani?"

"That sounds plausible," Tom said.

"Fouad was also at the conference," Sonia added. "He briefly greeted us, but then he disappeared. Maybe he left to follow John and Jolani."

"That might have been about the time I called to tell him Andrew was trapped inside the hospital," Nadia said. "He probably left because of my phone call."

"But why didn't he tell us about Andrew?" Mary asked. "Why did we have to come to Idlib to hear about the accident from Nadia?"

"Probably because he knew neither Nadia nor me would have wanted to see Sonia."

"Who's this Fouad you're talking about?" Tom asked.

"Deputy Director of Lebanon's Internal Security," Sonia explained.

"God! I wouldn't trust that lot," Tom said.

"I trust them over anyone else in the area," Sonia replied indignantly.

"I think he'd have a vested interest in John's whereabouts," Mary said.

"I agree, especially if he also suspects John's CIA," Nadia said. "The CIA has tried for years to destabilize Syria, and they're guilty of multiple assassination attempts in Lebanon. So was Robert, for that matter, and we have the documents to prove it."

"As an outsider listening in on this discussion, I'd have to say Andrew's theory makes the most sense," Tom said. "And while it's important you solve the mysteries surrounding John, it doesn't solve our cholera crisis. My concern is whether Jolani will agree to allow Andrew's project to go forward."

"If the CIA wants to prop Jolani up, they'll likely use this project to that end," Nadia said.

"To nudge it along," Mary said, "allow me to suggest a plan that will not only persuade Jolani but also his backers. Give me permission to write a story about the hospital bombing that'll include your proposal to Jolani. I've written a book about the war here, and I've got a publisher in London who will publish it."

"Well done, Mary," Tom chimed in.

"Yes, well I am actually pleased," she said, casting a glance at Tom, "but I only mentioned the book deal because it has stirred up a bit of publicity. So, I'm certain to find a media outlet in the States willing to carry a story about you, Andrew, and the hospital bombing. I realize those memories are still raw, and I wouldn't want to put you through any undue stress, but if framed properly, such a story could persuade Jolani to approve your project."

"I like that idea," Nadia said.

"So do I," Tom said. "Imagine Jolani doing something honorable. His backers will love it!"

"That's the plan," Mary said.

* * *

As the dinner hour approached groups of staffers strolled in, many of them only recently arrived due to logistic and weather-related delays. With the distraction of their lively chitchatting and the shuffling of tables and chairs, no one noticed the man with the white apron and cap who approached their table until he said, "Good evening, everyone, and welcome."

"Salim, how nice of you," Nadia said. "Friends, this is our amazing chef who manages to feed us every day no matter the challenges."

"Thank you, Sitt Nadia. You're much too kind. I wish I could offer a wider variety, but it all depends on what I find locally and what I can grab off the supply trucks from Turkey. But you're in luck. This morning, I got my hands on some okra and fresh tomatoes along with a generous amount of cilantro, so I prepared a nice stew. I also found some fresh greens for a change, so you'll have a salad as well. Enjoy."

"Salim, how do you manage to bring the beer in?" Tom asked.

Salim laughed. "It's a concession to staff here. The UN staffers in Damascus stay in a luxury hotel with wine and fine food so it's the least they can do for us here in the wilderness."

"God bless them!" Tom said.

"Now, if you'll excuse me, I have a bit more to do before I open the dinner line."

While they waited, Andrew and Tom served everyone another beer. When dinner was finally served, they fell silent and ate like hungry wolves.

"Best okra dish I've ever eaten," Tom said. "I wonder if there'll be enough for seconds."

Mary looked up from her plate. "I was wondering the same thing."

Everyone laughed.

"Anyone object if I start asking Andrew some questions?" Mary said.

"No," Andrew said. "Fire away,"

"I'd like to say something before we begin," Sonia said, looking at Nadia. "I know you aren't accepting apologies, but right now, we need to make this project work. For that to happen, we all need to be on the same side."

Nadia looked up and caught Andrew staring at her. He gave a gentle nod of his head as if to say, "It's all right, go ahead."

"Okay, we'll put it aside for now."

An audible sigh of relief took hold over the table.

Mary began her interview. "First question—I understand you spent months in the hospital recovering from a vicious attack."

"I can't talk about that," Andrew said. "Too painful."

"Understandable. Why did you decide to take a leave of absence from your Doctors without Borders clinic in Beirut to work in Idlib, the most dangerous place in Syria?"

"A better question," he said, and then relayed as much detail as he thought relevant to make the story a page grabber.

"You didn't mention the Arabic lessons," Nadia interjected. "To distract from his injuries, he studied one of the most difficult of languages, and he did it so he could work in the camp."

"How honorable, old chap," Tom said.

"He wanted to rescue Nadia, so he learned boxing to fend off her keepers," Sonia added.

Andrew put up his hands. "Stop. You're embarrassing me."

"No, I want to hear more," insisted Tom.

"Enough!"

"It's remarkable the number of challenges you've overcome the last ten years," Sonia said.

Andrew sat back in his chair, momentarily quiet, then said, "All the struggles and hardships Nadia and I have faced over those years you've had a hand in."

Mary jumped in. "You almost died, Andrew. You were literally buried alive. What was going through your mind?"

"Nadia," he replied. "I was thinking about the first time I saw her."

Mary kept her eyes down. Sonia sat back, annoyed, and Tom said, "Tell it, old chap." Nadia put her hand over her face.

Andrew turned to his wife and said, "As you danced to Arabic music, your long auburn hair swung back and forth across your shoulders. I was mesmerized by your beauty, your elegance. It was in that moment that I knew I would love you for the rest of my life. Do you recall how I came up to you? I didn't even introduce myself before I asked you to marry me."

Nadia nodded. "And I answered, 'I think we should get to know each other first.'"

"In that heap of rubble, I thought about our wedding day, the happiest day of my life, and as it got harder and harder to breathe, and I felt certain I was going to die, I focused on your face. Your image was the last thing I wanted to remember. You kept me calm, Nadia... until I was rescued."

Andrew drew in a long breath and exhaled slowly while Mary searched in her pockets for a tissue. When she couldn't find one, Tom handed her his hanky.

Mary said, "Do we need a time out?"

"No," Andrew replied. "Let's get on with it."

"Okay. Tell me about the actual rescue. Who were the men who removed the rubble and set you free?"

"Tom was part of the rescue mission. He volunteered even though it wasn't his job. The other man was Salim from the Syrian Civil Defense."

"You mean the White Helmets. That's their real name," Sonia said, "and they're not the squeaky-clean people they pretend to be."

"All I know is what they told me, Sonia. They could have been mass murderers for all I cared. I was seconds away from taking my last breath, and that man helped save my life. Yes, he was wearing a white helmet. Why is that such a big deal?"

"It's not," Mary chimed in to prevent another confrontation. "At face value, they're an unarmed group of some three thousand volunteers. They operate in opposition-held areas. Their job, after every chemical weapons attack and Syrian airstrike, is to dig for survivors, evacuate the injured and bury the dead."

"I can vouch for that, except in my case the airstrike was Russian, not Syrian," said Andrew.

"If it wasn't for those men," Tom added, "hundreds of wounded would die or still be buried under the rubble."

"I agree," Mary said, "and it's not the men who do the rescuing we question. The controversy around the White Helmets centers on its late founder, British intelligence veteran James Le Mesurier, and his employer, the Western intelligence contractor called Analysis, Research and Knowledge."

"Why would that be controversial?" Andrew asked.

"Since its founding in October 2014," Sonia explained, "the US State Department and the UK Foreign Office have supplied the White Helmets with about $70 million while additional millions have flowed into its coffers from NATO and other opposition sources. The Pentagon played a role, too, financing an Oscar-winning documentary promoting the White Helmets. The goal of the film was to drum up public support for a humanitarian group that opposed Bashar Assad."

"Assad's by no means innocent," Andrew said, "but he's being used as the bad guy for everything that happens here. I suspect those same contradictions apply to the White Helmets, even though they do vital work."

"They do, but they only operate in areas under insurgent control. This taints them in the eyes of the Syrian government," Sonia said.

"Doctors without Borders only operates in insurgent controlled territory," Tom said. "Does that make us tainted too?"

"There must be some reason for that," Mary said.

"It's partly due to security concerns," Tom asserted. "In mid-2013, when al Qaeda-linked groups moved into areas where Doctors without Borders were running their hospitals and clinics, the terrorists abducted thirteen members of their medical staff. The Syrians in the group were released within days while the internationals working under the Doctors without Borders banner were held for five months. After that incident, the organization withdrew its staff and closed its facilities in all ISIS-controlled territories. The Syrian government declared any clinic that operated in opposition-controlled areas to be illegal and legitimate targets for attack."

Andrew interrupted, saying, "That's why hospitals working with Doctors without Borders should never give GPS coordinates to either the Russians or the Syrians. It only opens them up to aerial assaults."

Mary steered the conversation back to the White Helmets. "Evidence suggests the White Helmets were implicated in the false claims that Assad used chemical weapons."

"What do you mean false claims? I've seen the photos," Tom said. "They leave no doubt as to what happened."

"We've seen them too," Sonia said. "Hear us out, and then decide if what we say has merit."

"Fair enough."

Mary and Sonia teamed up to explain what they had heard at the Damascus conference about a possible politically-motivated cover-up. As their explanation reached a crescendo, Sonia said, "Now there's new evidence to suggest the allegations of a cover-up could be true. If you're not familiar with how the OPCW collects its samples, the procedure's very straightforward."

Mary opened her bag and took out a notebook. Turning to a certain page, she read aloud, "The OPCW's chain of custody requirements are so stringent that any inspector who is not specifically assigned for evidence-related tasks is not allowed to deal with any item linked to an investigation site. According to its chain of custody and confidentiality code, the inspector must have physical control of the sample. The sample must be under continuous visual observation by an OPCW inspector and be kept under OPCW seal. If the integrity of a sample is questionable, the Inspection Team Leader must be informed. Such a sample will not be accepted for OPCW verification purposes."

"No room for error there," Tom said.

Mary responded. "When Western and Israeli officials began accusing the Syrian government of chemical weapons use—an alleged violation of Obama's so-called red line—the OPCW laid down its own red line. It would never get involved in testing samples that their own inspectors hadn't gathered in the field themselves."

Sonia picked up the thread. "In 2014, the watchdog sent a team to a town in northern Syria to investigate claims of a toxic bombing by the Syrian government, but the OPCW team never reached its destination. A roadside bomb hit the four-vehicle convoy. Armed insurgents opened fire. They kidnapped the inspectors, and the OPCW abandoned not only that mission but all other on-site deployments."

"I remember that incident," Tom said.

Sonia nodded and continued. "That's when the OPCW began to outsource its duties to groups still able to operate in insurgent-held areas, and where the White Helmets come in. They became an OPCW partner. They identified sampling locations. They collected and tagged samples. They gathered video and photo evidence. In some cases, they selected witnesses for interviews. Then they traveled to the Turkish border and handed their material to OPCW staffers operating out of hotels there."

"Okay, maybe the White Helmets aren't as impartial as they should be," Andrew said, "but their enlistment could be seen as a practical solution. They have free rein to move through insurgent-held territory without fear of attack."

"In principle, yes," Sonia replied. "But given their source of funding, it's clear they aren't impartial. More importantly, by using the White Helmets, the OPCW compromised itself. Look at it this way, Andrew. The OPCW-White Helmets arrangement is akin to the OPCW subcontracting external organizations founded and funded by the Syrian government's allies—Russia and Iran—to help investigate alleged chemical attacks that they then blame on the insurgents."

"I understand why you want to defend them," Mary said. "I'd do the same if they'd saved my life. But given how dirty this war is, and how implicated the West is, it's obvious who they're loyal to. Defending them overlooks the conflict of interest they have along with certain OPCW officials."

"Why would such an esteemed organization compromise itself?" Tom asked.

"Coercion from Washington," Sonia said. "The same kind of pressure they apply at the UN Surely, you know who pulls the strings there, Nadia."

Nadia nodded. "Of course I do."

"Three prominent witnesses accused the West of manipulating the evidence," Mary said.

"Who were they?" Nadia asked.

"The first was Ian Henderson, a veteran OPCW inspector," Mary explained. "When he tried to testify, he was verbally attacked by the US, the UK and French diplomats whose governments had bombed Syria over allegations of chemical use. Jose Boustani, former OPCW chief, attempted to testify, too, but he wasn't allowed to speak. The other witness was award-winning physicist Ted Postol, MIT professor emeritus and a former Pentagon adviser. And there's more."

"Go on," Andrew urged.

"At the hearing, Jonathan Allen from the UK said, and I quote..." She looked down at her notes. 'While we agree that the presidency of the Council should have space for proposed testimony, it must be relevant and knowledgeable to the topic under discussion. Unfortunately, this is not the case of Jose Boustani.' Boustani refused to be silenced. He recorded his statement and released it to the public. And he urged the current director, Fernando Arias, to let the other two witnesses air their suppressed evidence in a transparent manner."

"This is incredibly damaging evidence against the West," Tom said. "I raise my hat to you for pulling all this together."

Mary nodded her thanks, then said, "The French representative Nicholas de Rivière said it even more starkly in these words. 'At the root of today's discussion is the very simple and plain fact that the Syrian regime, in August 2013, gassed 1,300 men, women and children to strengthen its military hand, and this is not disputed by anyone.'"

"Except," Sonia said, "the Office of Director of National Intelligence, James Clapper, who told President Obama after the alleged chemical attack that the allegation of Syrian government responsibility wasn't a 'slam dunk.' Clearly, that this was a deliberate reference to the same kind of phony intelligence that had led to the Iraq war."

Mary said, "And then it was Ted Postol's turn to testify." She read his testimony. "The UN is an important international vehicle for enforcing international law, and if you people are not interested in facts, then there can be no justice. I'd also like to respond to a White House statement claiming intelligence findings about another alleged chemical attack, this one in Khan Shaykhun. I've reviewed the report, and it doesn't provide any evidence that the government of Syria was the source of that chemical attack. In fact, the evidence cited points to an attack that was executed by individuals on the ground, and it was either tampered with or staged. My own assessment points to the same conclusion. Considering these findings, I have grave concerns about the politicization of intelligence that seems to be occurring with more frequency.'"

"Explosive stuff," Andrew said.

"It's obvious," said Sonia, "that the US, UK and France wanted only one outcome to the investigations of repeated chemical weapons attacks, and if they had to use the White Helmets or faulty intelligence to get it, they had no qualms about doing it."

"It's the same old propaganda approach," Mary said. "Repeat an unproven assertion again and again until it becomes accepted wisdom. And it's worked perfectly in the case of Assad, who's been so thoroughly demonized. I should know. I'm responsible for some of that propaganda."

"Hey, look what's coming," Nadia announced, and everyone followed her gaze toward Chef Salim coming toward them with a platter.

"You've been discussing things far too seriously, so I thought you might want something sweet. It's nothing fancy, but it's good—my mother's lemon pound cake recipe."

After a round of applause for Salim, Nadia took charge of cutting the cake. Laughter broke out when everyone joked and teased the other for getting a bigger slice. Tom, gentleman that he was, offered Mary his slightly larger piece, betraying to the group how smitten he was.

How wonderful, after discussing the ills of the world, Andrew thought, *that we can smile and relax, with everyone speaking English and slipping now and then from English to Arabic with Lebanese accents, even with people we dislike.*

"Mary, your article will highlight the rescue mission and the camp project, nothing else, right?"

"Of course, and once it's written, you'll get final edit."

"Fair enough, thanks."

"Andrew, Mary and I have something to tell you," Sonia said.

"Can I eat my cake first?" Andrew asked.

"You'd better, because after you hear what we have to say, you won't have an appetite for much of anything." Sonia said.

"If you're that sure, maybe I should eat your slice too," and he grabbed Sonia's plate and put it in front of him.

"That's hardly fair," Nadia joked.

"Really?" and he leaned over and snatched her plate and put it in front of Tom.

"Hey, I'm not getting involved in your cake war," said Tom, as he slid his plate in front in Mary.

"And now you can give me back my piece," Sonia said.

"No way!" Mary laughed, and as she did Nadia snuck her piece of cake from under her nose and gave it back to Sonia.

"*Salope!* If I'd wanted it back, I'd have gotten it myself," she snapped and shoved the plate back in front of Nadia.

Andrew glared at Sonia. "Hey, you're the one who asked for a cease-fire earlier. Nadia has complied, so what's going on?"

"She didn't mean it."

"Not any more than I would have, had I agreed, but Nadia's a diplomat. If she wasn't, she'd have exposed you here and now for the monster you are. Shall I start naming your crimes?"

"I propose a truce," pleaded Mary.

"Listen up," Tom said, raising his voice. "I understand the knee-jerk reaction to Sonia's rude behavior, but I second Mary's plea for a truce."

Andrew looked at Mary and Sonia. "There was something you wanted to tell me?"

"It's about Omar," Sonia said curtly. "He killed Father Frans."

"No… no way," he said dumbfounded. "That can't be true."

"You never met Yacoub, the Syrian Army officer we befriended during the siege on Homs," Mary said. "After we were evacuated, he was charged with rounding up the al Nusra insurgents and sending them here to Idlib. Omar and his friend Hassan, whom you also know, weren't among them."

"He always said he wouldn't go to Idlib to live in a tent, but that doesn't mean he went to Raqqa," replied Andrew.

"Where else could he have gone but to Raqqa?" asked Sonia.

Andrew folded his arms and closed his eyes, thinking back over his conversations with Omar. Then he said, "I remember asking him once if he agreed with all the savagery he had seen. He said no and insisted there were other ways to serve Allah. I took that to mean he didn't support ISIS. He insisted Islam was a beautiful religion but agreed that parts of it had been hijacked and turned into something ugly and vile. When I suggested he return to Dearborn if he felt that way, he said, 'In the eyes of the US government, I'm a terrorist, so my only choice is to join ISIS. I may not be able to cut off limbs, but they have a media center and desk jobs for men like me.'"

"I asked if he could put a gun to a man's head and kill him. He said he probably could pull the trigger if forced to do so. I reminded Omar he had told me he couldn't kill anyone, but he then asked me, 'What if you were forced to join ISIS, and not given a choice about leaving?' As I recall, my last words to him were, "You always have a choice, Omar.'"

Andrew fell silent until Sonia said, "Omar didn't just kill Father Frans. He beheaded him."

Andrew buried his head in his hands. When he finally looked up again, he asked, "Are you sure it was him?"

"Mary and I interviewed three witnesses—nuns who had gone to the garden where I buried Joe, the place I showed you. It was there that Frans usually heard their confessions. They described a man who fit Omar's description, but more importantly, that man had spoken English to Frans with an American accent. From her hiding place, one of the nuns watched Omar take a knife to Frans's throat and slash it."

Andrew winced. "Did this assassin act alone?"

"No, he was accompanied by another man, probably his handler. According to the same nun, the accomplice gave Omar instructions, and when Omar didn't comply, the man got angry."

"Maybe Omar was forced to do what he did."

"Possible, but right now we're going on the assumption that this man accompanied Omar to make sure he carried out his initiation."

"Initiation?"

"Anyone who wants to join ISIS and rise in its ranks must perform a beheading," Sonia said.

Andrew shook his head. "This isn't something you do without a lot of practice."

"Andrew, I know you're not convinced it was Omar who carried out that crime. Why is that?" Nadia asked.

"Omar's a confused young man. He saw his father murdered and his mother raped by Shiite militiamen in Iraq. He claimed he came to Syria to take revenge on Shiites—nothing jihadist about that."

Sonia jumped in. "When I first met Omar in Daraa back in 2011, he had just come from Saudi Arabia where he'd been schooled in the destruction of Syria. I told him it was the Saudis who had supplied the weapons and paid the salaries, but the real masterminds behind the war in Syria were the same people who had destroyed Iraq. 'You're working for the devil,' I told him then. 'I know,' he replied, 'but the Americans don't understand the force we're about to unleash. We're unstoppable. We'll soon have our Caliphate, and even more jihadists will come.'"

Andrew looked eviscerated as he said, "Clearly, this is a contrast from the insecure man I thought I knew. That man loved poetry, for Christ's sake. And when I asked him to recite a verse from his favorite poem—an explicitly erotic one—he actually blushed. He carried on an affair with Hassan while in Homs and was terrified they'd get caught. He loved his mother. He was studying to become an engineer like his father and regretted giving all that up. There was deep remorse in that boy's soul. How could I have been so wrong? If he did commit this hideous crime, he must be held accountable, and for that you'll need irrefutable evidence, like a photo the witnesses can identify."

"I'm sorry, Andrew, but the nuns did identify him in a photo I showed them. We have an iron clad case. We plan to hand the information over to Yacoub, our Syrian Army contact in Homs. Once the authorities find Omar, he'll be remanded to US authorities and returned to the States to stand trial."

"When we told John we'd discovered Omar's real identity," Sonia said, "he insisted we hand the information over to him."

"We refused," Mary added.

"A smart move," Tom said. "So you two are the only ones who know Omar's real identity? And no one knows that you have a photo?"

"That's right," Mary said, "except for the nuns and Yacoub."

"And what about Omar?" Tom asked. "What if he finds out you've learned his real identity. Maybe he stayed behind and saw you at the scene of the crime talking to the nuns. If he did, he'd want to silence you."

"Extremely unlikely," Sonia insisted. "He would've wanted to flee the scene of the crime as quickly as possible."

"I agree," Andrew said. "I know Omar better than any of you—or thought I did. If he killed Frans, he'd have felt such shame and remorse, he'd have fled back to Raqqa as quickly as possible. It's unlikely he'll resurface unless flushed out."

"So, what happens next?" Nadia asked.

"We guard Omar's true identity until we turn it over to the proper Syrian authorities," Sonia said.

"And when the time comes," Nadia confirmed, "I could help you find the right person, someone who isn't a US agent."

"Yes, that's essential," Mary said.

CHAPTER TEN

When the US-led coalition announced a truce with safe passage out of Raqqa, Omar assumed this applied to the people who had endured a four-month-long siege at the hands of both ISIS and the US-led coalition forces. He was wrong. The coalition had not only agreed to a truce with ISIS, it had also granted their fighters safe passage out of Raqqa.

Astonished and outraged, Omar and Hammad stood on Raqqa's main thoroughfare on the day of their departure. They watched alongside the other stunned residents as the ISIS convoy rolled out of town. It was not even a quiet, sneak-out-of-town affair, and that's what infuriated Omar even more. It was a seven-kilometer-long parade, some four thousand people—both fighters and family members—in about sixty trucks, over a dozen buses and hundreds of ISIS-owned Toyota trucks. The faces of the fighters were covered as the men sat defiantly on top of the vehicles rolling out of Raqqa. The coalition did not want the retreat to look like an escape or a victory lap, so they stipulated there would be no banners or ISIS flags flown from any of the vehicles. Despite an agreement to take only personal weapons, ISIS fighters took everything they could carry plus ten additional trucks loaded with weapons and ammunition. As they made their way out of Raqqa, the convoy was escorted out by US-flown helicopters.

"K'lab (dogs)," Omar said, spitting out the words. "If the coalition intended all along to let those bastards go, why the hell did they have to destroy most of Raqqa and kill 1,600 civilians?"

"I'll repeat what I said before," Hammad said to Omar. "The Americans never intended to destroy ISIS. Their goal all along was to dismantle the country, one city at a time, and remove Assad from power. They're simply using ISIS to achieve their goal. They also knew they'd have no interference in Raqqa from the Syrian Army. Syria's soldiers were exhausted. Their resources had been depleted in Palmyra fighting, and it took them eighteen months to defeat ISIS there. Now we'll see the Americans set up their military outposts, take control of the oil fields and croplands, and no one will be able to stop them."

"I'm sure you're right, Hammad," Omar said.

Hammad continued. "Something I hadn't mentioned before is the water supply. Going forward, the US and its Kurdish forces will not only control Syria's three largest freshwater reservoirs, which are all here in the northeast, but they'll also control the flow of water from the Euphrates and all the electricity generated by the Tabqa dam. If you think we have water and electricity problems now, just wait till they turn off all the faucets."

* * *

On its website, Amnesty International published what Omar considered an accurate description of Raqqa. "Never has a city been so completely devastated. Not just in one neighborhood but in its entirety. Think Dresden and you'd be close." About 80 percent of the city lay in ruin. Aside from the astronomical number of dead, many more still lay buried under rubble, some still alive. Omar had heard their desperate screams and their pleas for help on his errand runs, but without the proper equipment, there was nothing he or any of the other onlookers could do except leave them to die agonizingly slow deaths.

That act of abandonment, however understandable in the abstract, took a weighty toll on Omar. Nightly, the voices of those suffering souls called out, admonishing him for forsaking them. Tormented nights propelled Omar into such a state of deep gloom that he could hardly speak when spoken to. He sought solace outdoors by walking alone in his neighborhood for hours each day. His relentless witnessing of so much suffering eventually pushed him over the edge.

Street by street, he observed the windowless, hollowed-out buildings—and those were the ones still standing. There were miles of what had once been apartment buildings literally pounded into particles so finite they looked more like gigantic mounds of crushed sandcastles. How many bombs had it taken to render a five- or six-story building into such a state of nothingness? He beheld utter ruin everywhere he looked. Roofs were knocked off, some hanging like lean-tos down to the ground. Slabs of concrete jutted out at wrong angles like fractured limbs bent beyond what a surgeon could repair. And there was no help available for anyone desperate to rebuild even the most rudimentary shelter. Omar saw entire families living in bombed-out husks of buildings and children, braving uncleared landmines to scavenge in the rubble for bits of steel and plastic to resell for food.

Then he saw a man three stories up on his heavily damaged roof, clearly heedless of any safety issues, blasting away with his jackhammer at oversized slabs of concrete that only high explosives or a wrecking ball could have adequately addressed. He seemed resolutely determined to do whatever he could to repair his home.

The downtown area around February 23rd Street with its restaurants, video arcades and shops, once a space of leisure, had been leveled in the first month, as had been the city's two main bakeries. The principal pipes that carried water from the dam to the city were heavily damaged, forcing many to undertake a perilous journey in the 100-degree July heat to search for water. The destruction was deliberate and systematic—schools, clinics and hospitals, the post office, five mosques, fifteen bridges, a funeral procession, even the ancient Abbasid Wall in Rashid Park that dated back to the eighth century lay in rubble.

Omar wondered how a city that lay so badly broken and agonizing could ever recover. But then he saw some scrappy local entrepreneurs collecting mangled steel rebars and then straightening them into long spaghetti strands to sell. He noticed a group of men drinking tea and smoking cigarettes as they discussed ways to reimagine ordinary urban domesticity in this postapocalyptic scenario. He walked past a giant cell tower near the town square, which had been struck by coalition bombing, now bent in half to resemble a monstrous praying mantis. Yet a crew was on hand to repair it.

A few days later, Omar glimpsed the jackhammer man again on his roof, still at his repairs in an act both futile and defiant. He was coming to believe that Raqqa could recover—one pile of rubble swept up at a time, stone after stone put back into crumbled walls, one pane of glass replaced after another. A partly refurbished bakery was already selling bread to long lines of hungry residents. Welding shops were again busy firing off sparks. Makeshift stands were now selling falafel and manoushe. Kids were zipping in and out of traffic selling chicklets from rickety bicycles. This kind of unity and determination boded well for the locals, but Omar wasn't one of them.

The coalition forces had just issued a ruling that any civilian who wished to leave Raqqa would be subjected to search and screening. This was another decree that made no sense to Omar. Why subject the same people who had suffered so cruelly at the hands of the US-led coalition to such a stress test when the coalition had just let the ISIS fighters leave town in a victory parade?

And there was Omar, an ISIS member left behind to wonder what his fate would be. Before it unfolded, he needed to send Hammad to his son in Aleppo, and then Aisha and the children to her family in Iraq. After that, would he be able to find a smuggler to get himself out, or would he be identified in some screening process as ISIS, and be shipped off to the nearby al Hol prison camp, a place far worse than anything in Idlib?

* * *

As had been their morning routine, Omar and Hammad still perused the multiple media sites even if they were too weary to comment on the egregious reports they read. The Amnesty International and the Human Rights Watch-Arms Division reports both stated that the US-led coalition had fired or dropped 4,400 munitions on Raqqa in the month of June alone, using everything from 250-pound precision-guided small diameter bombs to MK-80 bombs, which weighed between five hundred and two thousand pounds, and were all equipped with precision-guidance equipment to "ensure" precision bombing.

Omar finally turned all of his attention to his first task—getting Hammad to Aleppo. During the siege, escape under cover of night had proven too risky. Anyone seen on foot was deemed by the coalition forces to be the enemy and killed outright, leading the locals to think the offensive looked less like a battle against ISIS and more like a war on civilians, who were now trapped inside Raqqa.

When a semblance of calm finally reigned over the city, Omar set out to find a suitable driver to escort Hammad. With the rigorous search and screening policy in place, Omar dared not venture too far outside his neighborhood, which precluded a search for Abbas's whereabouts.

ISIS headquarters had been one of the first buildings destroyed, so Omar had no way to contact Abbas, if in fact he was still in the city. Rumor had it that some of the higher ranks in the ISIS structure had snuck out of Raqqa before the official evacuation. Maybe Abbas had been among them. Not knowing who else to turn to, he approached Salim, his local grocer—a man who had risked his life to provide him and his neighbors with fresh produce during the siege.

Omar said, "Salim, you know Hammad. You've seen him recently. He's a shell of his former self. He needs to get to his son in Aleppo. I want to help him do that. Do you have any ideas?"

"My brother Edgar still has his car. He was smart enough to have parked it in the tunnel on the other side of the park before the bombing campaign. He may be interested in earning some extra money. I'll let you know tomorrow morning."

The next day, Omar was waiting outside Salim's shop when he arrived.

"Any news from your brother?" Omar asked.

"He agreed, but only if Hammad meets him on the other side of the park. With all the rubble and debris, it's impossible to navigate anywhere around here unless you've got an armored vehicle like the ones the coalition forces use."

Omar didn't want to risk going himself and getting caught, so he asked, "How difficult will it be for Hammad to get to Edgar by foot?"

"It's an easy enough walk."

"Land mines?"

"I know a safe route. I'll draw him a map. It'll be much easier than explaining where to go."

Omar nodded. "Did Edgar say how much money he wanted?"

"Six hundred dollars."

Omar thought that was a lot for only one person, but he had decided when Amira died that he would dip into his savings and pay whatever amount was asked.

"We have a deal," Omar said, shaking Salim's hand. "Thank you."

"Have Hammad here tomorrow morning when I open."

* * *

When Omar and Aisha told Hammad they had arranged for him to go to his son's place, he collapsed into a chair and cried. "If only I could," he said. "I've wanted to go ever since I lost Amira, but I can't afford to pay a driver."

"You won't have to, Hammad. Aisha and I have taken care of it. It's the least we can do for you."

Aisha said, "Amira was my best friend. She delivered me a healthy baby. I will never forget her kindness. Omar and I are very happy we can do this for you."

With that news, Hammad jumped to his feet, grabbed hold of Omar and Aisha, and hugged them.

"It's settled then," Omar said. "You leave tomorrow morning."

"While you pack your things," Aisha said, "I'll finish preparing dinner and we'll have our last meal together. If you need help collecting your things, Omar will be happy to help."

* * *

With Hammad successfully on his way to his son in Aleppo, it was time for Omar to find a way to get his wife and children on a boat across the Euphrates to Iraq. Even before the siege, it had been unsafe to cross the river. On the erroneous assumption that every boat carried ISIS fighters and weapons, the US commander of the coalition forces, Lt. General Stephen Townsend, affirmed in a *New York Times* article that *"We shoot every boat we find."* By their own admission, the coalition acknowledged thirty-five airstrikes had destroyed sixty-eight boats and killed dozens of innocent civilians.

Omar had discussed the idea with Aisha several times, but each time she dismissed any notion of leaving without him. Omar knew she was speaking with her heart and not her brain, so he persisted, hoping she would eventually see the wisdom of getting herself and the children to safety.

Omar told her, "With the coalition's new screening policy I could be arrested and sent to the al Hol camp. If that happens, they'll come looking for you. Do I need to describe the conditions in that camp?"

Aisha sighed. "I already know. I've heard the women at the market talking."

"Neither of us wants that for our children, do we?"

"Of course not. It's just that… I worry I'll never see you again if I leave."

"If it were up to me, I'd move mountains to make sure we're reunited, but my priority right now is your safety and that of our children. Please help me make that happen, Aisha. If something happens to me, I need to know that you and our children are safe and with your parents. We both know there's no future for us here. I have money saved, so you'll have enough to live comfortably. You won't be a burden on your parents, and *Inshallah*, I'll find a way to join you."

The coalition forces had destroyed every bridge across the Euphrates. Because of the depth of the river, the only way to cross was in a shallow-draft boat powered by a mud engine capable of navigating shallow and hazard-filled waters. With debris from the destroyed bridges still floating in the river, this was the only kind of motor that ensured a safe crossing. By day, merchants brought their produce across in these boats. Despite all the drawbacks, it was terribly expensive. By night, these same merchants used their flat-bed boats to transport a limited number of passengers across the Euphrates for an even heftier price.

"Why a night crossing?" Omar asked Riad, the first boat owner he found. "Are the coalition forces still creating problems?"

"No, but it's always better to be cautious. A boat that transports produce is one thing. A boat full of people is a much more serious matter, and I can only take fifteen people at a time. I already have twelve for tomorrow night. How many are you?"

"My wife, a ten-year old boy and a four-month-old baby. How much would that be?"

"A thousand dollars each for your wife and boy, another five hundred for the baby."

"That seems exorbitant. Surely you can do better than that."

"The crossing takes about two and a half hours. We land in a small Iraqi village. Then, there's land transportation from there to Mosul, the nearest major city. I need to cover my overhead and pay my employees."

Omar knew the going rate, but it never hurt to haggle over the price of anything. It was expected with any transaction, so he waited to see if he'd get a better price.

After an uncomfortable silence, the boat owner said, "Okay! Two thousand for the three of them, and we'll settle now, if you don't mind."

Omar pulled out a wad of cash from his pocket, peeled off the asking fare and paid the owner. Riad, in turn, wrote up the three tickets and handed them to Omar.

"Wouldn't want you to think I wasn't a fair and honest man, the boatman said. "We've all been through a lot these last four months, and we deserve much more than we've received from the coalition forces. I thought they'd come to rid us of ISIS. Instead, they let those filthy pieces of scum walk free. Animals, the fucking lot of them."

Omar didn't know how to respond, so he remained silent.

"Sorry," Riad said, "I didn't mean to sound off on you. I lost most of my livelihood and most of my boats to those bastards. I hate them all."

"You're not alone, Riad."

The boatman nodded. "Have your wife meet me and the others at the clock tower tomorrow evening at eleven. I always suggest my passengers bring along some snacks and water. Tell your wife and boy to dress warmly. It gets cold on the river at night. You're welcome to accompany them to the boat landing. It might ease their anxiety to have you come along."

"I plan to. My wife's quite nervous about the trip."

"Reassure her that everyone will be wearing a life vest. To date, I've never had anyone fall overboard."

Omar shrugged. "I won't even put that possibility in her head."

The clock tower was a good twenty-minute walk from their apartment, so Omar allowed plenty of time to get Aisha and the children there on time. Once the group was assembled, Riad led them through the city, careful to avoid land mines and the mounds of rubble and debris.

Along the way, they passed dead ISIS fighters. One, seemingly too young to even be a fighter, was buried under the rubble of a concrete bunker, his small hand sticking out of its mangled remains. Omar diverted Anwar's attention in time so he wouldn't see him. Nearby, an older fighter's corpse lay in the grass with eyes open and a portion of its head missing, likely eaten by hungry dogs.

Omar and Aisha had discussed their final moments together many times. For Anwar's sake, there were to be no tears, she agreed. When they reached the river, Riad instructed them to take shelter under the ramp of the destroyed bridge until it was time to board as a precaution.

Omar had insisted Aisha remain brave. It was he who was a wreck, however, at the thought of saying goodbye to a family he might never see again. His stomach was in knots. He could hardly breathe. A large bird pounded furiously inside his chest, trying to escape.

Teary eyed, Omar took his wife's hand and kissed it. "I love you, Aisha. Thank you for bringing so much joy into my life. *Inshallah*, we'll be together soon."

Her eyes swelled, too, but she kept her promise and did not make a scene. But she did have one last thing to say. "I almost forgot to tell you. I'm taking my placenta with me. I'll bury it as soon as I reach my parent's home. This will ensure that Walid sets roots and grows into a fine man in his father's country."

Omar kissed his wife's hand one last time. "*Allah Maaki* (may God be with you)."

He helped his family onto the boat, placed their luggage under their seats and gave Anwar one final hug. Eyes full, Aisha glanced one last time at her husband before she busied herself making the children comfortable.

With a heavy heart, Omar watched as the boat left the Syrian shoreline. He waited under the ramp until they were out of sight and then made his way back to Raqqa, uncertain of his fate.

* * *

The coalition's commander, Lt. General Townsend, continued to insist that Amnesty's claims of massive casualties were "not supported by any verifiable evidence." Adding insult to injury, the newly formed Raqqa Civil Council, run by the same Kurdish forces who were partnered with the US coalition, operated their screening centers throughout the city to send displaced persons to places like al Hol prison while verifying their identity. The head of the Civil Council was quoted as saying, "There are only two kinds of people left in Raqqa—ISIS and thieves. Otherwise, why haven't they already yet?" This did not bode well for Omar.

Anyone above the age of eighteen who could not produce an ID ran the risk of arbitrary detention. The displaced persons who wanted to leave Raqqa also faced restrictions. They were required to have a sponsor who could verify their identity. Faced with such hurdles, Omar knew he did not stand a chance in hell of passing the screening process.

His fears came true when he foolishly ventured outside his neighborhood. The Kurdish forces who now manned every intersection spotted him as he turned a street corner. Before he could turn back, a soldier called out to him.

"You! Advance."

Omar considered his options. *Do I comply or do I turn and run?*

When he saw two soldiers with automatic weapons already advancing toward him, he had no choice but to surrender.

"Your ID," ordered the younger of the two Kurdish officers.

"I don't have any. I lost it when the building I lived in was bombed."

"Where was that?"

From his walking tours, Omar was familiar with just about every neighborhood. In a flash, he was able to produce an address."

"Who else lives with you?"

"No one. My wife and two children died when our apartment was hit."

By thinking about his departing family, Omar spontaneously produced tears.

"How is it that you survived?" the older one asked.

"I was at the market."

"How long have you lived in Raqqa?"

"I was born here."

As soon as Omar said that he knew he had made a serious mistake. After all this time in Syria, he still spoke Arabic with an American accent.

"No you weren't," the soldier said. "Your accent isn't Raqqawi. It isn't even Syrian. You better come with me." He grabbed hold of Omar's right arm.

"Where are you taking me?" Omar demanded in panic as he tried to wrestle free of the soldier's grip.

When the other soldiers saw the scuffle, they tackled Omar, threw him on the ground, grabbed his arms, forced them behind his back and handcuffed him. Then they yanked him up and marched him to their jeep.

"I demand to know where you're taking me."

"You're in no position to demand anything."

"Tell me, please!"

"First, to the processing center to be questioned. From there, I suspect you'll be sent to al Hol."

"What's that?" Omar asked, feigning ignorance.

"It's a detention center north of here," one of the soldiers said, laughing. "If we leave you in that hell hole long enough, I suspect you'll be more than willing to tell us who you really are and where you're from."

Omar remembered the callous words of the head of the Kurdish Civil Council—anyone still here was either ISIS or a thief— and knew he would get no special treatment. When they discovered his real identity and what he'd done, he dared not imagine what they'd do to him.

When Omar arrived at the screening center, he was dragged from the jeep. His handcuffs were removed before he was ordered to stand at the end of the line. The displaced prisoners were conspicuous by their age, dress and demeanor. The others, with long beards, straggly hair and bulging muscles under tight T-shirts, were sure to be screened for ISIS affiliation.

And here, among this motley mob, was Omar, a clean-cut man in his mid-thirties who had opened his mouth and said something stupid that could very well cost him his life.

As he stood in that long line, he had plenty of time to observe a man standing off to his left, about twenty-five feet away. When the man wasn't standing in place, he walked up and down the line seeming to scrutinize everyone else. *Who was he looking for?* Omar wondered. The man wasn't a local. From his looks, he wasn't even an Arab. He spoke with no one. Even more curiously, no one questioned why he was there. A baseball cap covered part of his face. His khaki trousers and a short-sleeved polo shirt were both unmistakably Western in style, but then Omar had dressed the same way when he had wanted to impress that American journalist, Mary O'Brien.

By his own calculation, Omar had been in line for well over an hour when he finally stood face to face with two Kurdish soldiers. One asked him to enter his name, date of birth and country of origin into a form. The other one played judge and jury by asking potentially incriminating questions. Just as the interrogation was about to begin, Omar again noticed the strange man with the baseball cap. The man had made his way back to the head of the line and was well placed to hear whatever Omar had to say.

You're being paranoid, Omar thought. *Worry about your interrogation, not that man.*

"Name?"

"Kareem, but I go by Omar." He gave his father's first and last name.

Omar happened to glance up at that moment and saw the stranger nod his head. *What the fuck! I'm not being paranoid. This man was waiting all this time for me to identify myself. Who is he, and why is he so interested in me?*

"Where were you born?"

"Raqqa," he replied, trying to imitate the local accent. He had heard it often enough from Hammad and thought he could fool his interrogator.

"I'll ask one more time. Place of birth."

"Iraq." He repeated his family name.

"How long have you been in Raqqa?"

"Since 2014 when I came here from Homs looking for work."

"Did you come here to join ISIS?"

"No."

"Why did you tell the soldier you were born in Raqqa."

"I was scared."

"Can you prove you're Iraqi?"

"No. My apartment was bombed. I lost everything."

"If we can verify your citizenship, your name will be put on a waiting list for transfer to Iraq. However, the list is long and getting permission is an opaque process, so you need to be patient. In the meantime, you'll be transferred to the al Hol detention center."

"Why locked up? Why can't I wait as a free man?"

"Next case," said the judge as a soldier grabbed hold of Omar's arm and led him to a waiting area surrounded by barbed wire.

As he was being shoved inside, he recognized one of the detainees. Omar tried to shield his face, but the man—a member of his media team—recognized him and called out Omar's name, then said, "So they got you too. Do you know where Abbas or any of the others are?"

As Omar was about to respond, he saw the stranger again, this time just outside the enclosure. The man's cold stare silenced Omar.

* * *

Omar was one of about fifty men who boarded a bus to al Hol. So far, he had not been identified as ISIS, and he hoped to keep it that way. But what was he supposed to do about that annoying young man from his media team, whose name he could not remember. Not only had he muscled his way to the head of the line, but he had taken a seat next to Omar on the bus where he again repeated the same damn question. "Do you know anything about the others?"

"No," Omar said, "and I suggest you not mention who employs us. Do you understand?"

"Got it."

"I hope so because if they find out who we are, we'll rot till we're dead in this detention center. Remind me your name."

"Abid."

"A piece of advice, Abid. Keep your mouth shut."

* * *

The bus pulled out of Raqqa and headed northeast for about two hours along a barren desert route. It was not unlike a similar journey Omar had taken five years prior when out of boredom he had initiated a conversation with a stranger by the name of Abbas. Unlike Abbas, a puzzle of a man, his current travel companion was an impulsive child/man. Still, how ironic that their conversation would begin with the same question he had asked Abbas.

"What do you know about this place we're being taken to?"

"Only what I just heard in the waiting area," Abid said. "That al Hol was initially set up to house about ten thousand Iraqis and Syrians fleeing ISIS. Recently, after the assault on Deir ez Zor and neighboring Baghuz, close to forty thousand women and children were sent to this camp, many of them hard-core ISIS supporters."

"All the more reason we need to keep a low profile."

The vast scale of al Hol could be seen from miles away as they approached from the west. It was an unwelcoming sight with endless tight rows of dirty, ragged tents.

Omar panicked and thought, *This was what the judge meant when he'd said permission to leave is opaque because once I get inside, I'll disappear in the legions of people who already live here and never resurface.*

"This place is a fucking time bomb waiting to go off," Abid said. "Thirty thousand people, or did the man say forty—some hard-core ISIS members—guarded by Kurdish forces who hate our guts. I'm scared, Omar. Please let me share a tent with you. I don't want to be left alone."

Omar was scared, too, but he didn't want to admit it. Instead, he joked.

"Alone? Abid, you'll be living with thousands of people."

"You know what I mean."

"Of course I do. And you can stay with me, if we're given a choice."

Upon arrival, each person received a case number duly noted in a thick ledger along with the assigned section of camp and a tent number. Each new arrival received a sheet, blanket, towel and cooking utensils. When check-in had been completed, the men were accompanied to their designated tents.

Omar pulled back the flap of his single-wall tent, walked in, and introduced himself and Abid to two men, Abdallah, the older one, and Amin, somewhere in his mid-forties. The floor of the tent was covered with a dirty, tattered carpet, a two-pot burner for cooking, two plastic containers—presumably for personal belongings—and four cots. A flap on either side of the tent allowed for cross ventilation.

"How long have you two been here?" Abid asked.

When Abdullah said ten years, Omar fought to hold back his tears. *Ten fucking years in this hellhole?* He recalled again the judge's words.

"How is that possible?" Abid asked, his voice shaking. "And you, Amin?"

"Five years and counting," Amin laughed. "After a while, all you can do is laugh about it. This camp is a scary place. It's crowded, under-resourced and very radicalized."

"It became even more so recently," Abdullah said, "when thousands of hard-cord ISIS sympathizers got sent here. In the last few months alone, there've been a hundred murders. Such things never happened before ISIS came."

"Were the murderers caught?" Abid asked.

"Where do you think you are, young man?" Abdullah asked. "This camp has only four hundred guards, and even with their AK-47s they're terrified of the residents and don't dare approach them."

"It's the women, mostly," Amin said. "When the guards go home at night, they move between the different sections of the camp. They're as bad as the *hisbah,* the religious police force that ensures residents uphold ISIS rules. The women forbid everyone, even the men, from smoking. God forbid you get caught talking to a woman you don't know. You'd be viciously assaulted, or worse."

"I've read about prisoner of war camps. This sounds just as bad," Abid said.

"There's no forced labor here," Abdullah sighed, "but the boredom is unbearable, especially for someone like me who was always so active."

"If there are women, there must be children too," Abid said. "How many?"

Amin replied, "Too many. Half the population is under twelve."

"Then they must attend school," Omar suggested.

The two men laughed. "I don't think you fully realize how bad conditions are here. No one cares about any of us, least of all the children."

"But I'm a schoolteacher," Abid insisted. "Maybe I can organize something. At least I'd have something to do."

"There are some schools in the camp, and they're run by aid organizations. But the ISIS women claim their curriculum doesn't conform to the traditions and values of Islam, so you'd better be mindful of who you talk to and what you offer to teach. And be careful not to appear to be collaborating with any camp personnel. That includes the aid workers. That's frowned upon by the hisbah too."

"Are we allowed to walk around the camp?" Omar asked.

"Sure, but there are sections you'll want to avoid, like the Annex where the most extreme women are located," Amin said. "Since they have arrived, the tenor in the camp has changed dramatically. Before, no woman covered her face. Now, you can't find a girl older than eight without a veil."

"Amin, shall we tell them about the other things?" Abdullah asked.

Amin gave his companion a puzzled look at first, then said, "You mean the abductions, the death by stoning and the beheaded bodies that show up occasionally in the sewage canals?"

"Not yet," Abdullah said with a chuckle. "Let them get acclimated first."

"Welcome to al Hol," Amin joked.

"Don't mind us," Amin said. "We're just having fun, not something we get to do very often."

"Abid, you asked if you could walk freely around the camp," Abdullah said. "You can, but keep in mind, this is a dangerous place. Those women I mentioned enforce Sharia law on everyone. If they suspect anyone of talking to guards or aid workers, you'll be targeted and labeled an infidel. This is a serious offense because in their eyes, infidels were the ones who brought down the Califate."

"The strict women also target what they call the renegades," Amin said, "those who no longer believe in ISIS and who regret having joined the group."

Why would anyone be foolish enough to reveal such a thing? Omar wondered.

"People who work with any of the NGOs in the camp are targets, too, and that could apply to you, Abid, if you want to play schoolteacher. So be careful. In fact, aid workers routinely need to change their mobile phone numbers because of the "death" messages they receive from ISIS death squads. And don't cozy up to any of the security guards. They're a constant target too."

This exchange of information filled Omar with dread and despair. He gave thanks to Allah that his wife and children had been spared this ordeal.

Omar said, "You've been very thorough in your introduction to Camp al Hol. I have one last question. What's the solution to all this misery?"

"That's an easy one," Abdullah said. "Disband the camp and return all of us to our home countries."

* * *

It was a month later, while Omar was in line to receive his tent's food supply for the week, that he saw the stranger again. The Westerner didn't approach Omar, but from a distance he followed Omar back to his tent. When he had delivered the food supply, Omar stepped outside and confronted him..

"Who are you?" Omar asked in Arabic. "What do you want from me?"

The stranger laughed and spoke in English. "Your Arabic isn't any better than mine."

"You're American!"

"Yes. My name's John, and I'm here to offer you your freedom."

"You don't even know me."

"Oh yes, I do. I know your affiliation with ISIS. I even know what you did in Homs."

Omar closed his eyes and dropped his head. *Mary and Sonia. They figured it out, but how? Did one of those nuns see me behead Frans?*

"If you know all of those things," Omar asked, "why would you want to set me free?"

"You have some valuable skills. It would be a pity to see them go to waste in some prison cell."

"And you want me to work for you instead?"

"That's right."

"I accept, but on one condition."

"What's that?"

"See to it that the three men in my tent are given their freedom. I don't deserve to be set free, but they do."

John gave Omar a broad smile, then said, "I like you, Omar. Consider it done."

CHAPTER ELEVEN

Andrew tried to give Nadia his undivided attention as she practiced a speech she was going to deliver to the UN Human Rights Council. He did his best to stay engaged, offering a slight clarification of something she had just said or a suggested rephrasing of a sentence to give it more relevance. The impact of Omar's unspeakable crime, however, weighed heavily on his mind, and the danger that Omar posed left Andrew breathless and confused. He had suspected Omar would join ISIS when Homs fell. That was inevitable, given Omar's slim options, but he never thought Omar would take a knife and cut off the head of a human being, much less Father Frans.

Omar's inexplicable act of barbarity betrayed the rapport he and Omar had established—admittedly, an uncommon rapport, given that he was Omar's prisoner at the time. Andrew understood that Omar was just a small part of a highly complex reality, but that didn't lessen the impact of his actions.

Heavy hearted, Andrew wiped his eyes. Jolani had finally endorsed his cholera protocol, and because of its success, he and Tom were prepared to travel to al Hol prison to implement the same therapy there. Perhaps he would find Omar in that horrible place. And if he did, what then?

Out of courtesy to Nadia, Andrew delayed their departure until after her speech. One of her duties as Special Rapporteur was to study the impact of the human rights abuses on Syrian society. Today, in a live-stream address from Idlib to the forty-seven members of the Human Rights Council gathered at the UN Palace of Nations in Geneva, she would present her findings.

Andrew accompanied Nadia to the staff meeting room, then took a seat alongside Tom and the members of her staff. Nadia gave Tom a gentle push in the chest and said, "You and Andrew must stay awake for this. I'll want a critique afterward."

Tom laughed and pushed her back, then said, "I'm British. I reserve the right to nap through Armageddon."

At the appointed hour, Nadia glanced over at Andrew, gave him a wink, then began.

"Distinguished members of this committee. Currently, 90 percent of Syria's population lives below the poverty line. They have limited access to food, water, electricity, shelter, cooking and heating fuel, transportation and healthcare. With more than half of the vital infrastructure either destroyed or severely damaged, the unilateral sanctions imposed by the West on key economic sectors have undermined efforts toward economic recovery and reconstruction. After a decade-long war, this travesty of justice should not be tolerated."

Andrew allowed himself to be distracted—he had heard this speech before. When he closed his eyes, the images kept repeating themselves—Omar gripping Frans's neck in a stranglehold, and Frans, terrorized, his brows furrowed, staring wide-eyed at the knife as it neared his throat.

Andrew's body shook.

Tom leaned in and asked, "Are you all right?"

Andrew nodded and put a shushing finger to his mouth.

Nadia continued. "…but the rehabilitation and development of water distribution networks for drinking and irrigation have stalled due to the lack of equipment and spare parts. These shortages create a serious public health crisis, which also impacts food security. Unilateral sanctions hurt women, children, the elderly and the sick. They perpetuate and exacerbate the colossal challenges the Syrian people have endured since 2011."

Andrew would forever remember that day in 2011 when a straggly-haired, cigarette-reeking, black-bearded man wearing a sweat-stained T-shirt named Omar stormed into his Shatilla clinic and forever altered his life.

"The West has imposed sanctions on anyone who wants to send money to a relative in Syria," Nadia explained. "This is of critical importance, because many Syrians count on family members from abroad to send them funds to survive. In this still-evolving humanitarian crisis, I urge this committee to demand the lifting of all unilateral sanctions, which are defined as restrictive measures imposed by an individual state against another state without any prior authorization from an international organization such as the UN Security Council. In the case of Syria, these western-imposed sanctions were never authorized by this body!"

Andrew wasn't listening to his wife. He was wondering under whose authority Omar had killed Frans. Clearly not the authority of the Qur'an, which explicitly stated that murdering the innocent leads to everlasting punishment. *May you burn in hell for all eternity, Omar.*

Nadia was still speaking. "In its National Defense Authorization Act, the US Congress recently incorporated the Caesar Syria Civilian Protection Act, a collection of both unilateral and extraterritorial sanctions on anyone who contributes to the reconstruction of Syria. While they recognize the destruction of Syria's railway system, its electric grid and its water supply and irrigation systems, they explicitly state Syria must rely on damaged infrastructure because acquisition of spare parts is forbidden. A government must have stable electricity and water pumps that function properly to deliver an adequate food supply to its people. In Syria, this is of critical importance because 60 percent of Syrians suffer food insufficiency, which means they skip days without meals. Another 2.5 million are considered food insecure."

Just as she had rehearsed, as she neared the end of her speech, Nadia slowed her pace to lend more emphasis to her closing remarks.

"By their own definition, the Caesar sanctions are extraterritorial. Under international law, a state may exercise its jurisdiction over indi-

viduals and entities only within its own borders. Unilateral, extraterritorial sanctions that have egregious impacts on the human rights of a
civilian population have no place in international law and should have
no place in a country's foreign policy. Freezing assets of a country as
well as its public institutions is a clear violation of the judicial immu-
nity of state properties. The designation of state officials as sponsors of
terrorism is a violation of international law.

"I have addressed these issues with European leaders. They admit
such restrictions interfere with their foreign policy decisions, but the
US gives them no choice. Either you trade with the US or the Syrian
government. I have made every attempt to contact US government officials, but I get no response. From this, I am left to conclude that the US
is using sanctions to pressure the Assad government to step down and is
unwilling to reverse its policy of never-ending sanctions. The only two
places that are sanction-exempt are Idlib province in Syria's northwest,
under the control of Mohammad Jolani—who is affiliated with both al
Qaeda and ISIS—and in the Northeast, where US troops are illegal-
ly stationed. This policy is explicit in its application. Those who are
against the Syrian government continue to be rewarded with supplies
and reconstruction material, while millions of peaceful civilians living
in government-controlled regions are kept in a constant state of suffering and deprivation.

"In a country wrecked by more than a decade of conflict, where 90
percent of the population lives below the poverty level, where more
than eleven million people rely on humanitarian assistance and more
than six million have been forced from their homes, such sanctions
have no place.

"You have before you a draft declaration on unilateral coercive measures and the rule of law. On the question of legality, the current draft
text asserts that sanctions are illegal if they purport to apply extraterrito-
rially and if they inflict undue suffering on a civilian population. I urge
unanimous and immediate passage of this document."

* * *

While the secret ballots were being tallied, Tom leaned over to Andrew and asked, "Will Nadia get the votes she needs?"

"Good job—you stayed awake," commented Andrew.

"That's more than I can say for you. You weren't even listening."

"I know her speech by heart. As to the votes, she only needs a two-thirds majority. She'll get them."

And she did. She thanked the Council for their prompt action and then joined Andrew and Tom to get their reaction. "How did I do?"

Andrew kissed her cheek. "You spoke from your heart, darling, and you were brilliant."

"I echo that," said Tom. "Where does it go from here?"

"To the UN Security Council for a vote. Sadly, the US will veto it, and that will kill the proposal."

"You've done what you can, Nadia," Andrew said, wrapping his arm around her shoulder.

Tom asked, "If it's defeated in the Security Council, what's to prevent it from going to the General Assembly?"

"The General Assembly can only adopt a resolution if at least nine of the fifteen members of the Security Council have voted in favor of it and no veto was used by one of the five permanent members."

Tom shook his head, "And the US will veto the resolution."

"That's right."

Andrew rubbed his face and shook his head. "So where is all this headed? No resolution in sight. More suffering for these people. I don't know about you two, but I'm having a hard time with all of this. For every step forward, we, our work, everything we do gets slapped back two."

Nadia kissed his cheek. "We both knew our work would come with setbacks. God knows we've each had more than our share, but we can't let them defeat us."

"But we have been defeated, Nadia. We've lost. They won—the power that be."

"Hey, you two, I've got an idea," Tom said. "Andrew and I have a bit of time before we take off for al Hol. Why don't we have a spot of lunch. After all that jabbering, you've surely worked up an appetite."

Nadia rolled her eyes. "It's more like a major headache."

"My dear Nadia," Tom said, taking her arm, "by the time we've had lunch and cheered you up, your headache will have disappeared." Turning to Andrew, he said, "And I want no talk of losers. You've had a big win, Andrew. In a two-month trial period, you've limited the spread of cholera across Idlib. No small accomplishment, my friend."

* * *

A round of applause from Nadia's staff greeted them as they entered the dining hall. She clasped her hands in front of her face and bowed her head. "Thank you," she said, holding back tears, "but this report is just the beginning. We need results, not just votes."

"Yes, but you made a strong case," Antoine said. "You showed the Council what we see and experience every day. Surely that will prompt them to do something."

"I hope you're right," Nadia said.

Lunch included a bowl of lentil soup and a selection of sandwiches. Choices made, they served themselves coffee and found a table in a corner of the dining room.

"I'll be right back," Nadia said, and headed to the restroom.

As soon as she'd left, Tom asked Andrew, "What's going on with you? You were mentally absent during Nadia's speech, and now you have a face as long as a camel's."

"I did listen—off and on—but it's Frans. I can't get his murder out of my head. I don't know if you made the connection when Sonia and Mary explained what had happened, but Omar, the man who committed this atrocity, is the same man who held me captive in Homs for a year."

"My God, no wonder you're upset."

"I knew this man, Tom. We had become friends, and I can't wrap my head around him plunging a knife into Frans's neck."

"If Omar was accurate and hit a primary artery, Frans went unconscious within seconds, so he didn't suffer very long. I've treated a fair number of stab victims back home. They all said they initially felt numbness. But they're the ones who survived to tell their story. I'm sorry, Andrew, but it's all I can offer in the way of consolation."

"Hey, you two," Nadia said as she took a seat. "Whatever you're talking about, it looks awfully serious."

Tom nodded Toward Andrew. "He's still obsessing over Father Frans."

Nadia reached out and touched Andrew's face. "You're going to have to put it out of your head, darling."

"What he really needs right now is a stiff whiskey to calm himself down."

Andrew smiled. "That would help."

"Well, now that we've settled that," Tom said, "I have a question. Who the hell is Caesar?"

"Caesar was the codename for a supposed Syrian military whistleblower," Nadia explained. "I've got no idea why they chose that name. All such operations have silly names, but this man named Caesar was part of an intelligence operation orchestrated by the US State Department and the Qatari government."

Tom rubbed his hands together. "That's a juicy bit of info right there. Go on."

"Apparently, a network of US and Qatari-backed regime change operatives, who marketed themselves as human rights lawyers, not only groomed the supposed whistleblower but managed his escape from Syria with a file of supposed incriminating photos."

"What's the connection with Qatar?" Tom asked.

Nadia responded, "The Emir of Qatar not only helped finance the war in Syria, but he bankrolled the fighters."

"Why would he do that?" Tom asked.

"He has close ties to the Muslim Brotherhood, which is the sworn enemy of the Assads. The Brotherhood declared war on Bashar's father when he came to power in 1970. By 1980, Syria had become the epicenter of Islamic terrorism. The Muslim Brotherhood owned the streets. Their mosques and schools were teaching jihad. By 1982, they had seized control of Hama, Syria's fourth-largest city. They attacked police stations and murdered every pro-regime party leader. In retaliation, Assad attacked Hama and killed some 25,000 Brotherhood members."

"Good Lord! That's a lot of dead people."

"It is, but back to Caesar," Nadia said. "A New York Times article claimed that Caesar fled Syria with photos of some 24,000 bodies, purporting to show torture at the hands of the Syrian government. The Times acknowledged that the Caesar photos were commissioned by Qatar. The article also mentioned David Cane, described as an investigator involved in examining the photos, but in fact, Crane was a veteran military intelligence operative who had previously held positions inside the Pentagon, including a stint at the Defense Intelligence Agency. Should I go on?"

Tom nodded, clearly fascinated by the story Nadia was unveiling.

"According to the article, Crane had already appeared on Capitol Hill multiple times to advocate for prosecuting Syrian government officials. The few photos that were released for public viewing could not be independently verified. In fact, outside investigators determined that at least half of the photos depicted bodies of government soldiers killed by the armed opposition. Human Rights Watch also had access to the photos. They were unable to definitively ascertain if the bodies had died in detention, or on the battlefield, or under other circumstances, confirming the findings of the New York Times. In the end, HRW did verify twenty-seven photos of people who had been arrested. HRW's findings were conveniently omitted in the final report handed to Congress."

"This whole thing is a sham," Andrew said.

"You're surprised?" Tom asked. "They had to preserve the narrative that the Syrian conflict was a one-sided, unprovoked slaughter of innocent Syrians orchestrated by Bashar Assad."

Nadia interjected, "There was another New York Times article about a non-profit group also associated with the Caesar dossier. It was called the Center for International Justice and Accountability, I think. Turns out it was a US and UK regime change-funded group that worked close-ly with extremists in Syria to collect documents from pillaged govern-ment offices, then spirited them out of the country. According to a piece in The New Yorker, this organization paid rebel groups and couriers for logistic support."

Nadia shook her head. "Every bit of this story smells. An article in Vanity Fair reported that Caesar's handler, Hassan Chalabi, claimed to be a Syrian academic when in fact he'd been running a shadowy intelli-gence network inside Syria that actively spied for the Syrian opposition as far back as 2011."

Tom whistled. "This could be something out of a John Le Carré spy novel."

"Or a Graham Greene," Andrew suggested.

"Or one of Eric Amber's," Tom added.

"I'll wait while you clowns carry on," Nadia said, amused.

Tom gestured for Nadia to continue.

"This man Chalabi," Nadia said, "told Vanity Fair he had arranged for Caesar to be smuggled out of Syria with the help of the CIA-created Free Syrian Army, the precursor to al Nusra."

Andrew interrupted. "I remember al Nusra from Homs. Jolani head-ed it then, and Omar ran their media center. When Jolani took control of Idlib, he simply changed the group's name to HTS."

Tom shrugged. "We already know that. Get on with it, Nadia."

She did. "When Caesar finally appeared before Congress, he was accompanied by a Syrian American who served as the director of the Syria Emergency Task Force, which was funded by the State Depart-ment, which in turn supports regime change. Caesar was shrouded in a blue Patagonia-hooded jacket. Audio and video recordings of his tes-timony were strictly forbidden, supposedly to protect his safety. Tes-tifying alongside Caesar's handler was David Cane, the author of the Qatar-sponsored Caesar report that accused the Syrian government of 'crimes the likes of which the world has not seen since Auschwitz'—that's close to a direct quote."

"It's sick to make mention of the Holocaust in that way," Tom said.

Nadia nodded. "I agree, but they obviously thought they could build public support by linking it to the Jewish genocide. By the way, no one was permitted to take photos of Caesar, and no one was allowed to ask him any questions. It was his handler who presented the case against Assad. He made no mention of the New York Times or Vanity Fair articles, or the Human Rights Watch report, which essentially undermined the entire Caesar narrative as a cynical lie. Nevertheless, Congress passed the Caesar Bill with zero opposition."

"Pretty nefarious," Tom said. "How could all those inconvenient truths have been ignored? They appeared in the New York Times, the paper of truth, for Christ's sake. Did those imbeciles in Congress even know what they were voting for, or just follow orders from higher up."

"I suspect the latter," Nadia said. "In an article in Politico, one of the Qatari-backed lobbyists boasted there'd be ever greater levels of destitution and famine because of the Caesar sanctions. Imagine that! And he saw the human suffering as an opportunity for the US to finally achieve regime change."

Andrew let out a heavy breath. "I'm sure there are some good people on both sides, but it's mostly bad people like this lobbyist making disastrous decisions that affect millions of innocent people."

"I know I'm an outside observer looking in," said Tom, "but I don't see where it matters who runs Congress, or who sits in the White House. Whether Trump, or Obama before him, US foreign policy objectives haven't changed. Libya, Iraq, still going on. Afghanistan, no changes there, either. Yemen—and now it's Syria's turn with the same old regime change plan, only this time Trump's going to pile on extra sanctions."

Andrew teared up a bit and looked at the ceiling. "Tell me how any of this gets resolved?"

"I'm not sure it does," Tom said.

"Nadia, you know so much about these sanctions," he continued. "The details need to be exposed."

"In my current position as Special Rapporteur, I can't do anything. But when I step down, I intend to write a lengthy article about this whole affair... every sordid detail."

Andrew sighed. "It's so tragic."

"Yes, and it's on such a massive scale," Tom pointed out. "People dying and starving and freezing to death for lack of basic shelter, and no one gives a damn. I don't imagine Andrew and I will find anything different in al Hol. Speaking of which," Tom said, looking at his watch, "it's already half-past one. If we don't want to arrive too late, we should leave now. It's a seven-hour drive."

"I didn't realize it was that far," said Nadia. "Why don't you stay here tonight and get an early start in the morning."

"No, tonight," Andrew said. *I'm too wired*, he thought. *I need to get out of Idlib. I need to do something to keep my mind busy.*

"Andrew's right," Tom said. "We get settled in there tonight and we're ready for clinic tomorrow morning. I alerted the al Hol staff that we'd be arriving late. No problem on their end. They're just grateful we're willing to come."

As they walked to the door, Nadia took Andrew aside.

"Are you going to be all right?"

He nodded and kissed her. "I just needed to sound off a bit."

* * *

Tom had hardly closed the door and started the engine in their beat-up old Land Cruiser when he started in on Andrew. "Okay! Out with it. What was going on back there? Are you suffering effects from the hospital bombing? You were minutes from dying under all that debris. Maybe you should have taken more time off."

"It's more serious. I've lost my will to fight. And to keep trying to make a difference seems futile. In the end, how many of these battles do we ever win? I'm tired, Tom. I count the days till Nadia finishes this assignment and I can get back to my clinic in Shatilla. I need a return to some sense of normalcy." He let out a forced laugh. "Whatever 'normalcy' means in this part of the world. Don't you ever think about such things? Maybe returning to London and resuming private practice?"

"Hadn't thought about it until I met Mary. I fancy her something chronic. I'd like to get her into my life, but she isn't responding as I'd hoped."

"I think she's still mourning the loss of her Joe, who was killed in front of her in Homs. And then there's the age factor. Aren't you about twenty years older than her?"

Tom nodded. "I'm pushing sixty, and Mary must be early forties."

"I'm not suggesting you give up. I'm just advising you to take it slow." Andrew said. "Now I'm feeling guilty for insisting we leave for al Hol tonight when you could have spent the evening wooing sad Mary."

Tom laughed. "She's one step ahead of us. She and Sonia left this morning for al Hol. They're going on the assumption that Omar was arrested and sent there after the fall of Raqqa."

"Holy Jesus, Sonia's the last person I want to see when we arrive tired and hungry."

"I know, and Mary also gets it now. We'll do our best to keep you two apart."

"I'll hold you to it."

Tom waited until they got onto Route 4 before he spoke again. "I assume you know precious little about the history of northwest Syria—and why would you since you've never been in this part of the country before. So, allow me. It's rather fascinating. Between Idlib and Aleppo, our halfway point, there are some seven hundred abandoned settlements called The Dead or Forgotten Cities that date from the first to the seventh centuries. They flourished because they were located along major trade routes. Historically and collectively, they illustrate the transition from the ancient pagan world of the Roman Empire to Byzantine Christianity, and perhaps that's why they were named a UNESCO World Heritage Site in 2011.

"We can't see any of these ancient cities from this highway, but just outside Aleppo there's the Saint Julianus Maronite monastery, which dates somewhere between AD 399–401. That's where the shrine of St. Maron is located. The Church of the Virgin Mary, which belonged to the late fifth century, is one of the most beautiful churches in northern Syria and among the oldest standing Christian churches in the world. Another is the half-ruined Late Roman Fafertin Basilica. There's also an Assyrian settlement from the ninth century BC and the site of a Roman temple that was converted into a church."

Andrew smiled and said, "If you ever decide to give up medicine, you'd make an excellent tour guide. But all kidding aside, this is fascinating stuff, even for an ex-Catholic. Most people would think of Syria as a Muslim country when in fact it's multi-ethnic."

"I don't know the latest stats, but pre-war, Christians made up 10 percent of the Syrian population. The largest denomination is Greek Orthodox, followed by the Maronites, then the Assyrian Church of the East."

"Didn't Christians suffer during Ottoman rule?"

"The massacres spanned from 1840 right through to the Assyrian genocide in 1933. Along with the Arameans, Armenians, Greeks and Nabateans, the Assyrians were among the first to convert to Christianity. Between 1899 and 1919, some 900,000 people from the Levant, which includes historical Syria, which includes present-day Lebanon and Palestine, emigrated to the US, and 90 percent of them were Christian."

"This region has never had a quiet moment, has it?"

"And Aleppo is a tragic example."

"Pre-war, wasn't it an important Syrian city?"

"Yes, in both industry and finance, with a civilian population of three million. They paid a heavy price from aerial bombing, shelling or snipers, whether from Russian air power or ISIS fighters."

"When was this?"

"It began in 2012 and only ended in 2016 when the Syrian government regained control. In Layamon, the major industrial zone, there were some 1,600 companies churning out textiles, pharmaceuticals and processed agricultural goods. The city still hasn't fully recovered so we'll have to bypass the center, but even from the highway you can still see overturned train cars and buses and industrial debris piled up along the sides of the roads. Now it's just a question of how, or even if, they can rebuild with so many Western-backed sanctions."

Andrew lay his head back and closed his eyes. Tom turned on the radio, chose a classical music station and adjusted the volume just enough so Andrew could listen to a lovely Bach concerto as he drifted off.

As Andrew would later recall, it was around seven that evening when he awoke to Tom's phone ringing. Tom put the call on speaker.

"We're about an hour outside al Hol, Mary," Tom said.

Mary interrupted. "But we're not there, Tom. We're in al Hasakah."

Tom glanced across at Andrew. Confused, he asked Mary, "What are you doing *there*?"

Andrew pulled his phone from his pocket. "I'll find it on Google Maps."

Mary said, "We came to al Hol looking for Omar so we could have him remanded to the Syrian Army. The prison official we spoke to refused to help, but one of the aid workers took us aside and said that Omar had left the prison."

"Who released him?" Andrew asked.

"He didn't know the man's name," Mary replied, but he showed up at the prison frequently. It was odd, the aid worker said, because he had never seen a prison official ask who he was or what he was doing there. The ISIS women didn't either, which was even more curious, he said, since they're the ones who really run the prison. The aid worker suggested we check the Hasakah prison. If we didn't find him there, he advised us to check the city morgue."

"Mary, this is Andrew. I just found al Hasakah on Google. We should be there in an hour."

"We got a late start this morning, so we've only just arrived ourselves. We're headed toward the Geweran neighborhood where the prison is located. We still need to find lodging and grab something to eat. Ring when you arrive and we'll rendezvous."

"Will do."

Tom shut down the call.

"Know anything about Hasakah?" Andrew asked.

"Not a thing. Ask Siri. She knows everything."

Siri responded, "Hasakah is in the northeastern corner of Syria on the Khobar River, a tributary of the Euphrates. It has an estimated 450,000 residents, predominately Arabs with large numbers of Kurds, the largest minority group in Syria, Assyrians and a small number of Armenians. Aside from three Syrian Orthodox churches, St. George Cathedral being the largest, there are also two Armenian churches, one Chaldean and one Assyrian."

"Thank you, Siri."

Tom said, "Now ask her for directions to the Central Prison. I have no idea where to go."

* * *

After reaching the prison and circling it twice to get their bearings, Andrew suggested they backtrack a few blocks to a restaurant he had seen on their way in.

"Good idea, I'm famished."

When they entered the restaurant, a bell over the door announced their arrival and a tall, slender, middle-aged man stepped from the kitchen.

When he saw all the empty tables, Andrew asked in Arabic, "We hope you're still serving dinner. My friend and I have been on the road for seven hours."

"*Ahlan,* my name's Boghus. I'm the owner. My usual customers come in early, but I'd be happy to serve you dinner."

"My name's Andrew, and this is my colleague, Tom. We're physicians with Doctors without Borders."

"Very pleased to meet you both," Boghus responded in English.

The restaurant had a dozen tables. The walls were clean, bare and white to match the tablecloths and cloth napkins. Boghus directed them to a table and handed them each a menu.

"I'll leave you a moment while you decide," and he returned to the kitchen.

"We'll both have the Kale Tabouleh," Tom said when Boghus returned. "We've never had it with kale."

"It's an Armenian specialty."

"We'll also have the beef kebabs with yogurt and cucumber sauce."

"Good choices. And if you don't mind, I'll turn on the TV. I like to listen to the evening news."

They were drinking coffee with their baklava when several explosions shook the restaurant.

"What was that?" Andrew asked as people started running past the restaurant.

"I don't know," Boghus said, "but the news will be on shortly."

"Call Mary," Andrew instructed Tom. "Maybe she'll know something."

Tom pulled out his phone and punched in her number. She picked up on the first ring.

"Where are you?" he asked. "Are you alright?"

"No, I'm not... and I'm scared. Sonia and I were walking toward the prison when we heard the explosions. People around us panicked and started to run. It was obvious to anyone looking at us that we didn't know where to go. That's when two women approached us and said we could hide at their house, which was nearby."

"Did you go there?" Tom asked.

"I followed them, assuming Sonia was right behind me, but then I heard her say something about Omar. Then she ran off before I could stop her. Maybe I should have followed after her, but I was...."

"Mary," Tom said, "you did the right thing. Just stay put. We're in an Armenian restaurant nearby. You can't be far away. We'll met up as soon as it's safer."

"I'll..." the phone's signal started breaking up.

"Mary, I didn't hear you," Tom said. "Mary, are you still there?" He turned to Andrew. "I lost her."

Just then, as the news came on TV, Boghus came running out of the kitchen and turned up the volume.

On the screen, a reporter was looking grimly into the camera as he said, "This just in from our correspondent in al Hasakah. 'The Syrian Defense Forces now estimate that at least 200 ISIS fighters, armed and wearing explosive belts, detonated two massive car bombs this evening. The first one targeted the prison's main gate while the second targeted a nearby fuel warehouse, most likely a distraction. Once inside the prison, they took over the watchtowers and set fire to fuel trucks just inside the prison courtyard. A video obtained from the SDF showed a truck loaded with weapons arriving at the start of the attack. Once inside the prison walls, weapons were distributed. Prisoners rioted and took seventy guards as hostages. In the initial battle, 200 SDF forces were killed. Eight hundred prisoners escaped while the remaining prisoners raided the armory and attacked the prison staff. Fires can be seen across the city coming from the direction of the prison. The city is in lockdown on orders from the mayor, and Apache helicopters hover over the prison as violent clashes continue.'"

Andrew asked Boghus, "How big is this prison to have so many guards and prisoners?"

"It takes up a full city block," he replied. "By all accounts, it's impregnable. Given what's happened, I don't recommend you leave here tonight. If you don't mind being so close to the prison, I have a small apartment upstairs. The bedroom is toward the back of the building, so it should be quiet enough."

"That's very generous of you, Boghus, but where will you sleep?"

"Tonight, I prefer to be down here. A precaution in case someone tries to break in. And I can also keep an eye on your Land Cruiser."

"Maybe by morning we can be of some use," Tom said, "either in the neighborhood or in the prison. We are pretty good at tending to the wounded. One more thing. How do I access the local news? Is there an app I can download?"

"Yes, the BBC, our local al Hasakah affiliate."

* * *

The next day, Tom and Andrew approached a Kurdish soldier near the prison and introduced themselves as physicians with Doctors without Borders.

"Sorry, sir," the soldier said. "I know you're here to help, but there's still active fire across the city, and no one's allowed in."

As Andrew and Tom turned to walk away, a TV crew pulled up and approached them, but when the reporter started in with a recap of events, Tom stopped him in English. "Tell us something we don't already know."

The reporter said, "OK… seems the Syrian Defense Forces have rounded up some of the escapees. Hundreds more are still at large, and we don't know the status of the hostages."

"How many hostages were taken, and who are they?" Tom asked.

"All we know is that the two sides agreed to release some of the hostages in exchange for treatment for the wounded prisoners."

"We're physicians from Doctors without Borders. We're ready to help. We can set up a field clinic somewhere nearby. Can you make that happen?"

"The SDF says some of the wounded have already died for lack of treatment, but there must be dozens more in need. I'll see if I can't get things moving."

"We already spoke with a soldier at the blockade. He wouldn't budge, said he had his orders."

"I know these men," said one of the reporters. "I'll talk to them."

The reporters walked over to the soldier. Andrew and Tom watched as they spoke.

"Sorry," the reporter said when he returned, "but just a few minutes ago, US fighter jets fired on the prison."

"Where the hostages are?" Andrew asked.

The reporter shrugged his shoulders. "Not sure about any hostages, but I know there are seven hundred boys and teens somewhere inside that prison."

"Are they children of ISIS members?" Andrew asked.

"In all likelihood. They probably got separated from their parents when Raqqa fell, or maybe were put in displacement camps with their mothers before being sent here."

"If you get another update, please holler. We'll be hanging out here."

Andrew looked at Tom and said, "I'd like to believe Mary is still safe with those two women, but I'd rest easier if I knew for sure. And where the hell is Sonia?"

"You talk as if you cared."

"I dislike her, but that doesn't mean I want to see her dead."

"Well, well, you have a tender heart after all."

Andrew rolled his eyes. "Try calling Mary again."

"I just did. No answer."

"So, we just hang out here?"

"You have a better idea?" Andrew asked.

"Actually, I do. Pull out your phone," Tom said. "There should be a news update in about…" He looked at his watch. "…about a minute."

A minute later, they were watching a news update. The reporter was saying, "Syrian Defense Forces estimate that around 120 to 200 ISIS men are still actively fighting inside the prison. There's no news on the hostages. The SDF has announced a curfew over the entire city to prevent ISIS cells from sending in reinforcements. This just in—An agreement has been reached. Fifteen hostages will be released in exchange for treatment of injured ISIS fighters."

"That's our cue," Tom said. "Let's go talk to that soldier, and the TV crew, and get us some live coverage. We're going to open a field clinic."

"Hold on," Andrew snapped. "We're in no position to do that."

"Why not? We have some supplies in the trunk, and we'll have the TV crew send out a call to all the doctors in the area."

Andrew nodded. "Okay, let's do it."

* * *

Hours later, the mayor allowed Andrew and Tom to set up a clinic adjacent to the prison. Tom had been right. A cavalry of physicians came

forward with medicine, even equipment needed to perform minor surgery. Andrew was able to push Omar out of his mind and do what he
did best.

They treated the injured from the prison riots until late into the night.
Finally, they returned to Boghus's apartment to collapse for a few hours
of sleep. Before closing his eyes, Andrew opened his BBC app to get
the latest update.

On screen, a reporter was saying, "This evening, US-led coalition
forces released a video of about three hundred ISIS fighters who surrendered, all of them on their knees and lined up against the prison wall.
According to their spokesperson, some twenty to thirty ISIS fighters
remain at large. Seven unidentified civilians were among those killed in
clashes today between the coalition forces and ISIS. According to the
mayor's office, there are six known instances of ISIS fighters breaking
into private homes and taking the residents hostage. Their status is unknown."

Tom looked up from the screen and glanced at Andrew. "ISIS fighters have moved their operation center into a dormitory that houses sev-
en hundred teenagers, some as young as twelve. This afternoon, their
spokesperson released a video that shows five civilians they intend to
use as bargaining chips."

Looking at the spokesman in the video, an electric shock jolted Andrew as he recognized Omar. One of his hostages was on her knees. She
had dark hair, and when she looked up, Andrew saw the patch over one
of her eyes. He nearly fell over.

"Holy Christ," Tom said. "That's Sonia!"

"Yes, it is."

CHAPTER TWELVE

From afar, Omar observed Andrew Sullivan as he tended the wounded, but he resisted getting any closer, for surely Andrew knew by now about the beheading of Father Frans. The meddlesome Sonia and her sidekick, the arrogant American journalist, had been seen strutting around, looking important. Sonia had been a thorn in his side since 2011 when they had first met in Father Frans's apartment in Homs, but now she was his prisoner. It had been quite the gathering.

* * *

It was a moonless night when the ISIS fighters, some two hundred strong, executed a near-perfect prison break, six months in the planning, by setting off two massive car bombs that blasted a hole in the exterior wall of the prison and killed a dozen Kurdish guards. Once inside the three-story cluster of concrete buildings, they set fire to two fuel trucks. The explosion not only lit up the prison compound, it produced an enormous smoke screen that allowed the fighters to sneak in a truckload of weapons. Firearms were distributed. Cell doors were flung open, and suddenly there were a thousand ISIS fighters on the loose. Some took the guards and kitchen staff hostage while others, to the envy of Omar, escaped through the prison gate and disappeared into the night.

Unbeknownst to Omar, John had been watching him. He approached Omar from behind. "Don't even think about joining the escapees," he said, handing Omar a map of the prison. "Study its layout. Learn it by heart."

After John freed Omar from al Hol, he had made it clear that Omar was to follow his orders. At the time, Omar thought this was a small price to pay to be out of that hellhole, but now he would have risked life and limb to have followed those fighters out of the gate.

John's map showed a high security section of the prison where the senior ISIS members were being held. "Free them," John said, "and if the guards put up a fight, take them hostage." He handed Omar a pistol. "In case you need it," he said with a grin.

"Where do I take the men?"

"Put them in the dormitory with Sonia and the boys until we can negotiate our way out of here. I'll post snipers on the roof and guards at the entrance. They'll be safe there."

Omar was about to cross the courtyard to the dormitory when a loud hellish sound filled the air. Seconds later, a helicopter hovered over his head. Omar suspected it was about to unleash something lethal and sought shelter. Even as he stood with his back pressed against an inner wall, the chopper's rotary blades beat the air around him so fiercely he felt like he was being flogged.

Omar had hoped the still lingering smoke screen would give the pilot pause, but the chopper blindly fired rockets into the courtyard. Bodies fell in heaps before Omar's eyes turned crimson. And then, as abruptly as the fighting had begun, the helicopter lifted upward and disappeared, leaving in its sudden absence a cacophony of screams from at least three dozen seriously wounded men. During what Omar suspected would be just a momentary lull, he enlisted some of the local ISIS fighters to take the wounded to Andrew's field hospital adjacent to the prison.

It was no more than an hour later that Kurdish forces gathered en masse at the remnants of the prison gate. The ISIS escapees saw them coming and took up positions around the inner corridors of the courtyard and upper floors. Once the Kurds were inside, about thirty of them in all, the ISIS fighters opened fire. Undoubtedly, the Kurds had planned for a quick takeover, but the shootout raged on for hours.

The next batch of Kurdish reinforcements arrived, this time with RPGs, putting the ISIS escapees and their AK-47s at a disadvantage. One RPG hit the column closest to Omar. He narrowly escaped death, reaching the next column just as the first one crumbled. Part of the ceiling then fell near him, and he was knocked out.

The Kurds and ISIS were still fighting when Omar regained consciousness. And then, just as quickly as the assault had begun, the Kurds suddenly stopped firing and pulled back. Omar stood up, and as he was about to cross the courtyard, he heard the unmistakable sound of fighter planes approaching. Suddenly, he understood why the Kurdish forces had pulled back.

Standing in the open courtyard, Omar was unable to accurately pinpoint the location of the jets. A loud buzzing filled the air as they suddenly swooped down. And then he heard it—a shrill whistle magnifying in sound as it approached. One second, two seconds...

"Take shelter!" he shouted to no one in particular. He dove toward a wall. An explosion cast a red glow over the otherwise dark corner of the courtyard. Then a second bomb fell so close it sucked the air out of his chest. A third bomb gutted the three top floors of a nearby building and sprayed large chunks of mortar and debris into the courtyard.

When it sounded like the planes were retreating, Omar rushed out of his shelter to catch a glimpse of the two planes arching their wings and soaring into the sky. He watched as the they became slim glimmers of silvery metal until they turned back toward them. *No time to run*, thought Omar, as he threw himself on the ground and rolled toward a wall. The attack was quick and precise. An entire section of the prison collapsed around him.

When the planes finally retreated and Omar assumed he had weathered the worst, he raced toward the other side of the courtyard to carry out John's orders. A bullet brushed past his face, so close the fuzz on his cheek stood on edge. The Kurds must have left a sniper behind. Clueless as to where he should hide, Omar instinctively zigzagged his way across the courtyard toward the dormitory. *That was too close*, he thought.

* * *

"You finally made it," John said as Omar pushed open the door.

"Fuck you! I almost died multiple times."

"But you didn't, so quit bitching."

Omar threw John a death gaze.

John ignored Omar and said, "The Kurds refuse to negotiate safe passage. I hoped to get us out of here tonight."

"You've had days to get things worked out."

"Your turn to try, Omar. Show me what you can do."

Omar shook his head and said, "And just like that I'm supposed to get one hundred fighters, a dozen hostages and seven hundred boys and teens out of here?"

"Weren't you in Raqqa?" John asked.

Omar threw him a questionable look. "Yes."

"Then you saw the convoy of trucks leave the city."

The statement startled Omar. "You organized that?"

Without answering, John said, "We'll do the same thing here. You find drivers and trucks. I'll take care of the rest."

It wasn't much of a plan. Omar wanted some direction, so he asked, "If they want to know where the convoy's going, what do I tell them?"

"You don't. Offer lucrative payouts and they won't care."

"And the money to pay them?"

From beside his chair, John pulled a leather briefcase off the floor and placed it on the table and unlocked it. When it was opened, Omar stared at stacks of crisp, clean hundred-dollar bills. He pulled out one stack, then another and another, calculating that the briefcase probably held well over a hundred thousand dollars. *Ya Allah. This is the kind of money that doesn't get taken to the bank and deposited*, he thought. It keeps changing hands and doing dirty deeds.

He returned the bundles to the briefcase and stared at John. *Who are you?* he wondered, *and what are you doing with so much money? Why do you care, Omar? It's dirty money. Play dirty too. Adjust the cost of the truck drivers upward by a couple thousand and send the money to Aisha.*

John closed the briefcase, locked it and returned the key to his shirt pocket. "Now find me those drivers!"

"I have a question about the boys and the teens. What do you intend to do with them?"

"Many of them have high value potential," John replied. "It'll be your job to develop that potential."

"If you're thinking along the lines of a Cubs for the Caliphate program, I'm not interested."

"You'd rather be in a cell in a maximum-security prison?"

"An upright and honorable man would have already sent me back to the States to stand trial, John. Instead, you got me out of al Hol because of the despicable things I've done. You don't have the moral high ground here. If anything, it speaks volumes about who you are. Maybe you haven't beheaded anyone like I have, but I suspect you're just as unscrupulous. Anyway, I'll do your dirty work. It just won't include turning boys into suicide bombers."

John nodded. "OK, for now, that's on the back burner."

And that's where it will stay, Omar decided. And then he said, "You showed me all that money for a reason. What was it?"

"The money's for various bills, salaries, compensation for work done well."

Omar smirked. "That's a given." As he was about to leave, Omar turned and asked, "Do you know Andrew Sullivan?"

"I do. Why?"

"He's here at the prison."

"What?" John blurted out. "Are you sure?"

"Positive. Another doctor's with him."

"Did he see you?"

Omar shook his head. "He was too busy tending to the wounded."

"Was the other doctor also a foreigner?"

"Yes, and come to think of it, Mary must be here too. Sonia's here, and she wouldn't have come alone."

"No sign of her?"

"No, she's probably still hiding. I suspect she and Sonia got separated when the fireworks started. If she reappears, I'll grab her."

"No," John snapped. "Leave her be."

Why such a reaction? wondered Omar. *Did John have feelings for Mary?*

"How do you know Andrew?" Omar asked.

"I bumped into him a few times, most recently in Idlib when he was working with that same group of doctors."

Why was John in Idlib? Omar wondered. As an American, John wouldn't have been welcomed unless he came as a volunteer like Andrew. On the other hand, he could have been invited to meet with Jolani, the most powerful man in Idlib, because he was American. When Jolani ran al Nusra in Homs, he was already a US asset. John's power and his dirty money were beginning to make sense.

"Enough with your questions," John said. "We've been in a fucking standoff with the Kurds too long. Find me those drivers and trucks."

* * *

John's convoy could wait. Omar wanted to see the boys and teens he had asked about earlier. John had shrugged off Omar's concern for the youths, claiming responsibility for their well-being belonged to the Kurds and their US partners. If last night's bombing raid was any indication, neither of those entities cared a damn what happened to the young people. And if he had not rescued little Anwar in 2015 when he'd been running the Cubs program, he would be among these boys.

Omar made his way to the section of the dormitory that housed the youths, climbing over stairs cluttered with rubble and debris to reach the upper floor. An ISIS guard gazed up from his phone when he saw Omar approach.

"I've been asked to check on the boys," Omar said. The guard reached into his shirt pocket and pulled out a key, handing it over. With his eyes, he steered Omar's attention to a solid metal door with a sliding observation panel in it at the end of the hall.

Omar slid the metal panel on the door sideways and looked in. A sea of tightly packed bodies, lying back-to-back, covered every available space on the floor.

"*Baddy Saadkun* (I want to help)," Omar said. "*Feeny fut?* (Can I come in?)"

The boys closest to the door understood they needed to stand so Omar could push open the door. Several rows of boys climbed to their feet to clear a path, and soon all the boys were standing. Omar unlocked the door and opened it, then fought back tears as he made his way through the staggering number of frightened, hollow-eyed faces, all of them mere children. They were standing shoulder to shoulder on foul-smelling mattresses wearing tattered clothes and staring up at him.

The boys were at most ten or eleven years old, Anwar's age. Maybe like Omar they had seen their fathers killed and their mothers raped, or had been abused or used as sex slaves, or had been obliged to witness executions to harden them for future acts of violence.

To Omar's horror and shame, any one of them could have been in his Cubs program. It was too late for the older teens, who had already gone on to become ISIS jihadists, but not for these poor boys. They broke Omar's heart, something he was relieved to discover he still had. Before he could clear his throat to speak, a weary voice pierced the silence.

"*Saadna min fadlak* (Help us, please)," a young boy pleaded. "We're starving and we have no water."

Omar turned to answer the boy, but before he could, another tiny voice spoke up.

"*Nahna Khayfeen* (We're scared)," the boy said.

As Omar looked around, he saw three windows just below the ceiling, each maybe two feet by two feet, barely large enough to allow in daylight. He saw electric sockets hanging in rows throughout the room, few with bulbs. At age ten Anwar was still afraid of the dark. What about these boys?

"How long have you been living like this?" Omar asked as he glanced at the dull, gray walls covered with years of grime and graffiti in multiple languages.

"We've been here since the prison was attacked."

"And the older boys?" asked Omar.

"They were taken to another part of the prison," said another. "I know because my brother was one of them. He was terrified he was going to have to fight. Some of his friends had already died."

Omar recognized the boy's native tongue wasn't Arabic, so he asked in English, "Are you American?"

"No, Canadian. Came here a few years ago with my parents. I was in another section when the helicopters struck. I got wounded in my head and hand. Nothing serious, but one of my friends got badly injured, and before I could find someone to help, he bled to death."

"A lot of us were somewhere else before we got dumped here," another boy explained. "We brought some of the wounded with us, but they need to see a doctor."

"Where are they now?" asked Omar.

"At the back of the room," someone answered. "We're doing our best for them, but they really need to see a doctor."

"Who transferred you here?" Omar asked.

"The Kurds, that's who," another boy said. "They called us ISIS pigs. Some of our parents were ISIS. That's why we're still here, but that doesn't mean we're ISIS."

A different boy spoke up. "They wouldn't let us bring anything with us, not even warm clothes. I have some back in my room. It's cold in here."

"At least we're all packed together, and that creates some heat," another said.

"Look," one of the boys said. "We don't want to make trouble. Most of us are Syrian or Iraqi. All we want to do is go home where we still have relatives."

"I may not be able to get you home," Omar explained in the one language they all understood, "but I will get you all out of here tonight, and I'll make sure you have warm clothes and food."

* * *

Omar had enough money to hire drivers, but where would he find them in a city he did not know? There was now a pause in hostilities as negotiations were taking place. Stores had reopened and farmers from outlying communities had arrived with fresh produce. For the first time in days, street vendors piled their carts high with greens and fresh vegetables, and that simple act produced a cacophony of shouting and haggling over prices, a semblance of normalcy. Omar quietly slipped out of the prison gate into that lively ruckus. He wandered the neighborhoods to acquaint himself with the city's layout and possible exit routes.

Finally, he settled into a quiet café and ordered a coffee. When it came, he said to the waiter, "I need a driver and truck. Know anyone who'd be interested?"

"Maybe, I'll ask around. How soon do you need them?"

"By midnight tonight. I can pay well."

Omar watched as the waiter went from table to table, pointing toward him during each brief conversation, until finally one man stood and walked to Omar's table.

"I'm interested."

"Take a seat," Omar said. "I don't need one truck. I need ten drivers and trucks."

"I'm still interested. How much?"

"Name a figure."

"What am I transporting?"

"Human freight, eight hundred in all."

"Are they fleeing prisoners?"

Omar nodded solemnly. "Children," he said.

The man stared at Omar. He sat quietly and watched the man process what he had just heard.

"So, let's talk details," Omar said.

The man took out a notepad and pen from his shirt pocket and cal-culated people per truck.

"Ten sounds about right. Destination?"

"Deir ez Zor. I'll also need coats and hats for several hundred boys. And food. They haven't eaten in a week."

"Bastard Kurds!"

The man went back to work and came up with a final figure, He showed it to Omar. $100,000, which was $10,000 per truck. Reason-able, thought Omar, considering the cargo and the risk involved. An additional $5,000 for food and clothing, and another $5,000 for Aisha and his children.

"We have a deal," Omar said.

They shook hands and the man called the waiter. "My guest would like a manoushe, with plenty of cheese." Turning to Omar, he asked, "Anything else?"

Omar shook his head. "You have a name?"

"Shammer. It's the name of my tribe."

"Your tribe?" Omar asked.

"You're not from here, are you?"

"Born in Iraq. Moved away when I was six."

Shammer said, "Hasakah has a large population of Arabs with links to different tribes."

Omar's manoushe arrived. As he bit into it, he asked, "You're not joining me?"

Shammer brought his two hands together in front of his chest and bowed. "Enjoy."

"Thank you," Omar said.

"Your hostages are from our tribe," Shammer said. We're very grate-ful you didn't kill them."

"That's why you agreed to help?"

"We stand with our tribes and against the Kurds. That's as plain as I can say it. They occupy our land. They've taken our property and try to recruit child soldiers from our ranks, and all of this with the backing of the US, their coalition partner."

"Valid reasons to dislike them." Omar took another bite of manoushe.

"Another coffee?" Shammer asked.

"Only if you join me."

"I will."

"I had an unpleasant run-in with Kurds in Raqqa," said Omar. "Are they from around here?"

"They're a stateless ethnic group from a region called Kurdistan. It spans southeast Turkey, parts of northern Syria, Iraq and western Iran. In Iraq, the US promised them a homeland in exchange for their help defeating Saddam Hussein. It never happened, and now here the Kurds have been promised the same thing—but on our land! All that has done is stir up problems with Turkey."

"I've heard about the border skirmishes with Turkey. I don't understand any of that."

"Turkey sees the Syrian Kurdish People's Party—the YPG that dominates the Kurdish ranks of the Syrian Defense Forces—as an offshoot of the banned Kurdish Workers Party, the PKK, which they consider a terrorist organization."

Shammer shook his head. "The irony is that the Americans consider the Kurds to be terrorists, too, yet they're happy to use them as coalition partners and dangle possible statehood to keep them motivated."

"Whatever it takes to defeat Assad."

Shammer nodded. "The trucks will arrive at midnight," he said. "I'll take care of everything, from neutralizing the Kurds around the prison to escorting the boys and men to the trucks."

"How will you get the trucks there undetected?"

"That's my problem, not yours. I know that area of Hasakah."

"What do you need from me?" Omar asked.

"Keep the hostages in a safe place. My men will find them and escort them to freedom. And I'll expect payment in full once we get everyone to Deir ez Zor."

"You're a trusting man."

"And you're a smart man. You don't need more enemies."

Omar smiled. He stood and shook Shammer's hand.

* * *

A sea of women, hundreds of them in black chadors flapping like birds' wings, made their way toward the prison. Omar watched these fearless warriors, equal to their men in fanaticism and grit. That was their power, their invincible armor, which was so mighty no one dared take them on.

Omar had experienced that zealousness firsthand. After accusing him of being disrespectful, had it not been for John, those women would have just as easily chopped off his head as beaten him to death. In al Hol, they had their own chat groups and a network of Telegram channels and money-making schemes, even their own PayPal account, which helped keep the insurgency and ideology alive and well-funded.

Omar found it almost comical to see how quickly people stepped aside when they saw the women, or rushed into the closest store, leaving the street vendors unable to move their laden carts to allow the women's boot-stomping passage.

The women had come to celebrate the prison break. Omar wished they hadn't. He had hoped to keep tensions at a minimum while John negotiated an exit strategy.

Omar approached the ISIS guards at the gate.

"See what you can do to break up this gathering," said Omar.

"Be my guest," one of them joked. "One of those women is my mother." He pointed out one of the women. "She's been on Telegram for days rallying local women to show up in support of their men."

"But we can't allow them inside the dormitory," Omar said.

"That's not their goal. They've come to celebrate their loved ones' freedom from prison. What we just did here has boosted ISIS's morale and undermined the credibility of the Kurds."

"I appreciate their enthusiasm," Omar lied, "but try to keep things peaceful. We're attempting to negotiate our way out of here."

Omar was about to update John on the truck drivers when he heard howls and screeches coming from the field hospital. When he arrived there, Andrew, his colleague, and Mary were all in the grip of an angry group of ISIS women. Andrew had not seen Omar since he'd left Homs. He was certain that Andrew knew what he had done and would not want to see him.

Given the intensity of the raging women's attack, Andrew felt a measure of relief when he spotted Omar coming toward him. "Do something, Omar," he shouted in Arabic, trying to fend off the women. "Explain we're here to help their men, not harm them."

Omar wrestled with two of the women, trying to free Andrew and his colleague, but a third woman grabbed him by the shoulder, spun him around, and within seconds put a knife to his neck.

"*Basbaa!*" Omar screamed loudly enough to catch her off guard. When the woman loosened her grip, he spun round.

"I'm the one in charge here," Omar said, glaring at her. "Not you."

She glared back, eyes on fire, refusing to stand down.

"Your son, standing over there…" Omar pointed toward the prison guard he had spoken to. "…told me you and your ladies came here today to celebrate a prison break. Not only do you sound like a flock of cawing crows, you and your women behave like them. You attack the very doctors who have spent the last five days treating your wounded men and saving their lives. And instead of thanking them, you try to harm them and herd them off like cattle to slaughter?"

Gesturing toward Mary, he said, "And this woman worked as a journalist in Homs. As an agent of ISIS, she was responsible for letting the world know Assad was killing his own people. You owe her your thanks too."

"They're foreigners, all of them, which makes them infidels," the guard's mother said. "You know what we do with such people." Turning on Omar, she said, "You claim to be in charge, but you speak a faulty Arabic, which means you're as much a foreigner as they are."

"I'm Iraqi born and just as Arab as you are! In Raqqa, I reported directly to the Caliph. You still want to question my loyalty and authority?"

The woman's eyes fluttered. Suddenly, she bowed her head and backed away.

Omar shifted to a calmer tone of voice. "I came to Syria to fight the infidels. In the service of Allah, I've killed my share, but this man…" He pointed to Andrew. "…served us in Homs by caring for our wounded, and now he and his colleague volunteer with Doctors without Borders. Since Assad doesn't govern this part of Syria, by ISIS decree these doctors are allowed to work here unharmed."

Omar turned to Andrew's friend. "What's your name?" he asked in English.

Tom replied in Arabic. "My name is Tom, and I've been in Syria for the last eight years helping the sick and wounded."

"You see," Omar explained, "these men are not only volunteers, but they speak fluent Arabic. That shows their dedication to their humanitarian work. They deserve to be treated as heroes, not enemies."

"You're right," the woman said. "But not this one." She pointed a crooked finger at Mary, who was still in the grip of two women. "Bring her forward!"

When Mary stood before her, the guard's mother said, "This woman is no friend of ISIS as you claim, and I can prove it."

What does this fanatical woman know that I don't? wondered Omar.

The woman addressed Mary in Arabic, "Why are you here?"

Mary shook her head.

"This evildoer does not even speak Arabic," the guard's mother announced. "I doubt she was of much use to you in Homs, unless you kept her around for some other purpose."

She looked around at her band of women and smirked, pleased with herself and her innuendo. "She is a spy!" she shouted.

"Explain," Omar said.

"On the night of the prison riot, she sneaked into Hasakah with another woman. A foreigner who doesn't speak Arabic wouldn't take such risks unless she was spying for the coalition and knew they would protect her." The woman paused and looked around at her mob. "Non-Muslims who work for the enemy are enemies of Allah against whom it is legitimate to use violence," she said.

Suddenly, Andrew spoke up. "That is nonsense, The idea of unrestricted conflict and violence is completely un-Islamic."

Omar remembered that Quranic passage from Andrew's conversation in Homs with the scar-faced elder, Omar's mentor.

Andrew recited the passage more or less. "Fight in the cause of God against those who fight you, but do not transgress against those who do not.' God does not like aggressors."

The woman stared at Andrew.

"You know the Qur'an?"

"Yes, I've read it, and I know Islam is a beautiful and peaceful religion. It abhors war and favors peace over violence. The idea of unrestricted conflict is completely un-Islamic."

"There are verses in the Qur'an called 'sword verses' that justify war against nonbelievers," she replied.

"As I understand it, those are radical interpretations not supported by most Muslims."

* * *

While Andrew attempted to negotiate Mary's freedom through debate, or at least calm the tensions, Omar hurried off to find John. When he found him standing idly by the prison gate, he said, "What the fuck? Why aren't you over there trying to appease those crazy women?"

"Because you're doing an admirable job."

"But I'm losing the battle. They want Mary. Do something! They'll listen to you."

"What makes you think they'll listen to me?"

"Stop shitting me, John. They listened to you in al Hol and spared my life."

"That was different."

"How so?" Omar shot back, until it dawned on him. John had saved his life because of his specific skill set. "Okay! Give them Sonia instead."

"Not an option," John said. "She's our ticket out of here."

"Okay, sacrifice Mary. But in exchange, let Andrew and his friend walk out of here as free men."

John stared at Omar.

After that uncomfortable pause, Omar said, "I suspected earlier there might be something between you and Mary. If you have feelings for her, you can free her yourself once we get out of here. If you don't, the women in Deir ez Zor will be happy to host both she and Sonia."

Omar again waited for John to respond.

When John said nothing, Omar continued, saying, "I get it. Your mission is to get the ISIS members safely out of here. Once you announce you have two hostages, one of them American, the standoff ends and we can leave. But you know what they'll do to Mary if they get their hands on her. It'll be too late to save her then."

"Is everything in order for tonight's departure?" John asked.

"It's set for midnight. The local tribesmen helped. They hate the Kurds."

"Good work."

"It'll cost you."

"Not my money. Have the guards at the gate bring Mary in but keep her separate from Sonia."

Omar hated Mary almost as much as he hated Sonia, but he did not want to see her die at the hands of ISIS. In a heated discussion in Frans's apartment in Homs, she had revealed her feelings toward him, her words ever more pertinent now as he recalled them.

"What don't you still understand, Omar?" she had said. "You're just fodder to your CIA bosses. You were taught to lead the charge, to create the desired level of havoc, and you carried it out brilliantly, beyond their wildest expectation. You're working for the devil, Omar."

Apparently, I still am, Mary, Omar thought. *But this time the devil has a name.*

* * *

"Take the foreign woman prisoner and put her in a room by herself."

Omar followed the guards to the field hospital and watched as they took hold of Mary. To their surprise, she broke free of their grip and ran toward Tom. Before she could reach him, a group of ISIS women tackled her and threw her on the ground. On their leader's orders, they tied her hands behind her back and stood her up.

"Omar!" she screamed. "Do something. Don't let them take me."

"You're in charge," Andrew shouted to Omar in English. "Order them to set her free."

"They're not taking her, I am," Omar said, rushing over.

"Why?" asked Tom. "She's not a spy, and you know it. She came here looking for—"

"Stop right there," said Andrew. "If even one of those fanatic women speaks English, you don't want to be saying what you were going to say. It'll give them another reason to believe Mary's a spy."

Tom nodded. "How do we convince them Mary's not a spy, or you, Omar, to let her go?"

"You can't," he said. "She's American. With her as a hostage, we negotiate our way out of here. Once we get to Deir ez Zor, we'll see about releasing her."

"That's not good enough," Andrew said. "Take me instead. I'm American."

"Or me," Tom said. "Brits are just as sought after as Americans."

"If I didn't know you were honorable men, I would appease these women and hand you over to them."

"Do it, for God's sake!" Tom insisted.

"Not going to happen."

"How do we know you'll release her once you get to Deir ez Zor?" Tom asked.

"You don't."

Omar was thinking, *Goddamn you, John, for putting me in this position.*

"Speak in Arabic," shouted the guard's mother. "You decide nothing about my prisoner without consulting me."

"A decision has been made," Omar said. "The prisoner comes with us to Deir ez Zor."

"No, she's ours!" She ordered her women to take Mary away.

"No!" Mary shrieked, her face scarlet with rage. "Make them stop, Omar."

Omar suddenly shouted, "Do you want your husbands and sons to reach Deir ez Zor?"

"Of course," the guard's mother said.

"An American hostage will ensure that the Kurdish forces won't attack us along the way."

The woman reluctantly nodded. "I agree." She instructed her women to cut Mary loose.

"No, leave her hands tied," said Omar. "Guards, take her inside."

Turning to Andrew and Tom, he addressed them in English, "These women still want someone's blood. I don't want it to be yours. Get in your van now and leave while I can still keep you safe."

As Omar was watching them leave, Andrew turned and said, "This is going to rebound on you big time, Omar."

"I know it will," Omar said. "Everything does."

Chapter Thirteen

"Have you warned Sonia she'll be leaving here tonight?"

Omar shrugged. "Let it be a surprise."

John laughed out loud.

"She's a bitch. I agree. She implied I had something to do with the assassination of the US Ambassador to Syria, who was my former boss. Coming from a prominent Arab journalist, those are dangerous accusations, especially since the investigation was shut down before it ever began. But that's not your business. Why do you hate her so much that you'd throw her to the beasts and let them feast on her?"

"Did you?" Omar asked.

"Did I what?"

"Kill the ambassador."

John's fiery glare sent a shudder through Omar's body. He turned and left the room.

* * *

From the doorway, Omar hardly recognized Sonia, who was shivering under a blanket in a corner of her cot. With her eye patch missing, her eye socket shone like raw meat. She looked like a scared animal.

Omar put his hand over his mouth and audibly inhaled to counter the pungent smell as he entered.

"What did you expect?" Sonia said, contemptuously spitting out her words in English. "I had to pee and shit somewhere."

"I gave orders to have you taken to the bathroom..."

"Cut the bullshit, Omar. You've had your fun. I'm cold and hungry and in need of a shower."

Omar shrugged. "You should have saved yourself this embarrassment and stayed away."

"We came for you."

"And instead of capturing me, you're the prisoner now."

"It was John who got you out of al Hol, wasn't it?"

Omar nodded.

"Sleazy, silver-tongued snake-in-the-grass," Sonia raged. "I told Mary not to trust him."

"She won't now," retorted Omar."

"What do you mean?"

"She's here too—on his orders."

"Omar, this has gone too far. Release us and you'll never see us again."

"What I can offer you is a proper toilet break, a cold shower and a change of clothes. Will an orange jumpsuit do?"

"You can't be serious. Me? An ISIS prisoner? This is John's doing, and you don't have the balls to stand up to him."

"I don't need to. I've waited eight years for this moment."

"What are you talking about?"

"When we met in Frans's apartment back in 2011, you asked me what would become of you and Father Frans. My response was, 'Your time will come.' Well, that time is now."

"Meaning?"

"I was going to send you to a special section of al Hol called the Annex where you'd have been the honored guest of a special group of women."

"You're scaring me, Omar. Those women are savages."

Omar put up his hand. "But John insisted you and Mary accompany us to Deir ez Zor. The ISIS women there eagerly await your arrival."

"You low life son of a bitch. I'll make sure you—"

Without waiting for more expletives, Omar turned and left, but not before ordering the guard to get her cleaned up. After he had descended two flights of stairs and exited the dormitory, he could still hear her cursing, this time in her beautiful Lebanese Arabic.

* * *

Omar met Shammer at the prison gate at midnight. "Take special care of the young boys," he instructed. "They've been badly treated by those bastard Kurds. And quite a few of them are injured. I won't be counting numbers when we get to Deir ez Zor, so if you know of people who can provide good homes for any of them, I'd be grateful."

"I'll see what I can do," Shammer said. "They're from our tribe."

"We have two special hostages I hadn't mentioned—two adult women. One speaks Arabic, the other doesn't. Separate them. I don't want them communicating."

Shammer nodded and Omar shook his hand. "Thank you. I'll see you in Deir ez Zor and we will settle up. I promise you."

He stayed long enough to watch Shammer's men load the former prisoners into the trucks. He paid particular attention when they brought Mary and Sonia out individually and placed them in different trucks. By the time he walked to John's car, John was already behind the steering wheel.

"What took you so long?" John asked as Omar closed the car door.

"Just checking to make sure the departure took place in an orderly fashion."

"And?"

"Would I be sitting here if it hadn't? Shammer expects to see us in Deir ez Zor with payment."

"No worries, I have the money."

* * *

They were some distance from Hasakah when Omar heard a helicopter. He rolled down the window and saw it hovering overhead, its navigation lights flashing against the night sky. When he pulled his head back inside, John was on the phone.

"Is something wrong?" Omar asked.

"The pilot's reporting in. The trucks have left Hasakah. At their current speed, we'll arrive well ahead of them."

"To have helicopters so close, the US must have a military base in Hasakah."

"In the province."

"Where are the other bases?"

"Where it matters."

That line of questioning didn't get me anywhere, thought Omar, *so ask something else.*

"How did you get all those fighters with their families and weaponry out of Raqqa?"

"You're full of questions."

"You can choose to answer them or not," Omar said.

"Under the pretext of ongoing fighting, we barred all outsiders, including the foreign press, from entering Raqqa for two days while we organized an exit convoy for the fighters."

"Why did you destroy the city if you knew you were going to let the fighters leave?"

"To prevent Assad from retaking it. His army had just spent eighteen months defeating ISIS in Palmyra. We knew they'd be too tired to take on Raqqa so soon after that. That's why we attacked Raqqa when we did."

Omar remembered Hammad saying the same thing.

"So, you fight ISIS to justify your presence when it's convenient. Otherwise, you let them do battle with the Syrian army."

"Perception is everything, Omar. You'll need to learn that for the work you'll be doing."

"And what is that?"

"You'll be told in due time."

Omar closed his eyes and dozed off. He woke up when he heard John call his name.

"What did you say?" Omar asked.

"Have you ever been to Deir ez Zor?"

"Multiple times—on gruesome media assignments. I hate the place."

"A lot of people do, especially the Armenians. They lost a million people there."

"Just across the border, the Iraqis lost many more," said Omar. "Why doesn't anyone commemorate them, or build them a memorial? Actually, I guess I know why that is. Because it was the fucking Americans who killed all those poor Iraqis, and they don't want anyone to know."

John's phone rang. He answered and said, "OK, thanks for the head's up." He closed his iPhone and told Omar, "We're being followed."

"Of course we are, by ten trucks."

"It's a Land Cruiser, according to the pilot."

"That would be Andrew and Tom," said Omar.

"Those motherfuckers don't give up, do they."

"They must think we have Sonia and Mary in the car. How far are we from Deir ez Zor?"

"About twenty minutes," John estimated.

"Pick up your speed. I saw their beat-up Cruiser when it was parked by the field hospital. There's no way they can keep up with us."

"In case you hadn't noticed," John said, "this Range Rover's just as beat up, and possibly even slower."

"Try anyway."

"Who's this Tom fellow?" John asked. "He seemed very protective of Mary when the women tried to drag her off." As if he was thinking aloud, he said, "When would she have had time to meet him? I just saw her in Damascus and—"

"Probably through Andrew," Omar suggested.

"How do you know Andrew? I only know what Nadia told me about him when we were in Boston for the ambassador's funeral, and then in Damascus, Sonia mentioned that he and Nadia had married."

"Happy to hear that."

"So, how do you know him?"

"I kidnapped him from his clinic in Shatilla and brought him to Homs to run al Nusra's medical clinic."

"So that's why the ambassador worked so hard to free him. Nadia must have asked him to. He adored that woman."

"Andrew should have hated me for kidnapping him, but he never showed malice. He took good care of my men and their families. A very honorable man. Easy enough to see why Nadia chose him," Omar said. "Apparently you made her choice an easy one."

Interesting, thought Omar. John didn't give me a threatening look this time.

The pilot called in again, and this time John put him on speaker. "They're not giving up," the pilot said. "What do you want me to do?"

"Stand by," John said, "but stay on the line."

Tom suddenly pulled his car alongside John's to block any oncoming traffic. Omar didn't care whether Tom was trying to see if Sonia and Mary were in the car It was a dangerous maneuver, one that could have cost them their lives.

John's response was immediate. He swerved his car near Tom's, and with the savviness of a race car driver inched closer and closer. Tom, for his part, kept his hands firmly gripped on his steering wheel while keeping up with John.

Quite a feat, Omar thought, but John was just as relentless.

Tom was left with two choices. Risk losing control and running his car off the road, which seemed inevitable given their speed, or pulling back.

John shouted into the phone. "Take it from here."

The pilot maneuvered his helicopter down and to the left of Tom's vehicle and hovered, allowing the downward rush of air from its rotors to make horrifically intimidating sounds until Tom wisely dropped back, allowing John to intentionally drive past the road they would have taken to reach Deir ez Zor.

"Why aren't we stopping there?" Omar asked. "I need to pay the tribesmen when they arrive."

"We'll be back in time."

"Where are we going that's so important?"

"We're going to pay Baghdadi a visit," John explained. "He asked to see you."

"Here—in the middle of nowhere?"

"Many of the ISIS fighters are holed up here in tents and caves along the cliffs."

"And all those fighters who left Raqqa—where are they now?" Omar asked.

"I don't know what news you followed, if any, when you were still in Raqqa," John explained, "but even before the city fell, Baghdadi had already fled with his top fighters."

"And he left the rest of us to suffer at the hands of the coalition forces."

John nodded. "A few months after Baghdadi arrived here in Baghuz, I think in early 2018, the US coalition began a series of ground assaults. They eventually corralled ISIS into this enclave. However, the coalition miscalculated. They hadn't realized how many civilians also lived here. To avoid a massacre, the coalition moved slowly, launching small assaults. At certain intervals, they stopped to allow surrendered fighters and their families and some civilians to evacuate through humanitarian corridors."

"And they ended up in al Hol," commented Omar.

"Thirty thousand of them, and that's not the only place the Kurds imprisoned the fighters and their families. They have twenty-five other pop-up prisons across northern Syria. Their protracted siege lasted a year until ISIS was left with this four-square kilometer God-forsaken parcel of land with a thousand of its most committed fighters."

"That's why the Hasakah prison break was so important, not only for the fighters, but for the seven hundred teens. They're the future of Isis."

"That's right."

* * *

The small village of Baghuz was a continuum of open, green fields dotted with a half dozen single story, crudely erected homes protected by surrounding stone walls. At dawn, John and Omar, accompanied by two guards, climbed the rough terrain, gripping ledges and grabbing hold of tree limbs for balance. At last they reached a small dwelling that clung to the edge of a cliff high above the Euphrates River.

They were escorted into a gaslight-lit, windowless room. The olfactory thunder of rank cigarette smoke and stinky, unbathed men attacked Omar's nostrils, and he gasped. Baghdadi, the once all-powerful but now haggard Caliph, sat cross-legged on a soiled mattress with a machine gun by his side. A dozen shabbily clad, armed men surrounded him.

"Welcome, Omar. Come sit near me."

Omar tried to sit a safe enough distance away, but Baghdadi waved him closer. As Omar turned to see where John was, Baghdadi waved his hand and said, "Never mind him. It's you I want to see."

Baghdadi dismissed John to the back of the room. *The mighty Baghdadi just took down the powerful John,* Omar thought with pleasure. What the hell was that all about? Didn't John, thanks to his official US government position, command respect from all lesser beings?

"I'm glad to see you made it safely out of Raqqa," Baghdadi said. "There wasn't time in all the commotion to get word to my team. My apologies."

"None needed, Caliph."

"Our defeat here has not disrupted ISIS's command structure or its operations. These were solidly constructed in 2014, as you know. You were part of those early years. We are still flush with cash reserves, and despite President Trump heralding our defeat, we still have close to twenty thousand fighters across Iraq and Syria. We've moved away from a centrally controlled operation to a movement that relies on decentralized and non-hierarchal networks. This ensures our movement will not be affected by the death of a central leader.

"Whether I live or die matters little," Baghdadi continued. "ISIS is an ideology, and the organization will outlive me because even in death the Caliph lives on as a martyr, especially if he's been killed. And if that happens, my death will be the ultimate recruitment tool. We cannot be defeated. That is our strength, and why I wanted to see you."

Baghdadi stared at Omar for a long time, as if weighing whether he should reveal certain information. Finally, he continued.

"The prison break was important. You freed some of our most valuable fighters, but the seven hundred boys and teens are even more important. They hold our destiny. They are in your hands to forge, Omar. You will have the funds and the weaponry and whatever else you need to make it happen. I trust you will not disappoint me."

"I will not, Caliph."

* * *

Omar and John returned to Deir ez Zor in time to watch the trucks roll in. The fighters were unloaded first and taken to nearby barracks. Next, Shammer unloaded the teens who were whisked off by local fighters to another set of barracks.

"As for the boys," Shammer told Omar, "I was able to arrange for a few dozen I deemed to be the most vulnerable to be taken to friends around the Hasakah area. They promised the boys would be treated kindly. I will make sure that happens. I delivered 675 boys. I hope I haven't delivered them to their death."

"I hope so too," Omar said somberly.

He was pleased to learn the younger recruits would be housed in new barracks with plenty of lighting and adequate showers and toilets. After what they had been through in Hasakah, he felt it important to ease them into their new role as future ISIS fighters.

Finally, Shammer unloaded Sonia and Mary. Temporarily blinded by the sunlight, they could not see the group of ISIS women coming toward them. With military precision, the women grabbed Mary and Sonia from behind, binding their hands and covering their eyes. As they were being led away, Mary screamed, her fierce voice full of rage.

"This is a mistake! I'm supposed to be set free. I was promised—"

"No, you weren't Mary."

"Sonia, is that you?"

"It is," Sonia replied, choking back tears. "John intended this to happen."

"May he burn in hell for this."

Omar watched with a heavy heart until the two women were loaded into a van and driven off.

* * *

Omar found John in his temporary office adjacent to the truck depot.

"Shammer's waiting for his money," Omar said.

John opened the top drawer of a metal cabinet adjacent to his desk. He pulled out the briefcase, set it on the desk and opened it.

"Take out what you need," he said as he left the room.

Omar counted out $110,000, then closed the briefcase. Before he invited Shammer into the office, he placed the money for Aisha into two packets and stuffed them into his pockets. Then he concluded his transaction with Shammer.

When Omar handed him back the briefcase, John did not question the cost of the operation or how much Omar had taken. *Like he said,* Omar thought, *it isn't his money. Why should he care?*

Later, with some time to himself and John nowhere to be seen, Omar hitched a ride with one of the local fighters to nearby Deir ez Zor. When they arrived, Omar said, "I'm looking for a Western Union office. Do you know where I can find one?"

"There are more discreet ways to transfer money if that's what you're aiming to do," the driver said.

"The recipient only knows this way."

"Their office is down this street one block, just past the pharmacy. If you want a ride back, meet me here in half an hour. And for your information, there are all manner of dark channels you can use in the future that can't be traced. I'd be happy to show you how to do that."

"Thanks. I'd appreciate it."

* * *

When he returned to Baghuz, Omar was astonished by the flurry of activity and sought out John.

"What's going on?" he asked John.

"Where have you been?"

"I caught a ride into Deir ez Zor. I wanted to check it out."

"Why?"

"After last week, I needed a change of scenery."

"A nap would have been more beneficial."

"Am I on such a tight leash that I can't go off on my own?"

"Until I say you aren't, you are."

Omar rolled his eyes. "What's up your ass?"

"Everyone's been ordered to gather just outside town."

"When?"

John looked at his watch. "In fifteen minutes."

"Do you know why?"

"Sonia and Mary are to be put to death."

"What? How is that possible? Who gave the order?"

"Baghdadi."

"But why?"

"To celebrate his men's release from prison."

"This is crazy. You've got to stop him."

"I don't interfere with internal ISIS decisions. Keeps me in Baghdadi's good graces."

In his good graces, like hell, Omar thought. *I saw how you cowered in his presence.*

Omar looked at John with disgust. "You didn't even try to save Mary's life, did you?"

John shook his head.

"And I thought you were the head honcho here," Omar said disdainfully. "How did I get that so wrong, John?"

"Why are you so upset? You were the one who wanted to give Sonia to the al Hol women."

"Yes, but not Mary."

"What can I do about it? Baghdadi wants to send a message to Washington. You know their spiel. 'Atrocities demonstrate power and induce fear, and that enables ISIS to control the local population.'"

Omar nodded. "Yep! The same message the Americans sent the Iraqis with their 'shock and awe' bombing blitz over Baghdad. I was young, but I still remember that awful day. Allow me to compliment you, John. You recite the ISIS ideology very well."

John ignored him and glanced at his watch. "It's time. Let's go. You drive."

"Why can't we walk there with everyone else?"

"Because I decided we're driving."

"So you won't be seen, is that it?"

Omar waited until after the throngs of townspeople had made their way to a clearing outside Baghuz before he started the engine and joined the crowd. By the time they arrived and parked on a site overlooking the clearing, the mob had been instructed to form a circle. When Omar opened his car door to exit, John told him to close it.

"We'll watch from here," John said.

Omar was about to protest when one of the men he had seen earlier with Baghdadi walked into the center of the circle.

"This is what happens when you defy ISIS," the Baghdadi associate said with a wave of his hand, giving the order to bring the prisoners forward.

A collective hush fell over the crowd as the doors on a van on the opposite side of the crowd opened and two women in orange jumpsuits were hauled out. Their limp bodies were dumped on the ground. The crowd parted to clear a path as two men grabbed each woman by the arms and dragged her into the circle.

Sonia and Mary were forced to their knees. At first, Omar thought they had been drugged because they were not resisting. But then he saw Mary's swollen nose and the bruises on her face and neck. Sonia's other eye had been gouged out. Mary had broken fingers and two of Sonia's were missing. After such torture, Omar supposed one welcomed death willingly.

When ordered to, the men tilted Sonia and Mary's heads forward and took up their swords. With a strength so fierce it left Omar breathless, they chopped off the women's heads in an instant. The onlookers, some only a few feet away, shrieked and recoiled at the horror, but not soon enough to avoid blood, sinew and bone fragments from splattering them.

The men picked up the heads and hoisted them in the air. The ISIS fighters cheered and chanted "*Allah Akbar,*" and the crowd was coerced into joining them.

It was only when the townspeople had dispersed that Omar noticed Tom and Andrew. They must have been there all along. They stood silhouetted against the late afternoon sun, the sole Western witnesses to this tragedy.

Omar watched Tom advance to the women's bodies. When he got close to Mary, he made the sign of the cross.

When John saw this, he snickered. Omar looked aghast at him. He found his reaction unconscionable. *What kind of a man behaves like this?* he wondered. Clearly, John's bravado was nothing more than a mask to cover his own weakness, Omar thought in disgust.

Shoulders shuddering, Tom sobbed uncontrollably, his long, piteous wail an ode to his grief and lost love. Andrew came forward and rested his arm around Tom's shoulder.

He eventually left Tom's side to bring their Land Cruiser closer. From the car, he took out two body bags and returned to the scene. He lay them on the ground and unzipped them. He and Tom delicately picked up the bodies and placed them inside the bags. They did the same with each head.

Before he zippered up Mary's bag, Tom lifted one of her hands and kissed it. The bags closed, they carried them to the van and placed them side by side in the opened trunk. Tom climbed into the passenger seat this time. Omar, still watching, assumed he must have been too upset to drive.

Before he opened his door, Andrew lay his head against the side of the van and let out a long sob. He finally pulled out a handkerchief from his pocket and blew his nose. Without looking back, he climbed in and started the engine.

Omar waited until their vehicle had disappeared in the dust before he drove back to Baghuz, his heart heavy and conflicted as he sat in silence next to the man who could have prevented Mary's beheading. He now realized that John was no more than an empty puppet. The deep rift between them that had begun in Hasakah had grown into a vast, irreconcilable chasm.

* * *

Two months had passed since Omar and his teens had arrived in al Tanf, a US military base under the command of Colonel Johnson. It spanned fifty-five square kilometers near the convergence of the Syrian, Iraqi and Jordanian borders. Since 2016, this garrison, in addition to housing hundreds of US troops, trained jihadists to wage war against the regional enemies of the US. Many of these fighters were ISIS members who had been escorted out of Raqqa. Others came from the ranks of the Hasakah escapees.

During the previous week, Omar applauded the arrival of some five hundred new recruits from Central Asian countries, guaranteeing him long-term job security because it was his responsibility to oversee their training in the use of rocket-propelled grenades, shoulder-launched rockets, anti-armor and anti-aircraft missiles. When battle-ready, they would be turned over to the US military for their various missions.

How fitting, Omar thought. *I've gone from being one of their mercenaries to training their new professional soldiers.*

Omar continued to insist the youngest boys be kept separate from the older ones and only gradually introduced to soft-core war simulations. Depending on their response to this exposure, they would be sent on for more rigorous training. This led to multiple arguments with John, who insisted they were a waste of resources and should be returned to Hasakah.

"And let the Kurds treat them like animals?" Omar argued. "If you'd seen how these boys were kept in the Hasakah prison, you wouldn't suggest such a thing. Do you have a family, John?"

"Me? Never considered it—not in my line of work. I don't know how you managed it in Raqqa with all your responsibilities. And yet you married and fathered a child."

"How'd you find out?"

"You're an open book, Omar. Sending money via Western Union. How naive. You didn't know those transactions were traceable?"

Omar looked up at the sky with a pounding heart.

"Since I know who you sent the money to and where she lives, I suggest you do what you're told. You're already strutting around here like you know everything. Do you need to be reminded of who's in charge?"

"Are you threatening me, John?"

John shrugged. He always took everything in stride. "Call it what ever."

"Maybe you're just jealous because Colonel Johnson comes directly to me when she has a question, without consulting you?" Omar sneered.

Omar assumed that John would have noticed this executive behavior. Undoubtedly, hard lessons had matured Omar over the last eight years. But aside from the ISIS savages, Omar had great respect for women, thanks to his upbringing, and easily slipped into an amicable relationship with Colonel Johnson, a robust, attractive woman in her early fifties.

"John, are you the one with thorough ISIS training or is it me? Isn't that why you got me out of al Hol? You said so yourself. I have valuable skills. I'm just putting all of them to good use like you wanted me to."

"And that includes getting those young boys into a Cubs-like training camp," retorted John.

"I already told you it won't happen until they're ready. You're not happy? Shoot me for insubordination," he said as he walked to the door.

"Omar, these youngsters aren't all like your little Anwar. Was he a weakling, or was he just too dumb to learn anything?"

Omar spun round and grabbed John by his shirt collar. "You son of a bitch. He's off limits."

"No, he isn't," John said angrily, yanking himself free. "Aisha and Walid aren't either. Now, do as you're told and get those youngsters into the program."

Beware, John, Omar thought, as he watched him storm out of the room. *I do not take kindly to threats, especially if they put my family in peril.*

* * *

Omar ultimately complied with John's orders. Based on his own experience as Director of the Cubs for the Caliphate program, he designed a more humane approach to radicalizing the minors.

As he explained to Colonel Johnson, "I'm convinced this strategy, in contrast to the rigid carrot and stick approach, will produce better trained, more intelligent and reliable troops. My goal is to deliver men who will be loyal to your mission, not unthinking thugs who only know how to carry out brutal acts."

"Clearly a noble goal, Omar, but can you deliver?" she asked.

"Children desire a sense of belonging and camaraderie. I can give them that. Do you have children, Colonel?"

"No. I chose career over family. Regrets? Yes. No husband, no children to go home to. At my age, that's a crusher. But I do have nieces and nephews I get to spoil."

"I'm sure that's a great joy," Omar said, wondering what else he could say. "As for the children here, social bonding also happens in the classroom, where they learn basic math and reading skills. All well and good, but that isn't enough. I also propose adding intensive English classes, which will allow them to better communicate with your troops. These youngsters are like sponges. They can soak up a new language more quickly than us adults."

"I echo that," she said. "My Arabic lessons are getting me nowhere."

"I'd be happy to help you, Colonel. Choose the time and place."

"How very kind, Omar. I usually take a coffee break in the mess hall every morning around half-past ten."

"That settles it. We'll begin tomorrow. Do you have a grammar book or are you more interested in conversational skills?"

"I need help with both."

"OK, they go hand in hand, and no worries, I'll make the lessons fun."
She laughed. "I'll hold you to that."

"Getting back to my idea, if I may. We're dealing with children, and
they need to be treated as such. A classroom setting motivates peer pressure conformity—what child wants to be seen as different? It also in-
stills a desire to be part of a group. Human bonding usually takes place
within a family. In lieu of that, as is the case for these youngsters, we
become their family and their trusted adult influencers, which ensures
their loyalty."

Omar knew his revised program did nothing more than sugarcoat
the exposure of these children to death and violence. It just did so in
a kinder, gentler way by reprogramming their acceptance to such acts
as a natural way of life. The idea of turning children into monsters still
unsettled him, but it achieved three goals. It ensured him continued em-
ployment. It brought him into the good graces of Colonel Johnson and
gave him more authority and freedom of movement, all of which infuriated John. And that was his third goal.

"Your ideas are solid and well thought out," she said. "You have my
blessing. Carry on."

For months, Omar had enjoyed the same recurring dream. In it he
hired one of those flat-bed boats and crossed the Euphrates to visit Aisha
and the boys. Now that he was in the Colonel's good graces, he mused,
his dream might come true.

* * *

Over the next few months, Omar was regularly awakened to the sound
of Russian planes flying overhead. According to Colonel Johnson, the
Kremlin usually warned Washington before they launched an attack on
ISIS. This allowed US ground forces to be moved out of danger. As
Omar discovered, sometimes there was no warning and vital manpower
was lost.

The incident a week earlier had come in response to a roadside
bomb attack his men had carried out against Russian troops some dis-

tance from al Tanf. Days before that, the Russians had deployed fighter jets to strike two suspected ISIS strongholds on behalf of their Syrian ally. That day, the Russians had pulled back their planes when the US had scrambled fighter jets into attack positions.

This night was different, one that Omar would never forget. He and John accompanied two US soldiers and four new recruits on a mission to locate what they suspected was a newly installed Russian position a mile from al Tanf. Omar and the others were holed up in an abandoned army barracks when Russian planes unexpectedly flew in, firing missiles close enough to blow out several walls and send Omar flying.

Momentarily dazed, it took Omar a minute or two to recover, and when he did, he saw sections of the barracks on fire and everyone still inside. On inspection, one of the soldiers was dead, the other seriously wounded. Two of Omar's recruits had also died; the other two lay unconscious. From another section of the barracks, he heard John's voice. He was lying in a pool of blood pleading to be helped.

Omar pulled him from the building and dragged him along the rough terrain, losing both his shoes along the way. When he saw the barracks roof start to cave in, Omar dashed back inside and pulled out the wounded soldier and the two surviving recruits. By then, Commander Johnson and her team had arrived with a medic, who immediately got to work tending to the wounded.

"Very commendable of you to have risked your life to save those men, Omar," the commander said.

"No less than they would have done for me, Colonel. How's John?"

"He's ready to be airlifted out. He's asking for you."

Omar found John on a stretcher. When John saw him, he called him in close and pleaded in a weak voice, "Don't let me die. This wasn't supposed to happen, Omar…"

"Don't worry, John. Our medical team is going to airlift you to a hospital in Iraq where they'll patch you up. You'll be back here in no time."

"Stay with me, Omar. I'm scared."

No need to mock such fear, Omar thought. *I've won.*

Omar glanced up at the medic tending John. When the medic shook his head, Omar understood John would not make it.

"I'm not going anywhere, John," Omar said, taking his hand. He was thankful that he knew where John kept the briefcase. Undoing the button on John's shirt pocket, he deftly slipped out the key to the briefcase. "I'm here for you."

A few minutes later, John took his last breath.

Colonel Johnson placed her hand on Omar's shoulder. "My condolences."

"Thank you, Colonel. John and I were as close as family. We've been working together for a long time."

"You did everything you could, Omar, not only for John, but for the others. The loss of a good friend is hard to deal with, and John was such a man. He was dedicated to his job, just as you are. And while this may not seem an appropriate time, I know you understand how vital our mission here is, and how urgent it is that a seamless transition in leadership take place."

"I do, Colonel."

"Can I count on you to step into John's shoes?"

"You can. I'm confident that's what John would have wanted too."

EPILOGUE

Syrians are a people proud of their history, their culture, their multi-ethnicity, their army. Despite the severe US sanctions imposed on every aspect of their lives, they remain resilient. Raqqa is being rebuilt, as are Aleppo and other major cities. While parts of their country remain under either ISIS or US occupation, they foresee a time when their country will finally be liberated and restored in its entirety.

For now, Nadia and Andrew remain committed to their work in Syria. However, they look forward to an eventual return to Beirut and to a "normal life," whatever that means in a place in constant flux and turmoil. Stay tuned!

ACKNOWLEDGMENTS

To my daughter Nayla who recommended important changes to the manuscript, and to my readers Sheila Perelman, Joe Golibart, Mildred Larson and Kim Landry Ayres. In researching this book, I wish to acknowledge the journalist Patrick Lawrence for his in-depth interviews with Sharmine Narwani, editor of *The Cradle*. Ms. Narwani was one of the few journalists on the ground in Syria. I also wish to acknowledge *The Grayzone*'s Aaron Maté for his thorough work on exposing the truth about the chemical weapons use in Syria, validating information the renowned journalist, Robert Fisk, wrote about before his untimely death in 2020; and finally, to my editor, Ian Graham Leask, who continues to support my effort to not only challenge mainstream media for its biased coverage of the Syrian conflict but the halls of power for their reckless attempt at regime change that has needlessly cost the lives of tens of thousands of Syrians. I also need to thank line editor and book designer Gary Lindberg and copyeditor Rick Polad, who worked overtime to get this book to the printer..

ABOUT THE AUTHOR

Cathy Sultan is an award-winning author of three nonfiction books: *A Beirut Heart: One Woman's War; Israeli and Palestinian Voices: A Dialogue with Both Sides, Tragedy in South Lebanon.*, and *Gaza: Changing The World and Opening Eyes. The Syrian,* a political thriller, was her first work of fiction, followed by *Damascus Street* and *An Ambassador to Syria. Omar's Choice is the* fourth of a quartet on the Syrian conflict. Sultan is also a peace activist who served on the Board of Directors of Interfaith Peace Builders (now Eyewitness Palestine) She took her first trip to Israel-Palestine in March 2002 and subsequently co-led five delegations to Israel/Palestine, including a trip to Gaza in 2012.

Sultan won USA's Best Book of the Year Award in 2006 for her memoir *A Beirut Heart;* USA's Best Book of the Year Award in 2006 in the category of History/Politics for *Israeli and Palestinian Voices. Tragedy in South Lebanon* was nominated for Best Book of the Year in the Category of Political Science in 2008; *Damascus Street* was a finalist for both the Eric Hoffer Award and the Montaigne Medal Award. *An Ambassador to Syria* won the Independent Press Award for Historical Fiction in 2022.

Made in the USA
Middletown, DE
13 September 2024

60856605R00156